D1603056

# THE
# SIREN'S
# REFRAIN

DENNIS JUNG

All the song lyrics attributed to Lou Ann Catskill were written by the author Dennis Jung

ISBN  978-1-66784-385-8 eBook 978-1-66784-386-5

ACKNOWLEDGMENTS: I wish to thank the usual suspects who suf fer through reading my first drafts and offer their much appreciated criticism and comments – this time around - Erin, Kerry and of course my wife, Kathleen who stoically endures my mood swings and the evil twin as she refers to my Gemini side. Also I would like to express my gratitude to Anne Mydia from Winning Writers for her professional critique and encouragement. And finally, I wish to express my admiration and gratitude to those who practice the art and craft of songwriting. The best of which are the spiritual scribes of the human experience in all its glorious and inglorious complexity and nuance.

-*Santa Fe*
*Winter, 2022*

Dedicated to all those who have lost at love, but have never forgotten its essence - its pleasure and its pain.

# FORWARD

THE SIREN'S REFRAIN is my ninth novel. I usually have at least a vague inkling regarding the genesis of my stories – how an idea evolved, or the source of my inspiration. In this case, those roots are not readily apparent. This one wasn't the kind of story that I typically brooded about for long periods of time before finally launching into a tentative narrative. It didn't evolve from an event or an article I might have once read. Nor did it grow out of an anecdote or story someone might have related to me. The only things that possibly comes to mind are the professions of the two main characters.

I have a deep affinity for music, the lyrics of songs specifically. I have always spent a great deal of my free time listening to songs and admiring the art and craft of song writing. In my acknowledgments, I referred to songwriters as "the spiritual scribes of the human experience in all its glorious and inglorious complexity and nuance." The character of Lou Ann Catskill owns that role of such a scribe, both in her songs and the arc of her life. The other main character, Leon Riser, is perhaps my avatar in respect to my being a frustrated travel writer. Stylistically, all of my novels embrace foreign and often times exotic settings and locales. So it felt natural to create a character that allowed my story to wander to and fro in those kinds of settings. Thus, these two characters were born.

As far as the story itself, its themes became clearer to me with every rewrite and revision, of which there were a fair amount. THE SIREN'S REFRAIN deals with aging and mortality, of love lost and rediscovered, and of regret. I would hazard to say that most people in my age demographic find themselves replaying seminal parts of their lives and the individuals that colored those chapters. All of which inevitably leads to a great deal of late night retrospection regarding the roads taken or not taken, and the friends and lovers that might have fallen by the wayside.

Then there is the ever present mirror of aging and mortality that we all eventually must face – the physical limitations, along with the loss of friends and loved ones. My character Leon faces not only middle age but terminal illness; two bogey men that draw into sharp focus his past, the present, and the future. The twenty-five year long on and off love affair between these two individuals forms the backdrop for these themes. The bonds of their relationship endure not only the passage of time but also the obstacles presented by two complex and disparate personalities who struggle with their own demons. I admit it was a challenge to reconcile a relationship between a turbulent woman-child dealing with Bipolar Disorder and fame, and a somewhat unconventional, lone wolf writer of travelogues.

Even though the fictional character of Lou Ann Catskill is a music artist of some note, this story isn't about music per se. I don't delve to any great depths into the art or the business of creating music. But I open each chapter with song lyrics that I attribute to Lou Ann. That was a challenging but enjoyable exercise.. I leave it to the reader to decide whether I pulled it off.

-*Santa Fe, 2022*

# PART ONE

# 1

*"You said love fades.*
*Fades in the wind*
*Fades in the tempest of our hearts.*
*You always said love fades*
*Yet when I call, you're always there".*

- Lou Ann Catskill
The Siren's Refrain

**LAKE COUNTY, COLORADO**
**APRIL 10, 2021**

Leon Riser leaned back from the eyepiece of the telescope, doing his best to avoid moving the tripod. Lifting his gaze, he squinted into the fading light of the late afternoon. It was impossible to make them out with the naked eye being that the tree line stood a good two thousand feet above the cabin's deck. He had been scanning the slope of bare talus through the scope when he spotted the goats, a billy and two females. The billy's shaggy white bulk dwarfed the two nannies loping in his wake.

He was quite familiar with that particular slope of jumbled stone and scree for he had once been forced to scramble down it to evade a July lightning storm. Leaning into the scope, he took another look. The two nannies appeared to be gnawing at the sparse lichen while the billy stood in what remained of the fading sunlight and stared down into the deep valley below.

He envied the goat. Not its diet of aspen shoots and lichen, nor the cold, harsh climate, but he did envy the billy's vantage point. On more than one occasion, he had climbed up to timber line and watched the sunlight fade across the valley. At this time of day, the patchy snow on the valley floor would be turning an orangey crimson that would soon fade into a delicate ice blue. All of it occurring in what seemed the blink of an eye. In that moment, he found himself wondering if he would ever again see the world from that vantage point.

"No wallowing," he muttered.

"*Nani?* What?" Fumiko said, not bothering to lift her eyes from the screen of her iPhone. Only her head and hands protruded above the water's surface. The two of them always took a soak in the hot tub at this time of the afternoon. A silent ritual of sorts that gave Fumiko time to read her email, and Leon the time to allow his mind to wander to and fro, editing fact from fiction, and more often than not, blending them.

"Nothing," he replied to her query. No wallowing, he thought again. Live in the present, asshole. Fumiko had scribbled something to that effect in her neat calligraphy at the bottom of their contract. He kept the document on his desk beneath his keyboard as a reminder. Her actual words had been, 'Pain is certain. Suffering is optional. It is your choice of how you live.' Her constant cue to that effect had undoubtedly helped his outlook, but even on his best days, he found her sage, unsolicited advice to be a thin coat.

Two weeks ago, his oncologist had pronounced him to be almost in remission. Leon took the qualifying word almost as faint recompense, and insufficient reason to entirely relinquish his well-honed pessimism. That being said, his improved prognosis seemed validated by the fact he actually did feel better. The pain in his back and hips had lessened, not to the point that it allowed a good walk, much less anything as strenuous as a hike. At least now he managed to crawl out of bed in the morning without gritting his teeth. His state of mind however remained another matter entirely. His outlook on life still seemed wholly proportionate to how often he turned on CNN, and to a greater extent, his degree of self-medication.

Think of your remission as an annuity had been the oncologist's parting words. It's good for the duration of the contract. Just realize you may not be around for the final payout, the doctor added. Leon assumed it was the doctor's way of reminding him that remission with multiple myeloma was common, but never permanent. In other words, no one gets out alive.

He leaned back from the scope, settled deeper into the hot tub, and allowed his gaze to take in the entirety of the vista before him. The cabin sat situated along a creek in the deep cleft of a valley that separated Mount Elbert, the tallest peak in Colorado at 14,400 feet, and the summits of the Twin Peaks and La Plata to the south. He had first noticed the place, a split level log cabin, while on a cross country skiing trip some twenty years before. When he received a more than generous advance on his third book, *Black Chrysanthemum, The Other China,* he bought the cabin on a prayer and a whim.

Most years, he was fortunate to spend two or three months at the cabin, usually in summer and early fall. His doctor had advised Leon against his usual winter migration to his rather remote second home in the Yucatan. So the autumn's first snowfall found him still at the cabin. At first, the long nights had taken a toll on his spirits, but after a while, the confinement seemed to be a fitting accommodation to his disability.

It would be another week or so before the higher elevation snow would begin to thaw in earnest and turn the stream beside his deck into a torrent. In the meantime, he enjoyed the faint trickling sound escaping from beneath the creek's half-frozen surface. For now, the only other sound was that of birdsong and the occasional cracking of the ice along the banks that bordered the deck. The pass leading to Aspen wouldn't reopen until Memorial Day, and as a result, this time of year the only passersby were the occasional car and snowmobilers taking advantage of the remaining snow pack.

"Take a look," he said, sliding back in the tub and nudging Fumiko's foot with his own.

She looked up from her phone as if she were noticing him for the first time.

"Come on. Just be careful you don't move the tripod or the scope."

She laid her phone on her towel with prim precision and slid over to the scope. Raising her hands in exaggerated compliance, she peered into the eyepiece.

"*Aree!* Oh, Leon. *Sugoi!*" she squealed.

"Rocky Mountain goat. *Oreamnos americanus.* You don't see them very often on this side of the mountain."

"So very white. It is very difficult to see them in the snow." She muttered something else that sounded Japanese.

Leon reached behind him and plucked the roach clip from the edge of a plate that held a rind of Manchego and an apple core. After groping around beneath a nearby towel, he found the lighter. He flicked it on and attempted to resuscitate the inch long stub of the joint. It took a while, but he managed one good hit before tossing the clip back onto the plate. As he exhaled, he squinted at Fumiko through the smoke.

"Don't even think it," he said in response to her all too familiar look of reproach.

"You know those little ends…*gokiburi*, a roach you call it…it has the most tar. The most carcinogens. If you must smoke you should use the vaporizer I brought you. There is no need for you…" her voice trailed off as she shrugged and leaned again into the scope.

"Old habits are hard to break," he muttered, his usual refrain. "That and I need it since you're so stingy with my hydrocodone."

She clicked her tongue and peered back into the scope. She finally pulled back and looked at him. "I am sorry to reprimand you, Leon. I am not your mother. Or a wife," she added. "But I am your nurse, and I… *yūkō*… enable I believe is the English word. I enable you quite enough already."

Fumiko's mask of disapproval failed to diminish the profound loveliness of her face. As a young woman in Japan, her countenance had graced many a cosmetic ad in the country's most popular teen magazines. Everything about her face was perfect; the porcelain white teeth, the mouth and nose that seemed sculpted to fit in perfect harmony with her heart-shaped face. And then there were the almond-shaped eyes; their inky black pupils peering from behind the upturned angle of her eyelids. It was only in the flare of some emotion that one could ever fully see her pupils. Even now, at the age of thirty-four, Fumiko Sato looked at least a decade younger, an attribute that gave Leon pause when he first considered employing her as his private duty nurse. He recalled thinking that only in some ridiculous male fantasy did a nurse resemble a runway model. On the two sole occasions that he had accompanied her down to the village, he had seen the reaction on people's faces. Add ridiculous old faun to his reputation as an eccentric hermit. In the end, he didn't really care.

"It hasn't killed me yet," he said, running his hand over his closely shaven scalp.

"Yet," she murmured in sullen agreement as she edged back to her side of the tub. "We should go in soon. There is still time before dinner for your infusion."

"In a minute. Tell me something. Am I really such a bad patient? I've told you more than once that you don't need to be out here all the time. I don't mind if you…"

"Don't be childish, Leon," she said, cutting him off. "And I have told you more than once. What would I do the remainder of the week? I have no desire to make home visits to some old man and clean his catheters and wash his dishes."

"Then I guess you should be grateful I don't have a catheter. As far as washing the dishes, I seem to do them a lot more often than you do."

She smiled and shook her head. "We are beginning to argue like some old married couple. I told you before that the problem is you pay me too well. Otherwise, I would not put up with you, old man. Now let us get out," she said, turning to climb out of the tub.

"Hold up," he said, cocking his head. "I think someone's coming down the drive."

He could just make out the crackling of tires on the gravel track that led to the cabin from the highway above.

"Are you expecting someone?" she asked, sliding back down.

"Not that I recall. It's surely not that widow woman from down in the village. You ran her off with your listing of my many symptoms, paramount of which were flatulence and erectile dysfunction."

"Why must you distort everything? I simply told her you were not feeling well. I did not mention any symptoms. Besides, all you two did that evening was quarrel about everything."

"We weren't quarreling. That was foreplay. I guess you cool and proper Japanese gals never engage in foreplay."

"That sounds vaguely racist."

"Why don't you do me a favor and go see who's at the door."

"I am not your maid. If they want to see you they can come around to the back. They will find us together in your tub and the lips will wiggle."

"Jesus, Sato. It's tongues. Tongues will wag. Besides, what's there to see? You're wearing a suit."

Fumiko always wore the same modest black one piece swimsuit; the kind with the little skirt that just managed to conceal her buttocks.. As for him, he always enjoyed his sauna in the buff. If she would ever happen to show up without a suit, his astonishment would surely overshadow any carnal urge. At sixty years of age, he was a long way from being dead from the waist down, in spite of his illness. His medications had indeed blunted his libido some, but still, he would have to be blind or on his death bed to fail to appreciate someone as alluring as Nurse Fumiko, as he liked to address her when feeling spiteful.

The chime of the doorbell gave way to loud knocking followed by a long minute of silence. Neither of them spoke in the hope the visitor had given up. It was only when Fumiko cocked her head to look past him that he realized someone had found their way to the deck. He turned to look over his shoulder at the unexpected visitor. A young woman stood at the edge of the deck. It took but a few seconds for him to recognize her.

"My God, do my eyes deceive me? Iris," he exclaimed in genuine astonishment. "For a moment there, I didn't recognize you. You know, with long hair the color of which actually resembles an earthly hue. Iris," he said again with obvious appreciation

Something approaching a smile appeared on the face of the young woman.

"Don't you ever answer your phone, Leon?"

Leon looked at Fumiko and shrugged. "The last I saw the phone it was out here on the deck somewhere. That may have been last week though."

The young woman stood there as if awaiting an invitation to come closer. She was tall and rangy in a way only certain women managed to carry off well. He remembered that bearing and how she walked, a dancer's gait, an attribute that had only grown more pronounced as she had edged into her adolescence.

He had forgotten how much Iris resembled her mother. She had the same deep set, piercing, blue gray eyes; the same coal black hair. And the same generous mouth and high cheekbones that hinted at some aboriginal lineage. Her mother, Lou Ann, always claimed her grandfather was a full-blooded Comanche. Iris's full mane of black hair lent credence to that claim.

Even from ten feet away he could see the emerald nose stud he had given her on the occasion of her sixteenth birthday. Her bulky parka partially concealed the Zia Sun tattoo on her neck. He had paid for that also.

"You said you called?"

"More than once."

She hesitated for a moment and then made her way warily to the edge of the tub almost as if she were approaching a hazardous precipice. She stopped and turned her gaze on Fumiko before looking back down at him. "It's about Mom. I think she's in trouble."

# 2

*"Running again*
*Don't know any another way*
*Running from myself*
*And always coming in second.*
*But it feels so clean."*

-Lou Ann Catskill
Isle of Hearts

A moment of silence passed before Leon said anything. "She's in trouble. Where have I heard that before?"

"I'm serious, Leon. This time it's different."

"Different how?"

"She texted me two days ago. She said she'd call me later that night. She said she needed to get away from Kevin and disappear for a while."

"Who's Kevin?"

"Her husband."

"I thought she was married to a Jake something or other. That jazz pianist."

Iris shook her head, obviously annoyed. "God, Leon. They divorced three years ago. Do you live in a cave?"

"Sorry, but my subscription to People magazine must've expired. You're forgetting your mother and I haven't spoken in… You know."

"Since you left. Seriously, you two really haven't spoken to each other in over five years?"

Leon didn't comment. Instead he started to pick up the roach clip before changing his mind.

"Anyway, she's not returning any of my calls. So I called Kevin to find out what was going on. Don't get me wrong. I'd be happy if she really did walk out on him. But why isn't she returning my calls? What?" she asked, reading Leon's expression. "Don't say it."

"Say what?"

"You were going to say she's probably just walked out on everybody again. Not just me. Everybody."

What he really wanted to say was that he could recall at least a dozen times Lou Ann had walked out on people. Twice that number if you counted people in the music business. Walked out and then disappeared. Once before, she had slipped away after a concert in Vegas and barricaded herself in a hotel room for two weeks during which time she refused to answer her phone. Her agent finally resorted to hiring a private detective to find her.

"Don't worry. She'll show up soon enough."

"What if she's dead? What if Kevin killed her?"

"Why would you think this Kevin guy killed her?"

Iris took a deep breath and then cocked her head in Fumiko's general direction.

"Should she be part of this?"

"This is Fumiko Sato. She's my nurse. Fumiko meet Iris Catskill, my… former step-daughter."

Iris snorted, more in disdain than amusement. "Nurse? That's a new one, Leon."

"I've got cancer. She gives me my chemo."

Iris's face went noticeably slack. Leon couldn't be sure if her reaction was one of mere surprise, a flare of empathy, or something entirely different.

"I will go set up the pump," Fumiko said as she wasted no time scrambling out of the tub. "But you should come in soon," she said, shooting him a stern glance as she wrapped herself in a towel before disappearing inside.

"Your mouth's open, Iris. You have to admit Nurse Fumiko is an eyeful, is she not? She's too old for you though. That and I don't think she's not of the tongue and groove persuasion. At least I don't think so. Then again, she hasn't made a move on me yet."

"Leon, Leon." Iris was grinning now. "You never change."

"Old habits are hard to break."

"As I recall, that's what you said when Mom found out you were sleeping with one of her backup singers."

"You mean Sue Mendez? Ancient history. Besides, you never knew the whole story. You were just a kid."

"A kid? I was almost eighteen. Yeah, a kid who shouldn't have been surprised at what the two of you so-called adults did to one another, much less to yourselves. And here I always hoped you would've turned out different," she added, hardly bothering to conceal the challenge in her voice.

"Well, I hate to rob you of your illusions, but a fair number of us so-called adults are assholes. And only some of us are sorry about it. Not to change the subject, but are you still hooked up with that tennis coach with the mullet?"

Iris shook her head. "You're still the same unevolved cretin you've always been."

"I'd never describe myself as unevolved. Besides, those were your mother's words, not mine. I always liked that gal. Mirna. Wasn't that her name?"

"Mariah."

"I liked her. She was authentic. She had this great laugh."

"And I've moved on. At the moment I'm, not involved with anyone. I'm too busy. I told you I was in law school in Austin, didn't I?"

"I believe you mentioned it in that sorry excuse for a birthday card."

"You have cancer," she said, more a statement than a question.

"Multiple myeloma. Cancer of the plasma cells in laymen's terms. It plays hell on the bones, too."

Iris folded her arms and clutched herself as if she were trying to ward off something more unpleasant than the cold air seeping up from the creek below. "Maybe you should go in. It's cold out here," she said.

"Then you better avert your eyes. Like I said, old habits are hard to break."

He boosted himself out of the tub with some difficulty. His usual state of fitness had been diminished by a year of unremitting pain and inactivity. Even now, with the pain lessened, he was unable to accomplish anything resembling exercise. He slipped into his robe and walked over to where Iris stood gazing down at the frozen creek. She turned to face him and he opened his arms.

"I should tell you. I'm safe," she said. "I had the Covid for Christmas," she said. "Even got the first shot."

"And they've given me every shot except the one for distemper." He took her in his arms. "It's good to see you," he said as she leaned into him, her head buried into the crook of his neck.

She allowed herself to be held and rocked for a moment before pulling away. Her eyes were glistening, and she seemed to study his face with the kind of clinical scrutiny he saw reflected in most people's faces whenever you mentioned you had cancer. There was always that mixture of concern and undisguised appraisal, as if they could see your prognosis tattooed on your forehead. It never offended him for he did much the same whenever he studied himself in the mirror. It was partially why he had stopped shaving. The beard concealed the fact he had lost weight as well as minimizing his sallow complexion. What he noticed most about himself were his eyes. To his surprise, they seemed to burn brighter. Perhaps, it was merely some final flicker before extinguishment.

Several weeks ago, for no other reason than morbid curiosity, he had pulled down his most recent book off the shelf and pondered the stranger posing for the publicity photo on the back of the book's dust cover. He had difficulty recognizing the fit, tan, roguishly handsome man with a full head of salt and pepper hair and the engaging smile. He marveled at the distance between the then and the now,

"I need you to help me look for her," she said, interrupting his thoughts.

He grunted in amusement. "Come on, Iris. Look at me. Most days, I have trouble walking up the drive to the mailbox. How do you expect me to help you find her? The truth is maybe she's out on a bender with some young buck on a sailboat. You know she's been known to do those kinds of things."

She offered a ghost of a smile. "So I've heard. I just thought maybe you would want to help is all."

He looked at her for a moment before patting her cheek. "We'll talk about it. Fumiko will have dinner ready soon. I hope you like raw sea urchins. I'm kidding," he added in response to her look of revulsion. "Tonight, you're in luck. Crab enchiladas."

"No way. God, I remember when you used to make those all the time. *Esos fueron los mejores.*"

"*Muy bien, chica.* I guess you learned a little something at that language school down in Antigua. I told you didn't I that one of the teachers there used to tutor me? Her name was Maya. Jesus, I haven't thought of her in years."

"She remembered you. God, you're an old goat. She had to be twenty years younger than you."

"Yeah, but I wasn't so old at the time," he muttered.

They started for the door, and she grabbed his arm. "Is that woman really just your nurse? I didn't think nurses would… you know," she said, nodding at the tub.

"Well, you know how the Japanese like their baths. I like them, too."

He opened the door and then paused to look up once more at the mountain where he had spotted the goats. By now, they would have most likely moved into the shelter of the tree line. Who was the lucky one now, he asked himself. Crab enchiladas and the company of someone he loved. Besides, his billy goat days were long behind him.

# 3

*"Seasons change*
*People change*
*Hearts change*
*And I still dream of you.*
*That never changes"*

-Lou Ann Catskill
Changes

Fumiko stood waiting for them in the doorway of an adjoining room, her impatience obvious by the manner in which she flapped her arms as soon as Leon and Iris stepped inside. Leon shot Iris a look somewhere between abject suffering and Zen-like acceptance before proceeding to edge past Fumiko and disappearing into the other room. Fumiko gave Iris a look of what seemed annoyance before slipping into the room behind Leon and closing the door.

Chemotherapy, my ass, Iris thought. She still hadn't bought into the idea that this Fumiko was anything more than a courtesan Leon had hired to feed his eccentricities. Or was Leon her prey? That room Fumiko had just led Leon into was likely her web. To a woman, a bedroom is either a trap one needs to avoid or the best place to set one.

She slipped out of her parka and studied her surroundings. Years ago, she had spent a week at the cabin. It was the summer before she was to start high school at an exclusive all girls prep school in Dallas. Her mother dictated the choice of school in the hope it might curb Iris's enthusiasm for a life much like Lou Ann's own dysfunctional adolescence. Fortunately, Leon managed to change Lou Ann's mind with the offer to home school Iris.

She still remembered Leon picking her up that summer at the Aspen airport and promptly taking her camping for three days. What she remembered most were the nights sitting around a campfire beside a mountain stream and listening to Leon pontificate on just about every subject other than Iris's mother. On that subject, he had resolutely held his tongue no matter how many questions Iris posed.

In many ways, Leon had been the father she never had. He became her non-judgmental confidante, a mentor, a partner in crime, and her compass for all things moral and immoral. He had guided her from her first post-pubertal infatuation to her first arrest for disorderly conduct. They were close until they weren't any longer, a denouement for which she never quite forgave him.

Back then, the cabin had been quite Spartan. Leon had since added some square footage. The living room in which Iris now stood was easily the size of a three car garage. Other than this room, all she could make out of the cabin was a dim hallway, the closed door leading to the room Fumiko and Leon had slipped into, and the large kitchen and dining area on an open raised split level. The ten foot high ceilings were dressed out in tight strips of bone-white aspen saplings, all of which were the uniform thickness of a sausage. Iris reached over to a side table and flicked on a lamp in order to better see the room in the fading light.

The walls consisted of chinked logs with a waist-high wainscoting of some blond wood. The only furniture consisted of a couple of espresso-colored leather sofas, their surface cracked with wear and age, and a recliner upholstered in coarse fabric of some ethnic motif. Rugs of various origins covered most of the planked pine floor. The wall to her left was taken up by a large unlit fireplace flanked on either side by Leon's mask collection. She recognized some of the masks as clearly Zapotec, others African. A dozen or so appeared to be of Balinese design interspersed with a trio of theatrical *kabuki* masks.

To her immediate right was an alcove dominated by a large picture window that looked out onto a thick grove of aspens, their bare branches and trunks a pale white in the shadow of the approaching dusk. As her eyes adjusted to the dim light she saw that most of the remaining wall space of the alcove was taken up by open shelves.

She fumbled for a light switch, and not finding one, settled instead for a pair of lamps on either side of the desk that sat in the center of the small room. The desk held a laptop and a notepad amidst a jumble of books and partially folded maps. She stepped over to examine the shelves. One entire wall appeared devoted to a large collection of vinyl record albums. A lower shelf contained a lesser quantity of CDs and DVDs.

The shelves on the remaining walls contained books. At first, there seemed no obvious order to their display. Nothing alphabetical by title or author, nor was fiction separated from non-fiction. Instead, the books appeared to be an eclectic assortment covering any and all subjects. After a moment, she could discern some apparent groupings; European history, autobiographies, ethnographies, Asian art books interspersed with travel books, a couple of thick medical books including a Physician's Desk Reference, and more than a few scholarly tomes on various scientific subjects. Grouped together on a top shelf were the books Leon had authored.

To the best of her recollection, he had written and published perhaps a dozen and a half travel books, an anthology of essays on the art of travel, and four novels, none of which were particularly well received, although one of them had been made into a movie starring Jeremy Irons and a French actress whose name escaped her. The film was a depressing drama about a couple living on a sailboat and the dissolution of their marriage. Iris had always suspected parts of it were partially autobiographical.

The top shelf also contained several dozen spiral bound notebooks and a row of bulging manila folders that appeared to contain newspaper and magazine clippings. Piled atop these were a half-dozen or so National Geographic magazines. She plucked them down and flipped through the covers until she discovered the one she expected to find. The cover depicted a tropical beach, its white sands marred by the rusty hulk of what might have once been a pickup truck. The overlay of the title read "French Polynesia – A Paradise in Transition." She squinted at the date. April 1996.

She tucked the magazine under her arm before replacing the remainder of them back on the shelf. As she turned to go back to the den, she startled at the sight of Fumiko watching her from the shadows.

"Jesus! You scared me. I didn't hear you."

Fumiko's stealthy approach did little to dispel Iris's reservations.

"He is resting. It will be an hour or so until he will awaken," Fumiko said, her tone matter of fact and almost clinical.

Iris nodded, unsure at first of what to say. "How often does he need the chemo?" she finally managed to ask.

"This was the last infusion for three or four weeks. He underwent a stem cell treatment a month ago. After today, he will be on oral medications. It is perhaps not safe for you to come here," she added.

"Because of Covid? I told him that I already came down with it a few months back. I even got the vaccine. Or did you mean something else? About this not being safe," she added, switching on another lamp.

"I only meant to say his immune system is weakened," she replied, retreating up the short flight of stairs to the kitchen. She opened the refrigerator, examined its contents for a moment, and then turned and asked, "Would you care for some wine?"

"Sure," Iris hesitated a moment and then joined Fumiko in the kitchen, taking a seat at the long pink granite kitchen island.

"So how is he? Really?"

Fumiko retrieved a bottle of white wine and a casserole dish wrapped in aluminum foil and placed them on the granite counter. "The oncologist thinks he may be in remission soon," she replied, handing Iris a glass from the cabinet. "We will see." She poured them each a glass.

"I thought nurses were supposed to project a positive outlook."

Fumiko didn't rise to the bait, but instead began fiddling with the oven. For the first time, Iris noticed that Fumiko was wearing a thin kimono-like robe, and from what Iris could tell, she wasn't wearing anything underneath. Iris took a sip of wine before glancing at the label. The words on the label looked Slavic. She examined the label more closely. It was Croatian and tasted quite good.

"So, you live here with him?"

Fumiko launched the casserole into the oven and turned and looked at Iris, her expression challenging.

"It is a matter of convenience. For Leon and for myself. At first, I lived in Buena Vista, but his condition required that I visit three, sometimes four times a week. It proved quite … burdensome I believe is the correct word. He was the one to propose I stay here. I cook and clean also, Remove the snow from the drive," she said with a measure of defensiveness. "I am not a *geisha* if that is what you are implying."

"I didn't mean it that way. Look, maybe we're getting off on the wrong foot," Iris said, drawing a look of confusion from Fumiko. "Why don't you tell me how you met Leon."

"We met at the hospital in Denver. He refused to continue going there for his chemotherapy. He is very stubborn, yes? So Leon arranged for me to give him his treatments. His doctor had little choice but to agree." She poured herself a generous glass of wine and took a long swallow before going on. "I am not sure how much to tell you. It is a matter of ethics. Patient confidentiality."

"HIPPA? I know all about it. There's an implied exception to patient confidentiality. Leon never explicitly said you couldn't tell me. I guess he told you I'm a lawyer."

"He said you were in law school."

"It's as good as actually passing the bar. Anyway, I just completed a course on medical-related law and ethics."

Fumiko gave her a long blank stare before going on. "He was difficult at first. Very depressed. I think perhaps even suicidal. He is much better now. But if you must know, he drinks too much. And smokes entirely too much marijuana."

"That's nothing new." Iris refilled her glass. "Do you know who my mother is?"

"Yes," she replied, offering her glass to Iris for a refill. "I saw her once at a concert in Tokyo in 2001. I was quite young. Fifteen years old, perhaps. I didn't really care for her music. Your father… Leon plays her music often."

"In case he never told you, Leon and my mom only began living together when I was twelve. They split up right after my eighteenth birthday." Iris picked up the National Geographic and paged through it until she found what she was looking for. She spun the magazine around for Fumiko to see. "This photo was taken when they first met in Tahiti in 1996."

The photo showed a man and a woman standing next to a crude wooden plank nailed to the trunk of a coconut palm. Scrawled on the plank were the words '*Papeete 60 kilometers and one island ovah*' and some other words in what appeared to be French. The photograph's caption listed Leon as the author of the accompanying article, but failed to mention the name of the young raven-haired woman standing a stride or so behind Leon. The woman appeared sun burnt and disheveled, her dark hair piled in a tangled heap on her head, her eyes hidden behind a pair of oversized mirrored sunglasses.

Fumiko examined the photo for a long moment before looking up. "He never speaks of her. He spoke of you once. He referred to you as his daughter. Though I must tell you at the time he was very intoxicated. "

"Has he been writing?"

Fumiko shrugged. "He often sits at his computer. Perhaps he writes. He told me once that he was writing an account… is that the right word? An account, yes? Of a time when he and two other men rode motorcycles across North Africa. When he spoke of it, it sounded too outrageous to believe. Is that the proper word? Outrageous?"

"Then you must not know Leon. The first book of his I ever read was *Black Chrysanthemum*. It was about China. Back then at least, a journalist was never allowed to travel around in China without an escort. A minder. Someone that was supposed to keep an eye on any foreigner on a government approved itinerary. Well, he gave his poor escort the slip and wandered around for three weeks posing as a mute beggar in this rural part of the country. The police finally caught up to him. He spent the next three weeks in jail before they expelled him and pronounced him persona non grata. It seems he wanted to write a book about the contrasts and disparities between urban and rural China. He figured that was the only way he would find out." She shook her head and smiled. "Can you imagine? Hell, I don't think he could even put three words together in Mandarin.

"I was fifteen when I read that book. It was like opening a window and letting in some fresh air. It wasn't so much about discovering another part of the world, but for some reason it made me feel certain things. It made me question things. My relationship with my mother, my friends, my sexuality, what I wanted to do with my life. Have you read any of his books?'

Fumiko gulped some wine and nodded. "I read his book about my country."

"*A Gaijin in the Land of the Rising Sun.* It wasn't one of his most engrossing reads."

"Oh, but I found that many of his observations about my country were very accurate. Or how do you say it? Right on. He was very observant and quite astute for a *gaijin*." A brief smile creased her face. "So, your mother is gone?"

Iris hesitated before replying. "Gone like she's run away. I'm sorry. That makes her sound like she's senile or something. No, she just decides to leave things behind. Her solution. Look, I shouldn't say more. Confidentiality and all that," she added with a smirk.

"I understand." Fumiko looked at her watch. "I must check on your father. I am sorry I keep referring to him as your father."

"I never had a father. Just Leon."

"He should be awake soon. Perhaps, you wish to light the fireplace?"

"Sure. I'd like to know something though."

"Yes?"

"Would you know if my mother ever calls him?"

"Leon rarely receives phone calls. And when he does, I am not in the habit of listening in on them. You also must realize I have only been here three months," she said, sliding the bottle of wine across the counter.

Iris nodded and watched Fumiko make her way down the stairs. Was it only her imagination or did Fumiko undo the belt of her kimono as she disappeared into the other room? She knew Leon and women. Her instincts told her there was more to Leon and Fumiko's relationship than met the eye. She would reserve judgment until she could grill Leon further. She poured herself some more wine and began paging through the National Geographic.

# 4

*"You hear me on the radio*
*I send you songs*
*And you think you know me.*
*You send me letters*
*And what do I know?"*

-Lou Ann Catskill
Woman Down

Leon paused with his fork halfway to his mouth, and with the index finger of his other hand traced the dark scar on the surface of the teak table where they sat. It had been there for as long as he could remember. But now with Iris's unexpected appearance, the blemish drew him back to a memory. The table where the three of them were now dining was a heavy teak affair from Indonesia that he had purchased at an auction in Hilo some twenty-five years ago. At the time, he was renting a house above Waipiʻo Valley on the Big Island, sequestering himself with the intention of completing his manuscript about Bali, hence the table.

Due to either sloth or convenience, the table ended up on the wide lanai where it served as his writing table, dining table, and general catch all. It endured countless rain storms and seemed to only become stronger in the way that teak does. However, the dry, high-altitude climate of the Rockies had not treated it well, opening up several deep fissures on two of the legs. The well-oiled surface bore a myriad of insults; dents, a constellation of circular water marks, the evidence of spills, knife wounds, and more than a few burn scars like the one beneath his hand. This particular insult bore the weight of memory.

One long ago night at Waipi'o, Lou Ann had allowed a joint to burn out on its surface, setting a magazine ablaze. She had performed in Sydney the night before and decided a stopover in Hawaii would fit into her hectic schedule. She had meant to stay only two days as she had a television appearance scheduled on Johnny Carson later that week. Instead, she had stayed for a week, paralyzed by angst and the doldrums of what she called one of her blue phases. She spent most of her time sleeping or simply staring out at the ocean, ignoring frantic phone calls from both her manager and her agent. Much of the time, she shut Leon out as well. It was his introduction to her demons.

He looked up and saw Iris eyeing him. "So are the enchiladas as good as you remember?" he asked.

"*Delicioso*," she mumbled, wiping some errant sauce from the side of her mouth.

"Fumiko made them. Under my exacting tutelage, of course. The Japanese do like their crab, but she's never been quite sold on the idea of slapping crab between a tortilla and goat cheese. Am I right?"

"Mine are much better than yours. It is the wasabi I hide in the chili sauce," Fumiko added, without looking up from her plate. She had changed into a pair of surgical scrubs for dinner. Leon assumed she was trying to convince Iris of something.

He wobbled to his feet and grabbed another Negra Modelo from the fridge. "So?" he said, dropping back down in his chair. "Let's quit dancing around. Tell me about your mother."

Iris looked over at Fumiko, who seemed to sense Iris's misgiving. Fumiko took her plate and started to push away from the table. "I will go."

"No, you stay," Leon said, his gaze fixed on Iris. "This time of evening I forget things. Fumiko will serve as my stenographer."

Iris shrugged and nudged her plate away.

"It would be one thing if Mom was just walking out on Kevin. By the way, do you know him? Kevin Riordan?"

Leon stared at her for a beat or two before replying. "Kevin Riordan?" Hearing the name again after all these years gave him pause. It had to be the same guy, he thought.

"What? You know him?" Iris asked.

"You're talking about the guy who used to be her manager back in the day? Tall lanky guy. Black Irish with a cracker accent?"

"One and the same. Mom did mention once that he used to be her manager."

"I'll be. She married that skunk. Jesus, what was she thinking?"

"Obviously, she wasn't. Under the influence is my guess. He's an asshole. A manipulative, duplicitous, oily asshole. And according to Mom, he's neck deep in all kinds of crooked shit."

"Such as?"

"All I know is that Mom told me it wouldn't surprise her if the cops came knocking on their door any day." She smiled in amusement. "She said Kevin was so crooked that the cops would probably have to turn him sideways and screw him into the back seat of their squad car. I know what you're thinking. If Kevin's such a prick, why did she stay with him, much less marry him?"

"So why?"

"She was…." Iris regarded him silently, as if she were editing things in her mind. "You know as well as anyone that Mom could never stand being alone. She always needed a man, someone in her life. I guess I wasn't enough. Then again neither were you," she said, shooting Leon a look that was intended as a direct hit below the water line. "After you guys split up, she went through her fair share of them. There was Jake, the pianist, and before him a British record producer and before him this guy named Sudd."

"Sudd? The keyboardist with the weird hair? She married that deadbeat, too?"

"God, no. They were never married. They just lived together. It didn't last more than three months. Mom said it was Platonic, or so she said.

Look, the bottom line is nobody ever did it for her. Nobody filled that big empty space she's always got." Iris made a snorting sound that was hard to discern if it was out of amusement or disgust. "Jesus, I swear those are lyrics from one of her shittier songs."

"I seem to recall that song. It was rather shitty."

"When she married Kevin she was broken is how she put it. Can you believe she told me that on the night before the wedding? As usual, she was cycling up and down. And she must've thought he was a safe bet for God knows whatever reason. She knew it wouldn't last. Like always, she didn't even want it to last. It was the same reason why she left Jake. The usual commitment crap. Jake wanted more. She wanted... Who knows what she wants from a man? So she marries someone like Riordan. You tell me, Leon. What quality does someone like him have that feeds her? I mean... Shit!" She looked at him, her eyes shining with tears.

"Is she off her meds?"

Iris hesitated and swiped at her nose. "Likely, but I don't know for sure When we last spoke two weeks ago she said she wasn't taking them. But she also told me she was going through one of her blue phases, like she always calls them. Her pilot light had gone out was the way she put it. On the bright side, she gave up drinking last Christmas. Or so she says. I have to admit she seems more together than she's been in a long while. Still, I could tell something was bothering her, but I couldn't get her to talk about it. I figured it had to be about Kevin. I know what you're thinking. She's not suicidal."

Leon's mind flashed back to a seedy motel room in the cedar breakes near the lake.

"Leon," she said, bringing him back.

He met her gaze but said nothing.

"She wouldn't do that, would she? She promised, didn't she?"

"How about her music?" he asked, changing the subject. "Any record deals?"

"A year or so back, she did one of those Best of Lou Ann Catskill kind of albums. She said she was offered a new deal, but she and the producers were butting heads. Seems they want some original songs, and she's not writing any."

Leon felt a pang of self-recrimination. Lou Ann wasn't the only one not writing.

"She hasn't gone on tour in five or six years. Maybe she's done a benefit concert here and there. Some asshole in Nashville tried to talk her into doing one of those fucking Christmas albums. You can imagine how that went over."

"So how do you know that she just doesn't want to be found? Maybe she's planning on holding up somewhere and writing."

"It's just not like her to not answer my calls. Apparently, Kevin even filed a missing person's report with the police in Santa Fe. You knew that's where they were living?"

"I told you, for chrissakes. We haven't spoken in five years. I don't know her anymore."

"I was hoping maybe you might know where she could've gone. Like you said, maybe she's somewhere writing. Or maybe fucking some asshole on a sailboat," she said with a touch of spite.

"Makes no difference. She's not my monkey, it's not my circus. Not anymore." Leon stared at his plate for a moment before going on. "You have to understand that she's burned a lot of bridges in Nashville and LA. People in the business. People that aren't likely to answer her calls. That's not to say there aren't people that owe her. Some of her old band members. Maybe Sue Mendez." He lost himself for a moment. "And then there's this guy who used to be her producer that owes her big time." He thought of JB Coonts and recalled running into him once at the Newark airport. This was long after Lou Ann and JB's relationship had soured. JB however still spoke of Lou Ann with a fondness bordering on adulation. Like most men, Coonts had been totally enthralled with more than just her talent.

"She saved this Coonts guy's career. Made him a lot of money."

"So where do I find this Coonts?"

Leon shrugged. "Dunno. Look. for all I know she could be in Mongolia. I had an assignment there once. She was going to come along. She liked the idea of going someplace where no one knew her. As I recall, some concert got in the way. Look, aren't you being a little premature about this? Give her some space, why don't you? She's running away from a bad marriage."

"Just tell me where she'd run to."

He thought for a moment. "Sue Mendez, maybe."

"The backup singer you were screwing?"

"Jesus. Okay, I plead no contest. That had nothing to do with your Mom and I splitting up. Anyway, I ran into Sue a year or so ago. She showed up at a book signing in Denver. Said she and Lou Ann haven't kept in touch. Sue left the band four years ago. I guess she still lives in Austin. You could always give that a try."

"And you'll come with me?"

"Iris, I can't go anywhere. I've hardly been out of the house in two months. Look at me. I'm not a healthy man. Ask Nurse Fumiko."

"His condition is still fragile. I believe that is the proper word," Fumiko said. "He requires monitoring for any adverse reactions to his new medications. He has blood tests scheduled for next week. I do not believe it is advisable for him to travel."

"See? Amongst all my other issues, Nurse Fumiko has diagnosed me as having chronic high maintenance syndrome with episodic bouts of immature response. Look, Iris. I can't imagine what help I'd be. I'd just be rooting through last week's garbage. I told you I don't know your mother anymore."

"Could you come with us?" Iris asked, turning to Fumiko. "To give him his medications and to monitor him?"

Fumiko looked at Leon. "I have no part in your family business."

"Leon?"

He took a sip of beer. "I'll have to think about it. Okay?"

Without another word, Fumiko collected their plates and began cleaning them over the sink. Iris offered to help, but Fumiko shook her head in refusal. Leon rose rather unsteadily and made his way down to the sofa in front of the fireplace. Iris waited a moment and then joined him.

They sat and stared at the fading embers for a while before Iris reached for his hand.

"I wish you two would've never split up," she said, resting her head on his shoulder. "You were good for her,"

He turned and looked at her. "Well, I'm glad someone noticed, but you don't know the half of it."

"You loved her."

"That I did. It just got harder, especially at the end." He shook his head at the memory of something. "She told me once that here she was this reputedly great lyricist. But for the life of her, she could never make the two of us rhyme. Lou Ann could tell any story in five minutes of verse, chorus and bridge. But she could never make our story come out right."

Iris glanced up at the kitchen where Fumiko was busy loading the dishwasher. "I haven't told you everything. The last time we talked she sounded afraid. And that's not Mom. You know her. She's not afraid of anything or anybody."

"Except herself. You know how she is when she's cycling up and down. She's beyond help."

"Well God knows, we've seen her at her worst. But I could tell the last time we talked she wasn't happy. Something was bothering her."

They sat in silence. Leon lost in recrimination, Iris most likely nursing her own.

"I'm going to bed," Iris said, giving Leon a peck on the cheek and pushing to her feet. "I'll understand if you can't help. I do," she said and turned and disappeared down the hallway.

Leon sat there another moment before joining Fumiko in the kitchen. She offered him her usual inscrutable stare.

"I do not claim to know anything about you and Iris's mother," she said. "It is not any of my business, this family of yours. But I am guessing there is much... unfinished business. Isn't that the right term? Wounds that have never healed. Perhaps, you should help Iris. That is all I will say on the matter. *Oyasumi*," she said, tossing the dish towel on the counter.

"*Oyasumi*, Fumiko."

They had grown accustomed to bidding each other goodnight in Japanese. He watched her walk off. It was only then that he noticed the National Geographic lying on the counter. He picked it up and opened it to a dog-eared page that depicted the image of a turquoise blue lagoon, its fringing reef resembling a necklace of emerald green and white and silver in the bright midday sun. For twenty-five years, that lagoon had remained fixed in his memory, fixed to a time and place so seminal, that seeing it in his mind elicited an amorphous mixture of emotion - pain, pleasure and a nostalgia that made him wince.

He paged through the article before turning to the index page and the photo of the two of them standing in front of the crude sign. Papeete. And the memory of her on that first day as she sauntered down the pier.

He told Iris that he would sleep on it. He knew better than to expect the likelihood of any sleep. He took the magazine and retreated to his study.

# 5

*"Oh, the storm in our hearts*
*The rising seas*
*Love dashed on the rocks*
*God, rescue us."*

-Lou Ann Catskill
The Storm in My Heart

**Papeete, French Polynesia**

**January, 1996**

Leon sat at the bar sipping a double espresso and gazing out the open porch at the comings and goings at the adjoining pier. He always made a point to absorb as much local color as possible before delving deeper into his subject. At this time of the morning, the only local color was a pair of elderly tourists standing on the pier and taking pictures of some fishermen untangling their netting. He recognized the couple as fellow passengers on the plane on which he had arrived the previous night.

It was almost midnight when the taxi driver deposited him at a cabana a stone's throw from the bar, its proximity a definite selling point. The bar didn't have a name. In his mind, the absence of any visible signage only added to its appeal. It was a simple, open air kind of affair with a corrugated tin roof, a rough plank for a bar, and tables made of discarded wooden cable spools. The owner served up an excellent espresso and his croissants weren't half bad either. It was French Polynesia after all.

He had come to Tahiti at the suggestion of his agent who had called in a favor with someone at National Geographic. Write about the changes, his agent suggested. Write about whether it's still the paradise of Gauguin or just another tourist trap. And if you leave right away, you'll be there in time for France's last above ground nuclear test, he added. Leon had found it difficult to say no once the magazine offered him an advance on expenses. So here he was, jet lagged and without a plan beyond another espresso.

*"S'il vous plait,"* he said in an attempt to get the bartender's attention. *"Un autre café,"*

The bartender was a grizzled older guy with the chestnut complexion of someone who had lazed his life away under decades of tropical sun. His laid back vibe was accentuated by the fact he was bare-chested and wore only a pair of faded cargo shorts. A large tattoo of obvious geometric Polynesian design snaked down his one arm.

While Leon waited for his espresso, he surveyed the pier where a string of sailboats and cabin cruisers of various sizes bobbed languidly on the bay's calm waters. A throng of what appeared to be tourists were piling onto a large catamaran. The lunch cruise, he guessed- mid-morning Mai Tais, lobster salad and perhaps an afternoon snorkel. He briefly considered signing up for the sundown cruise and just as quickly rejected the idea. Then again, the article he planned on writing did require a tourist's critical perspective. Maybe he should reconsider.

As he stared into the middle distance, he noticed a figure separate itself from the clutch of tourists and began walking up the pier towards the bar. It was a woman. She appeared to be quite tall, her long limbs set off by a pair of very brief cutoff jeans. The rest of her ensemble consisted of an oversize aloha shirt and a baseball cap. She walked with a loose, bouncing stride that caught the attention of the fishermen unraveling a pile of fishing nets at the end of the pier. They watched with more than casual interest as she climbed the gangplank leading to the bar.

The image led him to recall something his mother had once said about there needing to be a law against a woman walking that way. His mother was a pearl clutcher in the presence of anything vaguely risqué or beyond the norm. She suffered the misfortune of four years of convent schooling, this in addition to teaching at that very same school for most of her adult life. How it was that such a milieu allowed his mother the time or the opportunity to spawn remained a mystery not unlike that of the Virgin Birth.

"*Bonjour, mademoiselle,*" the bartender greeted the woman as he placed the espresso at Leon's elbow. The bartender sounded no less effusive in his pleasure at seeing her than the fishermen on the pier.

"*Bon jour,* Henri," she replied, flipping her oversize sunglasses onto the bill of her cap. She had long black hair that she wore in a single thick plait.

"You will sail today?" Henri asked.

"*Oui,* but only around to Paparā. One of my crew says there is a nice little cove there," she said, slipping onto a stool a couple of places down from Leon. "Do you think we can get there by the middle of the afternoon? I wanted to leave earlier but my crew didn't show up on time."

Her accent sounded banally mid-western American with just enough of an understated drawl that might suggest somewhere further south, Oklahoma, perhaps.

"There is a pleasant breeze today. You should be able to arrive for the cocktail hour at the very latest. *Café?*"

"*Oui,* please."

She glanced at Leon and offered a quick smile. She appeared to be perhaps in her late twenties, early thirties at the most. There was something about her face that looked familiar. It may have been the eyes. He always remembered a woman's eyes. She had an intense, measuring quality to her stare. He took a quick mental inventory of faces and eyes and drew a blank linking anyone to the woman sitting on the stool. He wondered if she might have been on last night's flight from LA, but he would've remembered her.

"Henri, I was wondering if I could get a case of Hinano to take along," she asked.

"*Bien sûr, Mademoiselle* Lou Ann."

"You will put it on my tab, yes?"

Henri raised his hand in acknowledgement and disappeared into a back room.

She again glanced over at Leon and offered him another smile. Lou Ann. The name, the face, the voice tugged at his memory. In that instant, it came to him. Lou Ann Catskill, The singer.

"You're a long way from home," he said.

She shot him a quizzical look. "I'm not sure what you mean." Her voice sounded huskier than it sounded on her recordings. Her eyes, the color of agate, seemed paler than what he remembered from the magazine cover he had seen at some airport newsstand.

"You're Lou Ann Catskill, aren't you?"

She grunted and glanced away for a second before looking back. "Busted," she said, flipping her sunglasses back down. "Do I know you?"

"Unlikely. I recognized you from your picture. On the cover of the Rolling Stone," he crooned the refrain from Dr. Hook's ode to pop stardom. "It said you're the new queen of the blues."

She appeared a bit chagrined. "Hardly. I'm more like one of those ladies in waiting. Etta and Koko still reign."

The article in Rolling Stone had heralded her for winning a duo of Grammys, one for Best Female Jazz Vocal Performance, the other, Best Female R&B Vocal Performance.

She smiled, more openly this time. "That photo on the cover wasn't my best profile," she said, turning her face from side to side. "My face is a bit asymmetrical. This eye is higher. See?" she said, pointing at her right eye.

"The French have a term for that. *Un défaut* érotique."

"Something tells me that doesn't mean uneven eyes. Do you live here? I mean your French sounds pretty good, but I still detect something else. East Texas? Or maybe a touch of some Louisiana coon ass."

"Coon ass. I haven't been called that in a long time. You're pretty good with accents. I grew up in Lake Charles."

"I recognize accents because I tour so much. Sometimes I like to mimic local accents at my shows. I did a concert in Lake Charles a couple of years ago. I did this hurricane benefit. Did you happen to catch it?"

"Nope. I don't get back there very often. As far as the French goes, I learned it in the French Foreign Legion."

She snorted in amusement. "Now there's a line I've never heard before."

"And I never used it before either so you should feel honored. I'm Leon Riser," he said, leaning over and offering her his hand.

She hesitated for just a second before taking it. "So you never said why you're in Tahiti."

"Like you, I travel a lot."

"Let me guess. You're a Bible salesman."

"Close. I sell fables."

She arched her eyebrows. "What sort of fables?"

"I'm a travel writer. You could say I feed people's curiosity. Indulge their fantasies about far off places. And I get to embellish an awful lot along the way."

"I don't read much anymore, and when I do, it's only trashy romance novels. Believe it or not, it's where I come up with a lot of my best lyrics."

"I can only imagine."

Henri placed an espresso in front of her. She nodded her thanks and proceeded to empty the tiny cup in one swallow. "So, are you writing about Tahiti?" she asked.

"I am. I came out here to catch the explosion."

"The explosion?"

"*L'explosion nucléaire*," Henri interjected, setting the case of beer atop the bar. "The nuclear detonation. They say it will happen today. Or perhaps, tomorrow."

"I didn't hear about any nuclear explosion. Where? Nearby?"

No. At Moruroa Atoll. It is perhaps twelve hundred kilometers from Papeete. A safe distance, yes? Still, those *bâtards* in Paris will do their best to despoil our islands. "

"But you'll be able to see it?"

Henri shrugged. "Perhaps. If you look for it. Moruroa is to the southwest."

"That's terrible. These beautiful islands."

Henri grunted and returned to his cash register.

"Well, maybe I'll see you around," she said, hoisting the case of beer onto her hip. "If there's any around here left after the big fireworks." She offered him another smile and headed out the door.

He watched as she sauntered down the gangplank and onto the pier. About halfway across, she stopped, set the case of beer on the pier and hurried back to the bar.

"Would you like to come along?" she asked from the doorway. "It's not a big boat and there's no extra berth, but you can sleep on the deck. We'll be back the day after tomorrow," she added, sensing his mild hesitancy.

"Sure. But I have to warn you I'm used to traveling alone. And I like to read a lot when I'm on the road. So just assure me I'll have access to your library of trashy romance novels."

"Sure. I've got some really good ones. We leave in a half-hour. Slip nineteen," she shouted over her shoulder as she hurried away.

# 6

*"My heart is open to pain*
*Is that any different than closed to love?"*

-Lou Ann Catskill
Regrets

Either the sailboat's owner had a twisted sense of humor or didn't mind tempting fate. The words *Lost At Sea* were painted on the ship's stern in bold black italics. From his limited experience with sailboats, he estimated the trim, single-masted sloop to be in the thirty-two foot range. It wasn't the kind of boat he would ever consider boarding for a trans-oceanic sail, but he guessed it was perfect for cruising the islands. As he stood on the dock taking measure, Lou Ann emerged from the cabin carrying two small burlap sacks. She acknowledged him with a smile and a toss of her head.

"Can you grab this?" she asked, struggling with one of the bags. A couple of oranges and a pineapple tumbled onto the deck.

"Sure," he said, hopping aboard and hurriedly taking the bag. "I should have brought some food. This was all I could come up with. *Jugo de maguey*," he said, holding up a bottle of Patron tequila.

"Oh, *señor*. That will go nicely with the fish I hope we catch," she said, mimicking a Spanish accent.

As she began stuffing food into a large ice chest, a young man who looked obviously Polynesian emerged from the cabin's hatchway. He was short, muscular and wore a San Francisco Forty Niners T-shirt. Lou Ann turned and nodded her head in his direction.

"Hamuera, this is Leon. The friend I told you was coming along."

Hamuera gave a slight nod of his head before accepting Leon's outstretched hand.

"Leon speaks French. That will make it easier, yes?" she said.

"*Oui,*"Hamuera replied simply and began checking some gauges on dash of the bridge.

"So I rented this boat for a month. I wanted to decompress. Maybe even get some writing done. I didn't realize the boat came with a crew. You'll meet Afa in a minute. He ran up to talk to the dock master. You'll find him more engaging than Hamuera. From what I can tell they're experienced sailors. And they sleep on shore," she added. "Afa," she yelled, waving her arm at the young man strolling on the pier towards them. "Let's go."

Afa also looked Polynesian, well-muscled, but taller. He grinned broadly and took Leon's hand in both of his and said, "*Welina.*"

"*Mahalo,*" Leon replied.

"What the hell? Do you speak Tahitian, too?"

"I read the guide book on the flight over. You know, it had useful phrases like how much for the coconuts? Where's the restroom? And how much for the toilet paper? Stuff like that."

Lou Ann smiled and shook her head. "Beer?" she asked, opening the ice chest.

"Maybe later."

Without awaiting instruction, Afa quickly cast off the ropes and hopped on board just as the sailboat's engine belched to life. They puttered slowly away from the dock and out of the harbor before Hamuera turned the boat into the wind. Afa began releasing the lines on the mainsail, and once clear of the harbor released the boom and began yanking on the halyard. As the sail began to billow, he began maniacally cranking the winch to increase the sail's tension. Almost at once, the sailboat seemed to leap forward. A minute later, Hamuera clambered down from the bridge and joined Afa to help set the jib.

The receding shoreline with its ragged fringe of palms gave way to the corrugated lushness of thick forest that rose up the steep up-sloping terrain. The offshore winds had already formed a dense curtain of gray clouds that cloaked the summit of what Leon assumed to be Mount Orohena, the tallest peak in Tahiti. Looking to the west, he could just make out the iconic, cathedral-like silhouette of Mount Tohivea on the neighboring island of Moorea some twenty miles distant.

Leon glanced over at Lou Ann who had settled on the opposite bench after stripping down to a bikini. The intense morning sunlight allowed him a better appraisal of her features. She was small-breasted with broad shoulders that revealed evidence of recent sunburn. The occasional flash of white skin from beneath her bikini top and the splash of freckles across her nose both suggested she had a pale complexion beneath her hint of tan.

She removed her cap and undid her braid with a couple of flings of her head. As she turned her face into the wind, her long raven tresses swirled around her head like a nest of serpents. A smile of obvious pleasure crossed her face as she closed her eyes and tilted her head upwards into the sun. She remained like this for perhaps a minute before Leon broke the spell.

"So are you writing any music?"

She opened her eyes and looked at him. Her eyes now appeared a brilliant blue in the sunlight.

"Some. But this place is almost too laid back. And back in the world life was a little too crazy to write. It makes me realize that a little edge helps when I try to write about the shit that life throws at you."

"There's always the trashy romance novels."

"Speaking of." She leaned over and began rooting in a large canvas handbag at her feet. "Here," she said, tossing him a paperback. "You can keep it. I finished it."

"Was it helpful?" he asked, studying the cover. A busty young blonde was leaning into a hunky Latin looking guy with one of those two day, celebrity beards. He held the book up to his face and began to carefully flip through the pages.

"What are you looking for?"

"I'm looking for the parts you might've earmarked. Those will be the best parts, right?"

She laughed and then seemed to grow serious. "I thought that out here I would try making it without my pills. Back in the world, I needed to be on them. To balance out. I don't seem to need them out here though. It's a different vibe than back home."

He was curious about the pills, but he held back and instead asked "So where's home?"

"These days it's hotel rooms, mostly. I figured I would come here and just laze around on a sailboat. Let all those thoughts and stories percolate and it would just happen. I wouldn't have the pressure of my agent or a producer nagging me for something for the next album. And I'd just compose what I wanted. Am I telling you too much? I mean we've barely met."

"And?"

"And what? The songs? I guess the romance novels don't cut it anymore. They're too far a stretch from reality. Like I said, I think I need the real world to write. Not all of it, but some of it. I guess I can't write just feeling and imagining things vicariously. It has to be right in my face. I have to live it. Does that make sense?" When he didn't reply, she glanced up at the sails for a moment before looking back. "I take Lithium. You know what that is?"

"To treat bipolar, right?"

She looked away and shook her head. "I don't know why I'm telling you this," she said, looking back at him. "You're not going to put this in one of your books, are you?"

"Travels With Lou Ann. A Conflicted Siren. How's that sound for a title?"

"I'm serious. I've been burned before for revealing too much. You know, spilling my guts to some journalist with a pretty face and no scruples."

"Don't worry. I don't have a pretty face. As far as any scruples?" He shrugged. "Depends."

She looked at him with that measuring gaze for a moment before going on. "When I don't take the Lithium, I do things that I usually regret. I either want to burn down the house or never leave my bedroom. It's hard for people to understand when…"

"My mom took Lithium," he said, cutting her off. "Or at least she was supposed to." He couldn't help but smile at a memory. "She called it the bitter pill. And if she didn't take it… Well, I'll put it this way. Her helping me with my homework could get real interesting. My mom taught French and Spanish at this convent school in Lake Charles. When she was manic, she'd only speak to me in French"

"So that's where you learned French?"

"Yeah, but I didn't learn any really dirty words until I was in the Foreign Legion."

She shook her head in amusement and smiled. "I think I'm going to like you, Leon Riser. So tell me more about your mother."

"Her name was Antoinette. She was Cajun. My father was a shrimper. Or so I was told. I never got to know him. He left my mom when I was just a baby. For calmer seas, I imagine. In some ways, that manic part of her served her well. Here she was, this single mother working as a nurse's aide while putting herself through college. But there would always come a point when the tank was empty. And then…" His thoughts drifted off.

"I can relate," Lou Ann offered.

"All in all, she was quite a remarkable woman."

"Does she still teach?"

"She passed about five years ago. Her tank was empty, I guess. Heart gave out on her," he lied. There was no way he would tell Lou Ann about his mother's suicide.

"I'm sorry."

Neither of them spoke for a minute or two, their attention diverted by the tourist catamaran passing nearby. A number of the passengers hailed them and hoisted their Mai Tais.

"What about your family of origin?" he asked.

"Oil field trash. Oklahoma, mostly. Wyoming. My mother had some Comanche on her side. Dad was a mongrel in more ways than one. There's not much to tell. No French lessons that's for sure." She didn't add more and instead slipped down into the cabin. A minute or two later, she emerged carrying a couple of plastic cups and the bottle of Patron. "So, my Legionnaire friend. What do you say we get acquainted with the Mexican muse?" she said, hoisting the bottle.

# 7

*"This is no place for beginners*
*Or a tender heart,*
*But it's somewhere to start before it ends."*

- Lou Ann Catskill
Changes

They motored into the lagoon just in time for a late lunch. Only one other sailboat lie anchored at the far end. After dropping anchor in a shallow cove, Afa and Hamuera promptly disappeared ashore. Shortly afterwards, Lou Ann emerged from below bearing a tray of cheese, roast chicken and slices of mango.

"A girl's gotta eat," she said, opening an ice chest and removing a bottle of wine.

By this point they had done serious damage to the tequila, convincing Leon to pass on the proffered bottle of Chablis. Lou Ann, on the other hand, dumped a good part of the bottle into a large tumbler. Over lunch, she talked freely about music, both the art and the business. Leon recounted a recent trip to Bali, and talked about the book he was considering writing about a motorcycle trip across North Africa. Afterwards, they swam and walked the beach and talked about places each of them had visited or hoped to still visit.

After climbing back on board, Lou Ann excused herself and slipped into the cabin. Leon took the opportunity to rinse off with the hose on the aft deck and change into fresh shorts and a T-shirt. As he awaited her return, he picked up a pair of binoculars and scoped out the other sailboat. No one was visible. They pretty much had the cove to themselves.

Thick stands of palm surrounded most of the lagoon, though from the vantage of their anchorage, they were still able to view an expanse of the open ocean. The lagoon reminded him of an Impressionist painting he had once seen in Paris that depicted a pastoral pond, all greens and blues of every imaginable shade. The mental image of that painting and the feeling it engendered settled over him. He could understand why Gauguin found it difficult to leave Tahiti. Leon had yet to come across any bare-breasted *tahinis* in colorful *pareos*. However, Lou Ann in her brief bikini, proved more than an adequate complement to his South Seas fantasy.

Several minutes passed before Lou Ann emerged carrying a tray with two cups and a coffee carafe. Without saying a word, she poured them each a cup of strong black coffee. He passed on the cream while she poured an ungodly amount into her own cup. He was beginning to realize the concept of moderation had passed Lou Ann Catskill by.

He no sooner had taken his first sip when she opened a small wooden box that sat on the tray. She reached inside, and with a flourish, produced what appeared to be a hand-rolled joint,

"First day on board, I was rooting around in the galley and found this inside a tin of granola. I decided to save it for a special occasion. So I guess you're in luck, sailor."

She lighted it, took a long toke and passed it to Leon who nursed a couple of cautionary puffs before passing it back. He had long ago learned to test drive his marijuana. He recalled an almost amnesiac episode after sucking on a hookah of hash in the tent of a sheepherder in the Moroccan hinterlands. The next morning, he awoke in a confused fugue. When he finally stumbled from the empty tent, he was pleasantly surprised to find his motorcycle still parked beside the tent.

They sat in silence for a long time, each of them entertaining their senses with the spectacle of the growing shadows on the glassy lagoon.

After an uncertain amount of time passed, Lou Ann disappeared into the cabin again.

Leon's mind drifted from thoughts of his unfinished manuscript to reveries of similar evenings on a long ago sailing trip off the coast of Kenya, and then to a sudden memory of his mother. Other than the occasional passing thought, his brief recounting to Lou Ann of his mother's biography earlier that day had been the first time in a good while that he had reflected on her passing. He raked through the memory of her poorly attended funeral, and how afterwards, he had sorted through and discarded many of her possessions, most of which were of no material or personal value. The spare amount of furniture and household items were ones that he had given her over the years. His mother had lived in the small, hard-shingled bungalow beside the lake for three decades, yet there was nothing that provided even scant evidence of the previous inhabitant - no photographs, no letters or favorite books, not a saved high school track ribbon. Nothing remained to mark neither her life, nor his for that matter.

He was unaware of how long he sat there mulling over the jumble of these thoughts. Dusk in the tropics tended to fall quickly, and in what seemed only the span of several minutes, the lagoon had receded into deep shadow. After several more minutes had passed, Lou Ann emerged from the cabin carrying a guitar and a lantern. She had changed into white parachute pants and a red tube top. After lighting the lantern, she dropped back onto the bench and began brushing her wet hair.

The marijuana had heightened his senses, and he savored the resulting ambiance; the dark waters of the lagoon, the faint orange smudge of sunset, the night birds chattering in the nearby trees, and the smell of Lou Ann's shampoo on the breeze. It made him realize what a mistake it would've been to have remained behind in Papeete.

"Be honest. Who's your favorite girl singer?" she drawled, bringing him back.

"That sounds like a loaded question. I have to say I really liked that one song of yours about sleeping under the stars in the desert."

She pulled a face. "I never wrote a song like that," she snapped.

"Relax. I'm fucking with you. I do like your music. I like Mitchell a lot. Lennox. Ronstadt. I listen to a lot of the old jazz singers. But the truth be told, I travel so much I don't have the opportunity to listen to much music anymore."

She tossed the brush onto the table and fluffed her hair with her long fingers. Without a word, she picked up the guitar and began strumming. At first, there was just the merest hint of a melody before the tempo of the strumming coalesced into an obvious melody. She began to sing, and he remembered the distinctive timbre of the voice he had listened to on regrettably only a few occasions. It was a song about a lover spurned, an affair soured by guilt and obsession. She paused for a beat before repeating the final refrain.

"You say love fades

Fades in the wind

Fades in the tempest of our hearts

You always say love fades."

He applauded and she beamed. A faint yell of bravo and applause erupted from the sailboat at the far end of the lagoon. Leon picked up the binoculars again. In the dim light of the dusk, he could barely make out what looked to be a man and a woman perched on the bow.

"I'm still working on that one," she said. "Any requests?"

"No. Just play."

Again, a long, inexact amount of time passed as she sang of uncertain love, frenzied love, life on the road, and bittersweet separation before she finally set the guitar down. The lantern had long since dimmed to a mere flicker. Her eyes shifted and glistened in the reflection before finally settling on Leon. She stared at him for a moment, as if again taking careful measure, before getting to her feet.

"I'm going in. My berth is the one on the right. But give me a minute."

He did as instructed before finally stumbling through the dark cabin until he saw the glow of a cigarette in the darkness off to his right. He caught a whiff of marijuana as he waited for his eyes to adjust to the darkness. There appeared to be an open hatch over the bed that allowed just enough light from the night sky for him to see her stretched across the bed. .

"Come into my web said the spider to the fly," she murmured.

He could see she was nude. He undressed and then lay beside her on his back. She handed him the joint.

"No. I'm good."

She rose to her feet and stuck her head out of the open hatch. She took a final hit and flicked the joint into the darkness. In the light of the stars and the sickle of moon, he could just make out the curve of her hips, the length of her legs, and the tangle of her long hair. She bent and crouched over him, settling with her face inches from his, the nest of her hair blocking out the faint star light leaking from the overhead hatch.

"Let's make some music," she said quietly before lowering herself atop him, her arms and legs straddling his hips.

As her mouth found his, he reached up and touched her face, his fingers tracing her jaw, the notch below her throat, her breasts. Her flesh felt hot to the touch, and in that moment, he envisioned a whole new, unexplored country that lay beneath his fingertips; with wild savannahs to cross, the unexpected sanctuary of a desert oasis, and the tension that came with realizing one might become lost in these unknown expanses.

He started to lower his hand and she stopped him. He sensed some hesitancy before she slowly moved his hand between her legs. She shuddered as he caressed the hot, slick moistness of her. She rose to her knees, her arms pinning his to his side, and then lowered herself onto him with a violence that felt almost punishing. He pulled her down and took one of her breasts in his mouth. She made a small animal noise and shuddered, but hardly slowed the rhythm and force of her gyrations. Grabbing her buttocks, he guided her until her thrusts were synchronous with his own.

She came a moment before him in a rush of agonal gasps and trembling. He tried to pull her down onto his chest, but she continued to rock as if driven by some primal instinct.

"Whoa. Stop," he said finally.

Her fugue spent, she collapsed on the bed beside him. Neither of them spoke, the silence filled by their ragged breath.

"Is there a chorus to that song?" he asked, rolling onto his stomach.

"Give me a few minutes. Wait. What the hell is that?" she asked, pushing up.

He rolled over and opened his eyes. The berth was bathed in a glowing light coming from the rhomboid of the open hatch. He struggled to his feet and joined Lou Ann who stood peering out the hatch.

"Look," she said, pointing to the aperture of open sea.

A reddish-yellow half-globe of intense light rose pulsing from the otherwise dark horizon. One could easily confuse the glowing orb with the rising sun if not for the column of white light rising above its center. The reflection on the clouds on the horizon seemed all wrong, their crowns a bruised silver. At first, he thought he only imagined the dark, nebulous shadow above it all, its mass laced with jagged splinters of lightning.

"It's the nuclear test," he said. "It has to be."

They stood watching in silence as the light slowly faded to an ember on the far horizon. All the while, the lightning storm above it seemed to gain intensity.

"Jesus, Leon. Not likely we'll forget this any time soon," she murmured, slipping her arm around his waist.

For once, he was at a loss for words, disoriented by what he had just witnessed and the emotion it engendered.

"How come we can't hear it?" she asked.

"It's going to take a while since it's…. What did Henri say? Seven hundred miles away? I bet it'll take an hour at least. Maybe more."

"What about a tsunami? God, do we need to run for the hills?" she asked with obvious amusement.

"It might be smart. You should maybe pack some things."

"You're not serious, are you?"

"Let me ask you something. If you had only one hour to live, what would you do?"

She turned and looked at him. "I'd write a song," she said without hesitation.

"And if you couldn't?"

She thought for a brief moment. "You asked if there was a chorus to that song. I'd say we already laid the rhythm down pretty good. Let's go spend our last hour working on lyrics," she said, taking his hand and pulling him back down.

He awoke sometime in the night to a deep rumbling like thunder that lasted for perhaps a minute, in its wake there remained an eerie silence devoid of everything but the faint clattering of the palms. Lou Ann never stirred. The next morning he would vaguely recall that sometime during the night the boat had gently rocked back and forth.

# 8

*"On Saturdays you had me*
*By Sunday, I've gone*
*Only a voice on the radio*
*Come closer*
*Don't you hear the lyrics of regret?"*

It was mid-morning before they managed to leave Leon's cabin. Everything from the final negotiations, to the preparations and packing had been impromptu, and despite Fumiko's best efforts, supremely ill-organized.

Leon and Iris had happened upon each other in the kitchen at first light. Over coffee and leftover enchiladas, he informed her he had decided to accompany her.

"Come with me where?" she asked.

His rejoinder "I'll come along only so far," was met with grudging acceptance.

The uncertainty of their destination was matched with his ambivalence regarding the possibility of encountering Lou Ann. All he knew was he couldn't allow Iris to carry on without at least a modicum of his assistance. He had spent the better part of a sleepless night balancing obligation with curiosity, guilt, and his depleted reservoir of fervor for Lou Ann. By dawn, everything was clear as mud.

In the end, he agreed to accompany Iris as far as Santa Fe since that was Lou Ann's last known whereabouts. Before Iris could press him as to the reason he had changed his mind, Fumiko appeared in the kitchen dressed in her usual scrubs, a duffel bag slung over her shoulder, and clutching a large Tupperware crate. Without as much as a good morning, she placed a typewritten list next to Leon's coffee.

"This is a list of essential items we will require."

He picked up the sheaf of paper and studied it. "I don't see a selection of fine liquors or my edibles. How do you expect me to…"

She stopped him with a wave of her hand. "One bottle only. You must choose."

He took her omission regarding his medical cannabis as a capitulation on her part. The remainder of the morning was spent packing clothes, accessories, books and music, and along with their lunch, Fumiko's extensive medical kit and pharmacy. They decided to take Leon's 4Runner, for Iris's rental car would hardly accommodate the freight.

Iris drove while he and Fumiko took turns napping in the cluttered back seat. At the first occasion that Fumiko settled down for her nap, Iris wasted little time in inquiring as to why Leon had changed his mind about coming.

He rummaged around the back room of his mind for a suitable answer. "Obligation, mostly. To you, not so much to your mother. I still don't know what I can do. I guess if nothing else. I'll be your *consigliore*. But if you think we're going to do some kind of intervention with your mother, forget it. I've been down that rabbit hole with her before. It never works."

They both fell silent as Iris slowed at the sudden appearance of a highway patrol car in the rear view mirror. The cruiser, lights and sirens ablaze, passed them by and continued down the broad expanse of the San Luis Valley until the lights finally receded in the distance. A particularly heavy storm system had recently passed through the broad, flat valley leaving the craggy mountain peaks to the east cloaked in snow. The weak light leaking from the heavy cloud cover rendered the valley, the peaks, and the sky itself a uniform ice blue.

"I'm doing this because she's my mother," Iris said after a minute had passed. "And you say you're only here because you owe me. There has to be more to it than that."

Again, he didn't have an easy answer, at least one he was willing to share. "I know you've heard it before, but it's complicated," he said after a moment. "Maybe one of these days you'll understand. Once you get a few more relationships under your belt. You'll find there are relationships you can walk away from with only minor wounds and without much baggage. And then there'll be the ones where all the scars and the accompanying baggage still won't be enough to keep you from making the same mistakes. You'll go back and walk over the same hot coals." He paused again to gather his thoughts.

"You may think you know things about your mother and I. Well, I doubt that any history either of us might've shared ever really listed all our little skirmishes, and what I used to call the winter offensives that we both knew we're never going anywhere. We'd have these détentes, these treaties that got broken There'd be these times when one or both of us thought we'd won something. It was more about losing though. And in between, when things were working, there'd be this high. This blazing, fucking synergy."

He allowed his mind to drift back to a string of bittersweet memories before going on,

"She had this ability to pull me under. Sink or swim was how it felt. Have you ever been there, Iris? No?" he said when she merely looked at him. "You will." He looked at the snowy expanse of the valley and shook his head. "Shit," was all else he could manage to say.

Neither of them spoke for a couple of miles. "This may turn out to be a long road trip," she said finally. "Maybe this would be a good time to give me some history lessons,"

"Wake me when we hit Alamosa. We'll need gas and a piss stop," he said, reclining the seat and closing his eyes. He wasn't ready yet to recount anymore stories. Last night's reveries about Tahiti had left him raw and reticent to dwell in the past. Then again, the past was all he had. It surely wasn't the future. And the present was entirely too nebulous a construct to anchor him. He fell asleep, his thoughts lingering in the only place they could – the past.

# 9

*"The good doctors always tells me*
*Yes, there's hope for me*
*Just me though. Not us."*

-Lou Ann Catskill
Woman Down

## SANTA FE, NEW MEXICO
## APRIL 11, 2021

It was late afternoon before they pulled up to the entrance of The Inn at Loretto. Their progress had been hampered by a freak spring snow storm just north of Tres Piedras that had sent an eighteen wheeler into the bar ditch. Despite Leon's admonitions regarding the hazardous road conditions and the reputation of New Mexico state cops, Iris had driven with sufficient zeal to keep them just ahead of the looming storm system.

The hotel, a cake-layer affair in a style the locals referred to as Pueblo Revival, had in the old days been her mother's favorite retreat whenever visiting Santa Fe. Iris had stayed there with her mother on several occasions. She still had memories of sitting in front of the fireplace in the bar and people watching while her mother stared out the window in obvious distraction.

Soon after crossing the border into New Mexico, Iris had called the hotel for reservations. Apparently, the nearby state legislature was in emergency session resulting in a scarcity of available rooms. The receptionist at first had difficulty finding three rooms. Fumiko finally chimed in from the back seat that she didn't mind sharing a room with Iris. Iris purposefully avoided looking at Leon, sensing his knowing leer.

After checking in, Leon announced he was tired and instructed them to awaken him for dinner. Iris wasted no time in dropping her bags in the room before informing Fumiko that she had some business to intend to and would be back in time for dinner.

*

The home her mother shared with Kevin Riordan sat snug up against the slope of Atalaya Mountain in a small gated community on the city's fashionable east side. She had decided not to tell Leon where she was going, confident that Kevin, being the insecure male that he was, would feel intimidated by Leon, and as a result, less than forthcoming with any information. Kevin had been an on and off again fixture in her mother's life for as long as Iris could remember, first as her mother's manager, then the occasional drop in providing unwanted advice about Lou Ann's career, and finally as her husband. Iris had never developed anything remotely resembling a superficially cordial relationship with him. Nevertheless, this antipathy had always managed to engender a brutal honesty between them. She was counting on that to find out if Kevin knew anything about where her mother might have gone.

Since her mother's marriage to Kevin two years ago, their interactions had been relegated to the unexpected and hurried nuptials and the handful of times Iris had visited her mother in Santa Fe. For her mother's sake, Iris struggled to maintain a façade of equanimity, but her dealings with Kevin had grown increasingly less comfortable, and even threatened to fracture her tenuous relationship with her mother. On one occasion, Iris had berated Kevin over his attempts to meddle and micromanage her mother's career. To Iris's surprise, Lou Ann had come to Kevin's defense, further deepening Iris's mistrust.

One night after Lou Ann had been drinking, and in a fit of spite, she revealed more than she probably intended about Kevin's past and present business dealings. She related the rumors that the seed money for Kevin's seemingly successful real estate business had come from a money laundering scheme involving a condominium development in Acapulco. She also hinted at an indictment for extortion in his hometown of Atlanta that had been subsequently dismissed when the plaintiffs backed out. Then there was a fraud allegation made against him in Santa Fe over a failed real estate transaction. However, Lou Ann insisted that Kevin was nothing more than an unwitting pawn in the machinations of his business partners. But with each listing of these supposed transgressions, Lou Ann grew more and more agitated, lending support to Iris's suspicions that all was not well in their marriage.

It was near dusk when she arrived at the enclave's ornate metal gate. The approaching storm was already whipping up a few light, windblown snow flurries, and the dark bank of clouds spilling over the ridge tops promised the weather would only grow worse. She started to punch in the security code at the entry box and then hesitated, remembering that Kevin wasn't the type who liked surprises. To hell with him, she thought, steeling herself to face his expected obfuscations. In the end, she decided showing up unannounced might prove more productive.

She tossed her concerns aside and entered in the entry code to open the gate. The house, a four thousand foot sprawl of muddy brown faux adobe, sat at the end of a dirt track nestled into a stony alcove hemmed in by a steep slope and thick pine. With the exception of the room she knew to be the den, the house looked dark. Even the walkway lights leading to the partially enclosed portal were dark.

Pulling up behind Kevin's Mercedes, she got out and made her way to the door. She rang the door ball and waited. The wind carried the faint smell of *piñon* smoke, indicating Kevin was likely home. She started to ring the doorbell again when suddenly the front door flung open, revealing Kevin standing in the semi-darkness. Even in the dim light, Iris could see the handgun he held loosely at his side.

He made no effort to invite her in, but instead craned his neck to look past her. "What are you doing here?" he asked in his soft Georgia drawl.

"Are you going to invite me in or not?"

He seemed to hesitate before turning and walking off, leaving her to usher herself inside. He paused in the hallway long enough to place the handgun on a buffet table, replacing it with a tumbler of what she assumed would be bourbon, his drink of choice. She unzipped her jacket and followed him into the den.

A large kiva fireplace dominated one side of the room, its flames and a small table lamp providing the room's only illumination. Her mother had always felt the room appeared overly decorated in what she called Santa Fe schlock, referring to the over abundance of Native American rugs and the generic Southwestern paintings depicting pastel buttes and Technicolor coyotes. Kevin switched on another table lamp and dropped into a leather recliner.

"Bar's open," he mumbled, nodding at a table that held an array of liquor bottles.

He was barefoot and wore a rumpled tracksuit with the Atlanta Falcons logo. It was obvious he had shirked his usual vanity, for his stylishly coiffed black hair was uncombed. It was also obvious he hadn't shaved in a couple of days, nor bathed gauging from his sour body odor. His eyes and his carefully sculpted face appeared puffy. Her own tastes and orientation aside, she had to admit Kevin Riordan was an attractive man, in spite of his disheveled appearance. His dark complexion and full lips lent him a certain sensuous appeal. Had that been Lou Ann's only attraction? Knowing her mother, there had to be more to it than the pleasures of the flesh. The allure of another bad boy seemed the most likely explanation.

She eyed the liquor selection before looking back at him. "What's with the gun?" she asked.

He held his drink to his mouth a moment before swallowing. He studied her for a moment before carefully placing his glass on the side table. "Didn't I tell you I would call if I heard from her?" His voice sounded slurred.

"That was two days ago. I've tried calling you."

His heavy, lidded eyes shifted away to the table of liquor before looking back at her.

"The cops called this morning. They found a woman's body out on the mesa by Grants."

He always had this way of smiling whenever he said something unpleasant, and now was no exception. Iris looked away, struggling to maintain her composure. She finally allowed herself to slump down onto the sofa.

"Burned beyond recognition," he added, seemingly indifferent to her reaction. "They're checking Lou Ann's dental records. I wasn't going to call you until I knew something." He drew his lower lip between his teeth and screwed up his face. "I don't think I'd jump to any conclusions though. Not until…"

"Goddammit, Kevin! Where is she?"

He stared at her, rehearsing his smile. "Like I told you, honey," he said in an exaggerated Georgia drawl. "Your momma comes and goes. Sometimes she doesn't want to be found. You oughta know that by now. I just have to give her credit for finally getting out of bed."

They both eyed each other for a long uncomfortable moment before he grunted something unintelligible and lighted a cigarette. He took a long drag and studied the spirals of smoke leaking through his fingers. "She left me a note," he said through a mouthful of smoke. "She listed all my high crimes and misdemeanors and said she was leaving."

"A note? And she didn't say where she was going?"

"And what would be the point of her telling me where she was going? I told you. She doesn't want to be found."

"If she left you, why did you report her as missing?"

He shrugged. "Out of pride, I guess."

"Where's this note? Did you show it to the police?"

He looked at her and laughed. "What do you think?"

"May I see it?"

He offered her a poisonous smile, and then picked up this glass from the side table and pushed to his feet. He lurched over to the liquor table and poured himself another tumbler full of brown liquor. After taking a long swallow, he made his way over to a desk and opened a drawer. With a flourish, he removed a piece of folded paper and shuffled over to the fireplace. He studied the paper for a few seconds before balling it up and tossing it into the fire.

"You bastard."

He turned and looked at her. "Guilty as charged. It was private. The note. For my eyes only."

Iris held herself in check, knowing there was little use in engaging him in open warfare. She glared at him for a moment longer before getting to her feet and zipping up her jacket.

"I don't know why you have to be such an asshole. Then again, you've always been an asshole."

Kevin dropped back into his chair and nodded vaguely. "You know I've known your mother longer than you have. At least, I thought I knew her. You know when we got married, I couldn't shake the feeling that it was like she was just changing the linens. Or trading in her car for the latest model. I should've known that."

In that moment, she almost felt sorry for him for he was right. Lou Ann never had any intention of making her marriage work. It was always her modus operandi after all.

"You'll call me when they know something? About the body they found?" she added as she turned to leave.

"Wait," he said, stumbling to his feet and reaching for her but missing. "I need to give you something." He pushed past her and disappeared down the hallway. A minute or so later, he came back carrying a clear plastic grocery bag. "If you find her, she might need these," he said, tossing her the bag. "Your mother's little helpers," he said with a smirk.

Iris could see the bag held a half-dozen or so small brown plastic bottles, the kind that held prescription drugs, "She didn't take any of these with her?"

"Hell, she's probably has enough of that shit in her system to last a year. Maybe you can use them," he added with the same inappropriate smile. "You know, like mother, like daughter."

"Fuck you," she said softly, and started for the door.

"There's something else you should know. She took off with some guy. He never offered up a name, but I'm pretty sure it was Sudd Kiehne, her old drug dealer."

She turned and glared at him. It took every bit of her self-control not to deck him.

"Yeah, Sudd kept calling for her. He called the day she took off." He stepped toward her and placed his hand on her shoulder. "You know you and I haven't been all that close. I guess what I'm trying to say is don't be a stranger."

She grabbed his hand and shoved it away. "Call me when you hear from the cops. After that, I don't want to ever hear from you again. Clear enough?" She turned and walked out the door.

It had started to spit a few small pellets of what people in these parts referred to as popcorn snow. She hurried to the 4Runner, and after crawling behind the wheel, turned on the ignition. She took a moment to fiddle with the heater controls and turned on the windshield wipers. As she waited for the heater to kick in, she remembered the bag of medications she held in her lap. She flicked on the overhead light and emptied the bag onto the passenger seat. She picked them up one by one, squinting at the labels. Lamictal, Ambien, Seroquel, Adderall, Lithium, Trazodone , and a smaller bottle with a piece of paper taped to it in place of a label. She struggled to read what it said, but it was too faded to read.

"Jesus, Mom."

She began to return the bottles back into the bag when noticed the blister pack in the bottom. She held it to the light. The pack contained perhaps a half-dozen or so small white tablets, She struggled to read the label. Dexedrine. She hesitated for a moment before punching out one of the Dexedrine tablets and dry swallowing it. Reaching into the bag, she searched out the bottle of Trazodone.

"What the hell?" she muttered as she secreted the bottle in the pocket of her jacket. She sat there a moment longer before stuffing the bag under the seat, and then backed out of the drive.

# 10

*"Please, convince me*
*To work this love*
*To want it, desire it.*
*Convince me.*
*Why is that so hard?"*

-Lou Ann Catskill
The Uneven Surface of My Soul

While Fumiko was showering, Leon had left them a message saying he would wait for the two of them in the bar. By the time Fumiko had dressed, Iris still hadn't returned, so she decided not to wait and instead try to intercept Leon in the bar before too much self-inflicted damage was done.

She paused at the entranceway for a moment, scanning the crowded lounge. To her surprise the place was decorated in a tasteful, minimalist style; dark leather furniture and mostly bare, white alabaster walls. A massive reproduction of a ram's skull loomed over the blazing fireplace. She couldn't help but notice the ceiling that was made up of panels of intricately cut, raised and painted wood overlays. The ceiling and the relative austerity of the setting reminded her of the interior of a bathhouse outside of Osaka that she had often visited.

The lounge bustled with conversation and boisterous laughter, its denizens mostly men. She spotted only a handful of women scattered among them. A political crowd, she guessed, remembering the receptionist's mention that the state legislature was in special session. A group of mostly older men had taken over the cluster of leather sofas in front of the fireplace. None of them, she noted, wore masks. Upon arriving at the hotel, she had seen the sign posted at the entrance to the hotel stating that even though masks were no longer mandated, the hotel still recommended social distancing and masks whenever possible. So much for public health precautions, she decided.

She spotted Leon slumped on a sofa by himself in the rear of the lounge. He failed to notice her entry, his attention focused on the snow streaked windows. She had seen him preoccupied before, but not to the degree since Iris had arrived. It wasn't difficult to guess what he was pondering. Prior to yesterday, he had never once mentioned the name Lou Ann Catskill. It was a chapter of his life that she assumed he deemed off limits. Not that she was totally unaware of the fact that Leon and Lou Ann had lived together for six years, and from all other accounts, that they had been somewhat involved in each other's lives for much longer than that.

Before agreeing to take the position as his nurse, she had taken the time to Google him. Her research also led her to Lou Ann. From what Fumiko could ascertain, the nature of their relationship had been tempestuous, and thus explained his obvious reticence to discuss her. From what she knew of Leon, she had difficulty reconciling the attraction between the volatile diva and the reclusive writer of travelogues.

During the drive to Santa Fe, she questioned her motives for agreeing to accompany Leon and Iris. It was partly out of what she felt to be contractual and professional obligation. She could have predicted Leon would decide to go with Iris, and realized that at that point she had little choice but to accompany them. Not only would her absence disrupt Leon's treatment regimen, but any fallout due to complications would fall on her head.

It had proven difficult enough to convince the oncologist in Denver to agree to their unusual arrangement. However, Leon was headstrong, and in the end, threatened to simply discontinue treatment unless he got his way. And now Fumiko knew it would be highly irresponsible on her part if she abandoned him now. She also realized that it made little difference if she administered the medication at the cabin or in some hotel room. Besides, she had the oncologist on her speed dial.

But there was a whole other reason that she wanted to come along, and that was merely because of simple boredom. She had been naïve when envisioning what her life would be like living for three or four months in an isolated cabin in the middle of a Colorado winter with only Leon and spotty satellite television for company. Her life at the cabin was in sharp contrast to her previous life in Denver. There she had friends, her dance class, her professional relationships, and access to all the distractions of a large city. She had exchanged that existence for the day after day routine of living in the wintery isolation of the mountains. If the truth be told, she actually welcomed Iris's intrusion for it dangled the prospect of experiencing something of the world beyond the cabin.

She had to admit that, Leon's mood swings and disabilities aside, he had proved to be at times a lively conversationalist who could expound on almost any subject. With time and his clinical improvement, these interludes became more frequent. In spite of her utmost efforts to maintain a professional distance, she had grown fond of him, although she did her best to project nothing but professional concern for his well being.

She had tried her best to bolster his spirits, to aid him in achieving what in her culture was referred to as *ikigai* or purpose in life. At times, it seemed her efforts were successful, at other times nothing seemed to breach his melancholia. Leon remained a work in progress, and thus a challenge to her personally and professionally.

As she stood there watching him from across the crowded bar, she noticed several of the male patrons standing at the bar had turned to scrutinize her. She had exchanged her scrubs for a pair of tight, boot cut black jeans, red Western boots, and a gold cashmere sweater, her ensemble topped off with a black silk face mask embroidered with a small red chrysanthemum. She had gathered her long black hair in a ponytail.

She was used to men's open appraisal. It always engendered the kind of self-conscious awareness only attractive women would ever admit to experiencing. She would be the first to admit to a sense of guilty pleasure in knowing the men's eyes were tracking her every move as she weaved through the tables. As she approached Leon, he turned and gave her the once over and frowned.

"Why is it that I never get this look?"

"Perhaps, you should wear something besides those filthy flannel uniforms and I might honor you with something other than my scrubs," she replied, slipping off her mask and dropping down onto the sofa. Leon grimaced as he scooted to the side to make room for her.

He admired her for another moment longer before tilting back his martini glass. "So where's Iris?"

"She has not returned from her errand. Is that your first?" she asked, pointing at his glass.

"She didn't say anything to me about any errand," he replied, ignoring her question. He raised the empty glass and waved it in the direction of the bar, the effort obviously causing him some discomfort.

"I know nothing of where she went. Have you taken anything for your pain?" she asked, noticing him shifting uncomfortably.

"For now it's just juniper juice, not that it's helping all that much." He winced as he stretched his back. "It's that same little gremlin with the ice ax who wants to drive a piton in my spine."

"I could go to your room and get you something," she said just as the waitress, a stout young woman in a black pantsuit and matching mask approached the table.

"A glass of white wine, please. A Chardonnay if you have," Fumiko said, smiling up at her.

Leon handed his empty glass to the waitress to signal a refill. "She went to see Riordan, didn't she?" he asked, turning back.

"I cannot blame her for wanting to spare you the aggravation of having to speak to this Riordan person." She pronounced the name Reedon. Like many Japanese, Fumiko had some difficulty always pronouncing the letter R correctly.

"No, she's just the same stubborn and headstrong little shit she's always been."

Fumiko couldn't help but smile. "I find Iris to be an interesting young woman. Please, tell me about her."

Leon started to say something, hesitated, and started over. "You have to realize she didn't have much of a childhood in the conventional sense. Lou Ann used to take her along with her on the road. She'd have these gypsy nannies that would come and go. Sometimes Lou Ann would just leave Iris back at the hotel with some roadie to keep an eye on her. Her father... her biological father that is, was never in the picture. To this day, I don't know for sure who Iris's father is. Lou Ann would never say, although she did deign to inform me on more than one occasion that Iris wasn't mine," he added with obvious bitterness.

"When Lou Ann and I got back together, Iris had just turned twelve. Hormonal storm and a lifetime of living with Lou Ann as a role model didn't make for a well adjusted adolescent. But I did my best. Like I said, she was headstrong... wild. By the time she was fourteen, she already had her share of vices." He paused as the waitress brought their drinks.

"She had this pretty skewed world view that called for some major therapy. Instead, I did what I do best. I took her traveling with me. Places like Bali. Mexico. Spain. I tried to show her the world was more than just a reflection of how you see it. It is what you make of it. That's what I wanted to teach her. I'm sermonizing, aren't I?"

Fumiko gave a noncommittal shrug. "And? Did it make her see the world differently?"

"I thought it did. Then it fell apart again when Lou Ann and I split up. Iris blamed me. She thought I had walked out on her. On both of them. We've become estranged, for lack of a better word. To be honest, and to my great regret, I really don't know who she is anymore."

"Nevertheless, I can see the two of you are very close."

He nodded. "Yeah, we were close." He took a sip of his a martini. "You know she's gay?"

Fumiko nodded. "I assumed as much. You are surprised? I am more worldly than you might think, Leon Riser."

"Meaning?"

Fumiko shook her head. Even after three months of almost constant companionship, she wasn't prepared to share any intimate details about her life. "You do not give me enough credit. It is my duty to understand people. Or in your case, to at least attempt to," she added with a smile.

"Speak of the devil," he said, nodding with his chin.

Iris stood in the entranceway speaking to the waitress. Fumiko waved to get her attention. Iris waved back and weaved through the throng of men at the bar. She seemed to generate the same amount of attention that Fumiko had received earlier.

"Hey," she greeted them, slipping out of her jacket.

She swiped at her red nose and sniffled. Her eyes seemed to blaze with an intensity Fumiko couldn't help but notice. She might be wrong, but from what she could tell, Iris's pupils appeared dilated.

"What are we drinking?" Iris asked, dropping into an armchair. "I already ordered myself a tequila." She turned and gave the lounge the once over.

"You went to see Riordan, didn't you?" Leon asked, not bothering to wait for her to offer an explanation of where she had been.

"So what? He wasn't going to talk to you," she replied with perhaps more edge than she intended, for she quickly grinned at Leon. "He wasn't much help anyway. All he said was that the cops found a woman's body out by someplace called Grants," she said with what seemed an inappropriate smile. "He wants me to think Mom is dead out in the desert somewhere. It isn't her though. Couldn't be. Mom would never end up going out like that. Right, Leon?"

Fumiko and Leon exchanged glances.

"He said they found a body? And they're not sure if it's her or not?" Leon asked, sliding his gaze back to Iris.

"They're checking dental records, but… " Iris choked back her tears.

"Look, you're probably right. It's not her," Leon said, leaning across the coffee table and taking her hand. "So? That's all he knew?"

"He said she might've gone off with some guy named Sudd."

"Holy crap," he muttered.

"Kevin is a useless asshole. She never should've married that creep. Nothing would make me happier than to know she walked out on him, And I would never let her go back to him. I mean…"

"For god's sake, Iris. Take a breath and slow down."

She shot him a look of confusion. "You're right. We don't need his help. We'll find her."

The waitress brought over Iris's tequila. Without waiting for the waitress, she snatched the shot glass off the tray. "*Salud*," she muttered and wasted no time in downing it. She set the empty glass back on the tray. "I'll have another, please."

Fumiko took a sip of her wine as she studied Iris. Her pupils were definitely dilated. Her agitation, the rapid speech was all it took to convince Fumiko Iris was high on something. A memory of the Tokyo years rose in Fumiko's mind. Days and nights when she and her friends would stay up for endless hours snorting and gulping pills and listening to techno music and playing Pokémon. She also remembered crashing and burning.

"Perhaps we should eat something," Fumiko said with a side glance in Leon's direction.

"You know, I'm not hungry anymore," he said. "I think I'll just go upstairs and crash. You girls are on your own."

"No way, Leon," Iris said. "You promised me a history lesson. I want one of your best stories about you and Mom," she pleaded, her voice slurred. Iris turned to Fumiko. "You know the only story about them I ever heard him tell was how they met on that sailboat in Tahiti. Mom told me once the whole blow by blow. No pun intended," she added with a grin.

"Yeah, I'd give anything to hear that version," he said as he glanced around the bar. "But maybe some other time."

"Please," Fumiko said, surprising herself. "You are always such a wonderful storyteller. But it must be a happy story," she added when she saw him look away. She felt a sudden twinge of shame that quickly gave way to her over abiding inquisitiveness. For once, she wanted Leon to expose himself. She wanted to know Leon Riser. She waved at the waitress for a refill.

# 11

*"Dance me round the fire*
*See me canter and twirl*
*See the color of my soul*
*Or isn't that enough?"*

-Lou Ann Catskill
The Siren's Refrain

"Leon."

He looked at each of them in turn. Iris offered him a look of bleary expectation while Fumiko merely stared at him in her usual unfathomable manner. Iris took his hand and leaned in towards him. The intensity in her eyes led him to hesitate before giving into some amorphous sense of longing. It was as if he were once again losing himself in Lou Ann's eyes; the desperation of her gaze reflected in the mirror of his memory.

The bar chatter seemed to have lessened, allowing him to hear a faint melody of a woman singing. He recognized the tune. 'These Foolish Things' by Dinah Washington. He cocked his head to listen. He felt light-headed. Maybe it was the two martinis. Or perhaps it was the tab of hydrocodone that he popped just before Fumiko had arrived. Or maybe it was merely the buzz he felt just being out of the cage he had become accustomed to these past few months.

"Come on, Leon. Give us a story," Iris pleaded.

He grimaced. Why the hell not, he thought. Go ahead and lance the wound. Isn't that what this whole misguided journey was really about?

"So your mom told you about Tahiti," he said almost to himself. He cleared his throat before going on. "We spent two weeks on that sailboat getting to know one another. The truth is I'm not sure I really knew a whole lot more about her afterwards than the day we first met. I admit to knowing every nook and cranny of her body. I found out she liked to swim nude in the mornings. I learned how she liked her coffee. How she liked her eggs. But I'm not sure I really knew anything about the real Lou Ann. No back story and only the sketchiest of innermost thoughts. It seemed the more time we spent together; the less forthcoming she was. But, she'd sing. That's all she offered up. Her songs."

He looked up blankly at the waitress as she brought another round of drinks. It would've been too easy to rehash the story about Tahiti. But if Iris really wanted to know their history, she would have to know her mother in the years that he had first come to know her. The years he spent winking at the tiger as a Burmese friend once described his own misspent youth.

Now he wondered if he was really up to the task of expounding on that time. He took a slurp of his martini in the hope it might ground him before his soliloquy.

"After Tahiti, I didn't see her for six… seven months. I wrote her a couple of long letters that I recall being these sorry ass mournful expositions that I indulged myself in back in those days. She never answered them. I figured she had written me off." He tilted back the remainder of the martini before continuing. "And then one day I happened to be in San Francisco for a book signing. I saw this handbill that said she was playing in LA at the Greek Theater that very night. So I caught a flight figuring I'd make it there in time for the show. Well, for whatever reason, weather or something, the plane was late getting off the ground. So I get into LAX late and I ask this cabbie to break every law he felt comfortable with. So as I'm sitting in the cab in this crappy LA traffic, I start second guessing myself. Wondering why she blew me off. You have to realize I was sort of a fool for women back then. Up to that point love had cast a cold eye on all my romantic endeavors. But I figured. I'd either score or I wouldn't. So, I walk in just as the show was ending. And I catch one last song."

# 12

*"These seven long nights*
*I wake to the song of your sleep*
*I wake to the tide of your breath*
*And I wish the dawn would never come."*

-Lou Ann Catskill
Hoping the Dawn Never Comes

**LOS ANGELES**

**JULY, 1996**

He slipped the cabbie a hundred and hustled up the steps to the amphitheater's entrance. No one was manning the gates. No one seemed to be leaving the concert yet either. He could hear the audience chanting for an encore. He pushed past a throng of spectators standing behind the last row of seats and edged his way to an aisle. The amphitheater lay in darkness except for the stage which was spotlighted in cones of wavering blue light. The crowd continued their chant, their chorus now punctuated by whistles and rhythmic applause.

"Lou Ann. Lou Ann," a couple of women behind him shouted over and over.

A cheer erupted as two men began wheeling a piano onto the stage. Someone sailed a seat cushion onto the stage and the chanting grew louder as a couple of guys clutching guitars strolled onto the stage. A moment later, a roar erupted from the audience as Lou Ann emerged from the shadows at the edge of the stage, followed by a couple more musicians, one of them carrying a saxophone.

She wore a pair of skintight black leather pants and a flowing white blouse. Her hair was braided in one long strand that reached to her waist. She stood there a moment in the spotlight, arms outstretched, basking in the adulation before turning and sweeping her arms in the direction of her band. The crowd cheered, the volume of their cries only growing louder as Lou Ann walked over and sat at the piano. She waited a moment for the audience to settle before leaning into the microphone.

"Thank you LA," she shouted to more raucous applause. She waited for it to die down before going on. "I'm going to play something from my new album. The album is called Seven Nights, Seven Dreams. I wrote this one particular song earlier this year during a break I took. I really needed that time off," she added with a smile. "It's called Hoping the Dawn Never Comes." Someone in the audience yelled something and a few others in the crowd whistled. "I hope you like it," she said as he began to almost absently stroke the piano keys.

The melody, at first tentative, took shape, the tempo gradually rising and then falling before her voice broke in with its familiar timbre. A contralto on steroids is how a Rolling Stone journalist had once described her voice.

"These seven long nights," she began before pausing a beat before breaking into the rest of the chorus.

"I wake to the song of your sleep.

I wake to the tide of your breath.

Hoping the dawn never comes"

And then the saxophone came in, its wail almost drowning out the whistles and cheering. A second later a spotlight revealed the saxophonist, a wiry, Latin-looking kid in a sleeveless T-shirt.

Leon started down the aisle, his eyes never leaving the stage. A scrum of exuberant fans had crowded in front of the stage, elbowing the few security guards trying to hold them back. He pushed his way through until his progress was impeded by a low metal barrier. One of the security guys was engaged in what looked like mortal combat with a young woman who had one leg straddling the barrier. The woman had a pink shag of hair and wore a beaded and fringed leather jacket, and from what Leon could tell, little else.

"Oh, and I wish the dawn would never come," Lou Ann sang before breaking into an exuberant chorus about another long night. The audience roared their approval. A young woman beside Leon began dancing, her wild gyrations so infectious that several other people nearby began joining in.

As Lou Ann ended the chorus, her eyes swept over the wildly exuberant audience with obvious glee. She saw him then, or at least he thought she had, for she appeared momentarily confused before breaking into a smile and a shake of her head. She held his gaze for what seemed an indeterminable amount of time before she broke into the last chorus.

She ended the song with a dramatic swipe of the keyboard before leaping to her feet and blowing kisses to the crowd. She took a long deep bow and began to edge her way off the stage, but not before once more meeting Leon's eyes. She waved to the crowd for one final time and paused at the curtain's edge where a tall black man handed her a plastic water bottle. She appeared to lean into the man's ear and then pointed in Leon's direction. The man nodded and looked at Leon as Lou Ann slipped out of sight. Leon stood there a while, taking in the crowd. He suddenly felt a tap on his shoulder and turned to find the black guy at his elbow.

"Mistah Riser," he yelled in his ear. "You com wid me, mon." He took Leon's arm and pulled him through the crowd.

He led Leon past a couple of security guards and up some stairs and through a throng of what appeared to be crew and production people. Lou Ann was nowhere to be seen. It wasn't until they stopped in front of an elevator that the black guy finally released Leon's arm.

"Boss say you get highball treatment," he said, turning and smiling at Leon.

The accent was Jamaican for sure, Leon thought as he took the opportunity to study the man. The loose fitting *guayabera* the man wore failed to hide a coiled physicality. His shaved head shined in the fluorescent lights that rendered his complexion a shade lighter than a tobacco leaf. He had the open, agreeable face of a salesman and the intense gaze of a first closer.

"Are you her security?" Leon asked for lack of anything else to say.

The Jamaican guy gave him a look of amusement as the elevator door opened. He punched the button for the basement. "I am boss lady's manager. One of 'dem."

"One of them? So how many managers does Lou Ann have?"

"Boss requires a lot of management."

"I can only imagine. What do I call you?"

"I am Jimmy. Jimmy the manager," he said with a grin.

The elevator door opened to a small parking garage. Jimmy nodded for Leon to follow. He stopped beside a vintage black Mercedes, then opened the passenger door and popped the glove compartment. After a few seconds of rummaging through it, he pulled out what appeared to be a small brown envelope.

"Follow me, mon," he said, leading Leon out a garage exit that opened to a small parking area where a large tour bus sat parked. As they walked towards it, Jimmy handed him the envelope and offered him a broad smile. "Boss say you nevah come empty handed," he said and turned and walked back to the garage.

Leon hesitated a moment and approached the bus. He was almost to the door when it abruptly swung open. The interior light revealed a man with a long white beard and wearing a baseball cap slouched behind the steering wheel reading a magazine. As Leon began to step up, a couple of young women pushed past him, cackling like hens, their words unintelligible. He waited to let them pass before climbing on board. The driver acknowledged him with a slight nod and returned to his magazine.

Leon started down the dimly lit aisle to the rear of the bus. None of the seats appeared occupied with the exception of one row taken up by a couple of indeterminate gender who were ravenously dining on each other's face, their bodies cocooned in a sleeping bag. At the rear of the bus, he brushed aside a curtain to reveal a closed door. He could hear a man and woman's voices on the other side. He hesitated, and then knocked on the door, and a few second later the door flew open.

"Yeah? What do you want?" the man standing in the doorway yelled.

Leon could tell from the man's expression that Leon wasn't who he might have been expecting. Leon craned his neck and looked past him and saw Lou Ann wriggling into a pair of blue jeans. She wore nothing on top but a red lace bra.

"Dammit, Leon. You caught me with my pants down," she shrieked in mock embarrassment. She rushed over to him, shoving the man in the doorway aside. "Get in here," she said, pulling him into the room. She gave him a kiss on each cheek. *"Mon amour. C'est si..."* she stumbled for the words. *"si beau... de te revoir."* She laughed. "I tried to learn some French in case I ever saw you again. How did I do?"

*"Tres bien. Alors que pouvez-vous dire déautre?"*

"Don't be a shit and embarrass me," she said, buttoning her jeans. She clapped her hands and grinned, her eyes locked on his. "Sudd, hand me that blouse from behind the door."

The man grunted in annoyance and grabbed a silky red blouse off a hanger and handed it to Lou Ann.

"Leon, this is Sudd," she said, slipping on the blouse. "He was just going. Weren't you, Sudd?" she added when Sudd made no effort to leave.

Sudd's face stiffened and he sneered at Leon. He was a short wiry guy with a springy violent shock of black hair and sideburns that resembled commas. He had dark half-lidded eyes, groomed eyebrows and the kind of a handsome chiseled face that harkened back to a 1940's matinee idol. Leon thought this guise had gotten the guy plenty of action in high school, and for that reason alone, Leon took an immediate dislike to him.

'Don't pout, Sudd," she said, buttoning the blouse. "We'll talk about it later."

Sudd picked up an iridescent, silver-colored sharkskin sport coat from the bed and slipped it on. As he slipped on the jacket, Leon noticed what might be the butt of a handgun protruding from the waist of his jeans. He shot Leon a look of disdain before storming through the door.

Lou Ann shrugged in response to Leon's look of bemusement.

"Did I just see a gun in his pocket or was he just glad to see me?" he asked.

"Sometimes he's my security detail. He's my keyboardist, too. And a good one, which is the only reason I put up with him. Tonight he's just a piss ant." She smiled at him. "I can't believe you're finally here. I was starting to give up hope."

"I wrote you a couple of letters."

She pulled a face. "I never got any letters. I've got someone that goes through all my mail. Seems the only things anyone sticks in front of my face these days are checks that need signing." She put her arms around his neck. "Are you going to tell me what you wrote in those letters? Maybe the postal service saw they were smokin' and had to hose 'em down."

They kissed chastely at first, a peck that turned into a long, deep French kiss that always made him feel like he was moving against an outgoing tide.

"Jesus. That mouth of yours," he said. "Who taught you to kiss? Whoever it was deserves a seat on the right hand of God."

"Are you hungry?" she asked, breaking away. "I want some fried chicken," she added without waiting for his reply. She broke from his embrace and flung open the door. "Tommy," she yelled. "Take us to Smithy's."

"That's clear across town, boss" the voice yelled back.

"Let's roll, Tommy. A girl's gotta eat." She turned back and looked at Leon and noticed the envelope in his hand. "Did Jimmy give you that?"

"Jimmy the manager. One of many from what I understand."

"It is what it is. I've got one who calls himself my road manager. I'm not sure what he does. Then there's a guy that books the hotels, another one runs my road crew, and then there's someone else to handle my clothes and hair. You name it. I have a manager for it." She pulled him close again. "I sort of liked it when there was just one person I needed to take care of me."

She opened the envelope and slipped a joint into her palm. "Good old Jimmy. He's what I call my night manager. He's been with me since back in the Houston days when I mostly played clubs down by the refineries. He's been a good friend." She held up the joint for his inspection. "One puff, then we go and gnaw the bone," she said, trying to mimic Jimmy's accent. She directed the joint toward her mouth and then changed her mind.

"Just talk to me," she said, tossing the joint on the nightstand. "Transport me, Leon Riser. Tell me about some place where no one knows me. That's all I want. Take me away somewhere."

# 13

*I write the songs*
*You hear them on the radio*
*But then what?*
*You think you know me?*
*I don't know myself."*

-Lou Ann Catskill
Woman Down

Smithy's turned out to be an all night soul food diner in South Central LA. It sat between a Phillips 66 gas station and a Goodwill store on a narrow street lined mostly with what looked like auto repair shops and tire retailers. The parking lot attendant rolled the gate open to an almost full parking lot that was hemmed in by a ten foot high chain link fence topped with concertina wire. Even with the attendant's help, it took some effort before Tommy managed to maneuver the bus into the lot.

"What can I get you?" Lou Ann asked Tommy, pausing at the bus's door.

"The usual will do," Tommy replied.

Smithy's was one of those classic sort of diners with Formica topped tables and cracked red naugahyde covered benches. Waist-high, round swivel stools covered in the same naugahyde lined the counter. The floor was a checkerboard of scuffed and faded black and dingy white linoleum. Posters of concerts and club bills covered the walls, the featured performers predominantly black.

The juke box sitting at the far end emitted a faint melody of a familiar R & B hit, the name of which escaped Leon. The place was almost full with a mix of what looked to be people coming off shift work or young people feeding a post-clubbing craving. Almost all the customers were black with the exception of a couple of young Asian women sitting at the counter. Lou Ann led him to the empty booth next to the jukebox..

"For this is a hangout of mine," Leon crooned in his best Willie Nelson imitation.

"Matter of fact, it is," she said. "Every time I come to LA, I get this yearning for some fried chicken. My Mom used to make the best fried chicken." It seemed like she was going to say more on the subject but the approach of the waitress interrupted her.

"Miss Lou Ann," the waitress crowed. She was a black woman sporting a short Afro. Leon guessed her to be in her late forties, but she could have just as easily been a decade or so older or younger. She cut Leon a look of critical appraisal.

"Miss Ruth. How've you been?" Lou Ann said, looking up at her and grinning.

Ruth shrugged. "What do they say? Quiet desperation and all that accompanying bullshit. How about yourself, hon?"

"Depends on what day you ask me," Lou Ann replied rather somberly.

"What can I get you?"

"Two of the baskets. Make mine all dark, And coffee."

"Lord, I do love a woman who knows what she wants," the waitress said, giving Leon another look before walking off.

Lou Ann took both his hands in hers and gave him a wistful look. There was something different in her eyes that might have been nothing more than fatigue. They looked under water, less luminous. She continued to stare at him for a moment and then smiled.

"What?" he asked,

"You look older," she said.

"I am older."

"You're what? All of thirty-four? That makes you four years older than me.""

"Does that make a difference?"

She shrugged, seemed to think for a moment, and then grinned. "I mean if you were really old, like maybe thirty-six, then I'd have to think twice about this."

"This? You mean sharing some fried chicken?"

"This… feeling I've got." She smiled as different waitress brought them their coffee. Lou Ann spooned an obscene amount of sugar into her cup, took a swallow and sat back.

"I did this concert in Vegas a couple of weeks after Tahiti. It was then I realized what was special about those two weeks. It was the fact you didn't need anything from me. For the first time since I can recall there was nobody needing me. Or running my life for me either. Nobody asking me for things or telling me what to eat, what to wear, what to sing. I didn't have to be always giving people what they wanted, and not what I wanted. You heard the audience tonight. It's the same with them. I give them what they wanted." She shrugged. "The thing of it is, I like performing. It's just all the other shit that comes with it. And I guess I'm okay with it."

"You guess you're okay with it? That's not exactly a life affirming endorsement."

"Now you're sounding like my shrink. He talks like that. What I was trying to say was that back in Tahiti, everything was so different. It was scary. Nice, but scary."

"What was scary?"

"You. Us. A different kind of life."

The emotion in her voice left him uncertain of how to respond. He took a sip of his coffee to buy some time and edit what he wanted to say.

"You know, a lot of times I have to make a living writing about places and experiences like Tahiti. The romantic sailboat cruise through the islands. Or the walking safari, the gin and tonics in the luxury tent camp.

Fantasy vacations. The kind most people only dream about ever taking." He saw her stiffen.

"What are you trying to tell me? That those two weeks were just some fantasy? Just background for one of your bullshit articles? Is that what you're saying?"

He could tell she was angry and he reached for her hand, but she pulled away and turned her head. The juke box started playing an old Al Green tune. 'Keep on Pushing Love'. How apt, he thought. He took another swallow of coffee before going on,

"No. What I meant was I write those articles to feed my wallet, not my soul. Writing them doesn't give me the same high as riding a motorcycle on some back road in Egypt. Or sitting under a full moon in a rice paddy in Bali and listening to the frogs. What I'm trying to say is those two weeks we were together was like that. It fed something in me. Am I making sense?"

She didn't say anything, but merely stared at him, her expression guarded. He took a swallow of his coffee before going on.

"You and I really aren't so different, you know. We both make compromises for the things we love doing. But I figured out some time back that compromise doesn't work in the long run. It keeps you from ever getting to a place where you don't have to compromise any more. To reach a point where you're finally able to get off the horse, so to speak. I guess what I really want to say is those two weeks felt real for me, too. And yeah, that can be scary."

Lou Ann still said nothing, her eyes fixed on his. They held each other's gaze and allowed All Green to fill the silence.

"Is that the closest I'll get to you admitting you like me?" she asked after the song ended.

"It's not like I'm proposing, for chrissakes."

"I wouldn't accept anyway. Not that I haven't daydreamed about running off with you. I can imagine myself straightening up your desk every night before bed time. Maybe I'd buy us some his and her bath towels."

He laughed. "Funny, but I don't quite see you as the domestic type. On the other hand, that might make an interesting sequel to the Tahiti piece. I figure I'd call it 'The Domestic Siren.'"

"Promise me you'll never write about me. About us," she said, her face suddenly somber.

He sipped his coffee and didn't say anything. He realized there was so much about her that he didn't know. The possibility that he might never really know her only made her more appealing.

"I need another break," she said, interrupting his thoughts. "The problem is I've got these shows lined up back to back until freaking Thanksgiving. Then back to the studio." She hesitated a beat. "Could you come with me?"

"Where? On tour?" He thought about it for a moment. "Maybe I could get Rolling Stone to pay me to write about it. I have to say that four months on a concert tour doesn't appeal to me in the least. I can ride a chicken bus across southern India with a case of dysentery. But a concert tour? Not my kind of scene."

"You'd have me all to yourself when I'm not on stage. You could be my new manager of…. Let's see. How about you become my manager of internal affairs? Yeah," she said, licking her lips. "I like the sound of that."

"The problem is I just rented a house on the Big Island. I need time to work on a book."

She slumped in disappointment.

"But there's not to say I couldn't catch up with you at least a couple or three times. And then maybe once you have a break, we'll go somewhere."

"Some place where they don't know me." Her face grew somber. "Some place where I don't need my pills. You know? Not Africa though. I don't do roughing it. Not unless I can lounge around in one of those luxury camps you write about. Gin and tonics and eland steaks every night. The white hunter sneaking into my tent after dark. Are you serious though? About meeting me on the road?"

"Sure. Why not?"

She squealed just as Ruth brought their chicken. Ruth gave her a sly look.

"We don't allow that kind of business here. I gots to see your hands on the table at all times," Ruth said, arching her eyebrows.

"Ruth, this precious man just agreed to become my manager of internal affairs."

"Hon, you need to show me that job description. Maybe I'll go find myself one of those kinda managers," she said, refilling their coffee.

"And bring us three slices of pecan pie to go."

"Tommy's needin' his pie, yeah?"

As they ate, they listened to BB King and guys like Morris Day, The Fabulous Thunderbirds, and Etta James. And again, they talked about music and places Leon still wanted to see. And places she wanted to see with him. Afterwards, Tommy drove them to the hotel and found a deserted part of the parking lot, grabbed his pie and left, locking up the bus behind him. It was close to noon when Tommy showed up again bearing coffee and croissants.

# 14

*"Come in slow, come in close*
*Closer, closer yet,*
*Come lose yourself in the uneven surface of my soul.*
*Come into wrongdoing."*

-Lou Ann Catskill
Wrongdoing

**SANTA FE**

**APRIL 12th**

Iris took a long sip of her Americano as she watched a couple of young women in hiking clothes stroll by. One of them caught Iris's eye and smiled.

"I'm sure there are laws in this city prohibiting lascivious trolling," Leon said in a tone that sounded only vaguely admonishing. He sat slouched in what looked to Iris to be a decidedly uncomfortable position, his face awkwardly cocked to catch the morning sun. She looked at him as she tried to gauge his mood. His mouth gave nothing away and his aviator sunglasses concealed his eyes from the bright morning sunlight.

They had decided on a third cup of coffee after their hotel breakfast. They found a corner coffee shop with outside tables across the street from the hotel. The previous night's dusting of snow had all but melted, but still offered a reminder that winter's hold hadn't entirely receded. In the narrow greenbelt across the street, a few ornamental fruit trees along the creek's banks displayed their optimism, their otherwise bare branches girded in sleeves of pink and purple blossoms.

"You're just pissed because I have more hooks on my line than you do. And I have a lot better bait," she said.

"Yeah, but I've been to a lot more fishing holes. My pole and tackle are my only problem."

Iris couldn't help but laugh. "You know there's a pill for that if you don't mind having a face the color of a watermelon."

Leon didn't so much as break a smile. Instead, he reached over and took her hand. "Are you okay with this?" he asked.

"With what?"

"Meeting with this cop? I mean, why are we doing this anyway?"

"I really liked that story you told us last night," she said, ignoring his query. "It was sweet. It made me…" She paused as if lost somewhere. "I wish I could've known Mom before I came along. By the time I became cognizant about much of anything beyond the etiquette of where was a suitable place for little girls to piss, it was too late."

"You know that's a line I used in one of my novels," he interjected.

"Huh, I could've sworn I just made that up. Anyway, the Mom I knew seems different than the woman in your stories. You know I still look at some photos of her when she was younger. Like when she was maybe my age. I can't help but be curious about that person. Lou Ann the diva, the prey. And the predator," she added. "That's how she put it to me once. A woman is either prey or predator, and more often than not both. She used to tell me about the games women of a certain age have to play. The point I'm trying to make is that she must've been different when you two first hooked up."

"And in her defense and speaking from personal experience, we… Well, some of us." He started over. "A lot of us follow these screwed up trajectories in our lives. You ride along out of pride, excitement, out of ignorance. Or habit. Or artifice. Sometimes fear. And you always think you're the one in the driver's seat until you realize you've gone way off the grid and lost your way somewhere along the line." He looked at her and grinned. "You owe me a hundred dollars for that brilliant insight. Any useful advice will have to be extra."

"Your point being?"

"Have some empathy for your elders. We're not perfect."

"Still, I would've liked to have known her back then," Iris said. "It took me a long time to accept what little part of her she ever let me see. You know. I've forgiven Mom her sins."

"That couldn't have been easy."

"You remember that therapist you hooked me up with when I was seventeen? I still see her."

Leon looked at her but didn't say anything, his eyes hidden behind the ramparts of his sunglasses.

"I get the feeling that some of your stories about Mom aren't exactly going to be all wine and roses. But I don't care. You can tell me anything."

"The cop. Why are we meeting up with him?" he asked again.

"Because I don't believe a word Kevin tells me. He says he filed a missing persons report out of pride. That's bullshit. There has to be some other motive. I just thought maybe the cops know something more." She checked her phone. "It's almost ten. Let's mosey down to that so-called river," she said, pushing away from the table.

"I don't get why this cop couldn't meet us in the lobby or up in one of our rooms."

"Hey, before I could even suggest that he said he'd pick us up at the first set of tables on the river just down from the hotel. If you're cold, we'll tell him we want to go inside."

"No, I'm fine. That cop choosing where to meet is their way of putting us off balance. It's an interrogation technique. I'm serious. This cop I knew told me that once."

"Don't worry. Leon. You have your attorney with you. Let's go."

The detective in charge of Lou Ann's case had returned Iris's call promptly. Ahrens was his name and he didn't offer anything but the time and place of their meeting.

As they waited to cross the street, she dug in her purse for her bottle of Advil before remembering she had taken the last of it soon after awakening. Thanks to the combination of the altitude, the tequila, and the Dexedrine, she had a throbbing headache. The half of a Trazodone tablet she had taken at 3AM had at least purchased her four hours of sleep. Three cups of coffee later and she still felt underwater.

Over breakfast, Leon had reverted to his paternal role and questioned her obliquely, no doubt recognizing her hangover was not just a result of the tequila. She in turn blamed it on fatigue and the old standby, menstrual cramps. They both knew each other well enough for her to realize Leon wasn't buying it. Still, he didn't push her further.

While still up in their room, Fumiko had announced she was forgoing breakfast to explore the plaza. She seemed reserved and almost terse when Iris attempted to engage her in the most basic conversation. Iris suspected that Fumiko had seen through her mania the night before. She also assumed Fumiko had noticed her rifling through her coat pockets in the middle of the night and the distinctive rattle of a pill bottle.

The Santa Fe River was really nothing more than a creek that maintained a decent trickle for half the year. A series of stone picnic tables lined the river's narrow greenbelt. They had no sooner reached the first of the tables when Leon grunted and nodded with his chin at the black Ford Escape that had pulled to the curb a short ways in front of them. A man climbed out from the driver's side and waved his arm in greeting as he approached them. He was a tall, bulky man who walked with an obvious limp. He wore badly rumpled khakis and a light down vest over a chambray shirt. The vest did little to conceal the badge on his belt or the holstered handgun.

"Miss Catskill? I'm Detective Ahrens," he said approaching them. He started to extend his hand before dropping it to his side and stepping back, the handshake still obviously a pre-Covid custom.

"Thanks for seeing us," she replied. "This is Leon Riser, my mother's former... partner. My stepfather," she added.

Ahrens nodded. He looked to be in his forties although his face argued the guy might be older. It was the kind of face that appeared sun boiled no matter the season. He wore thick bifocals and his buzz cut hair looked freshly barbered. Even from three feet away, Ahrens smelled of aftershave. His smile betrayed some discomfort.

"We can sit in the car or maybe better yet, take a walk. I just thought… you know. Social distancing. And privacy." His voice was high-pitched and squeaky, belying his bulk

"The car is fine," Leon said, glancing at Iris for her approval.

"Leon isn't feeling well. Maybe the car is better."

"Sure," Ahrens said. "I've been vaccinated. How about you folks?"

"We're bullet proof," Leon replied.

Ahrens nodded and led them to the car and opened the back passenger side door. Iris chose the front seat. Leon crawled with some effort into the back seat. Ahrens climbed in behind the wheel and pivoted in his seat, his back against the door. "I assume Mr. Riordan informed you that the remains of the woman they found outside of Grants were not your mother's. The dental records were conclusive."

"No, I didn't know that," Iris said, shooting Leon a glance over her shoulder.

Ahrens appeared confused. "Mr. Riordan called me this morning and informed me of your visit last night. I thought he would've told you then. I notified him yesterday morning that it wasn't your mother's remains. He didn't tell you?" he asked in a way that sounded more like a statement than a question.

"That bastard," Iris said, unable to restrain herself. "He let me think… You're sure it wasn't my mom?"

"Positive." He waited a beat before going on. "Let me just say up front that our investigation hasn't turned up any evidence that would suggest any hint of tragedy, or foul play either for that matter. You are probably aware, Miss Catskill," Ahrens started to say as he unscrewed the lid of a thermos he retrieved from the console. "Would either of you like some coffee?" The thermos was one of those metal and ceramic ones they sold in stores dealing in vintage and second hand items.

"Sure. I'll take some," she replied. Leon shook his head in amazement. Iris was like her mother in her seemingly lack of moderation.

Ahrens pulled out a small tin cup from the console and carefully poured a full cup which he carefully handed to Iris. "Sorry, but I don't have whitener or sugar."

She took a sip, and decided it wasn't half bad. Her estimation of Ahrens rose a notch.

"So I suppose you are aware," Ahrens started over, "that Mr. Riordan filed a missing persons report. He seems to think there's a possibility that your mother may have been abducted. He even provided a name of a suspect. A Sudd Kiehne. He said this guy had a criminal record for drug dealing. Is there any chance either of you know him?"

"Yeah, I know him," Leon replied. "He used to play in her band."

"Do you have any sense there's anything to his claim?"

Leon shrugged. "Can't say."

"Like I said before, everything we've been able to find out points more to your mother having left on her own free will. And just because no one's heard from her might just mean she doesn't want to be found."

"She doesn't want to be found," Iris heard Leon mutter under his breath.

"We also have a witness, a neighbor, who says she was out walking her dogs when she saw your mother leave the morning she supposedly disappeared. This neighbor said your mother left in a white camper van driven by a man. The van slowed down long enough for your mother to roll down the window and smile at her and wave. So the neighbor thought nothing of it at the time. Since we have no reason to doubt her account, it leads me to believe we're not dealing with a missing person. That being said, I'd welcome any insight you might have," Ahrens added, draining the last of the thermos into an insulated cup.

"What do you think of Kevin Riordan?" Iris asked, blowing on her coffee.

Ahrens appeared somewhat caught off guard by her question. "You mean as a witness? Or a claimant?"

"I mean as anything other than an asshole," she replied. "He's a compulsive liar for one thing. Look, I also think she just left him. I just want to know where she went. Do you have any other leads?"

"Believe it or not, Riordan still has a land line. We were able to trace recent calls. There were two of them to a Sue Mendez in Austin. From what we can tell by the duration of the calls, your mother either hung up or no one answered. Do you know this Mendez woman?"

"She used to be one of my Mom's backup singers," Iris said, resisting the inclination to look back at Leon.

Ahrens grunted. "Huh. This is all beginning to sound like your mother's band might be getting together for one of those reunion tours. Sorry. That sounded sort of flippant. Look, I know you're worried about your mother. I promise I'll keep an eye on Riordan."

"It doesn't sound like you're a fan of Riordan," Leon said.

Ahrens only shrugged. "Let's just say that I question your mother's choice in husbands." He caught himself. "Sorry, I wasn't referring to you, Mr. Riser."

Leon held up his hand. "No, you're close to the mark."

"You said you've left your mother messages but she hasn't replied. Did you tell her you were up here looking for her?"

"No, not yet. She probably thinks I'm still in Austin."

"Do you think that's where she's headed?"

Iris shrugged. "Maybe."

Ahrens turned and looked back at Leon. "I read one of your books, Mr. Riser, The one about the aftermath of those wars down in Central America. I was laid up with a broken leg and had this pile of books a friend left me. I went down to Guatemala a few years back. It was your book that made me want to go and check it out."

"And?"

"It was an interesting place. Beautiful country. People were great, but there was this undercurrent of sorts. This veneer of normalcy covering up all that bad history was how I believe you put it. Like somebody had white-washed over the shit smeared on the walls."

Leon nodded. "I tell you what. You keep us in the loop, and I'll leave a few of my books for you at the hotel desk."

Ahrens smiled. "I'd like that."

"All right then," Iris said, downing the rest of her coffee and placing the cup on the console. "I assume you'll keep me informed if anything shows up," she said, removing a business card from her bag and handing it across the seat to Ahrens who studied it for a moment and nodded.

"I'll do that. Good luck with finding your mother," he said.

They crawled out of the Escape and watched Ahrens drive off.

"So, are you satisfied?" Leon asked.

"I'm satisfied Mom walked out on Kevin. I just don't know how she's doing. How she's handling all this. You know how she can get when things get out of hand. And I still think Kevin isn't telling us everything."

"Stay away from him. Okay?"

Iris nodded.

"I'm curious," Leon asked as they started back to the hotel. "What's on the business card?"

"Iris Catskill, Attorney at Law."

"That's a bit presumptuous, isn't it? And unethical. And illegal to boot."

She stopped and took his arm. "I've got a confession, Leon. I dropped out of law school. Or at least I didn't go back last fall. I took a job selling Audis. Don't be angry."

"Why would I be angry? I hate lawyers almost as much as I do car salesmen. Or should I say salesperson? Don't ask me to get the pronoun right. I was hoping you'd take up something like anthropology. Or something sordid like writing fiction."

She pulled him close and laid her head on his shoulder. "You're sure you're not even a little disappointed in me?"

"Glass houses. I just wouldn't be passing out anymore of those cards."

"You'd be surprised how handy they are."

"I can only imagine."

"So now what?"

"I'm guessing your Mom is heading to Austin. She probably thinks you're still there. And Sue's there. It'll be spring in the Hill Country. The bluebonnets and Mexican Hats will be out. I could handle that about now."

"Okay. Austin's a good twelve hour drive if we need to stop often. We'll leave in the morning. Are you sure you're up to it?"

"I'll manage. You forget I have a private duty nurse. And I'll let you break the news to her. She'll want to stock up on snacks. Shrimp crackers, dried seaweed, the ubiquitous sea urchin if she can find one."

"Guess I'd better stock up on beef jerky and Mountain Dew," she said, taking his arm. .

# 15

*"I take off my watch.*
*My earrings. My clothes*
*I take down the walls*
*The ramparts of my fear*
*Now can you see it?*
*The uneven surface of my soul?"*

-Lou Ann Catskill
The Uneven Surface of My Soul

Leon awoke to a knock on his hotel room door. He lifted his head and glanced at the clock. It was almost six. He had told Iris to wake him at three. With some difficulty, he rolled to a sitting position and sat there for a moment. There was the knock again.

"Hang on. I'm coming."

He faltered getting up before creeping to the door and opening it. "I thought I told you…" He stopped when he saw Fumiko standing in the hallway.

"Oh, even better. The night nurse," he said, limping back to the bed.

Fumiko lingered in the doorway for a moment before following him. "I have a reservation for a private tub at six thirty at a Japanese bathhouse. I thought you might also wish to come."

"Why Nurse Sato, that sounds delightful. By the way, did Iris tell you we're driving to Austin tomorrow?"

"Yes. We will leave early so we can take many breaks."

"Is she coming with us to this bathhouse?"

"No, she said she wasn't feeling well."

"Caffeine overdose is my guess. Okay, give me a couple of minutes and I'll meet you in the lobby."

Ten Thousand Waves sat atop a stony, juniper and *piñon* studded ridge in the foothills just a few miles north of the city. Leon's handicap permit allowed them to bypass the lower parking lot and avoid climbing what looked to be the steep and winding, proverbial stairway to heaven. The spa's lobby reminded him of a similar bathhouse he had often frequented in Bali; all wood and rock and running water and the scent of something pleasingly unfamiliar. A middle-aged Hispanic woman behind a Plexiglas screen greeted them, checked their reservation, and gave them each a towel and a robe before passing them off to a willowy young blonde whose face was almost completely hidden behind an elegant, Asian motif mask. She nodded and asked them to follow her.

The private tub turned out to be almost the size of small swimming pool. It came complete with a waterfall, a cold plunge, and its own separate changing rooms and showers. It sat in the center of a large flag-stoned patio shrouded by pine and juniper. The beauty and serenity of the setting gave him pause. The tub made his simple Jacuzzi look quite pedestrian. He disrobed, showered and made his way to the tub.

Without waiting for Fumiko, he climbed down the steps into the pool and promptly submerged himself up to his chin. He turned as Fumiko entered his peripheral vision. She slipped out of her robe and made her way to the pool's steps.

To his astonishment, she was nude. For a moment, he thought of turning away, but found himself captivated by the figure before him. Not surprisingly, Fumiko's body proved to be every bit as delicate and beautiful as her face. She was small-breasted and high-hipped in a way that complimented her long slender legs. It wasn't until she had slipped into the water with graceful precision that she met his gaze.

"I did not bring my suit. I did not think I would need one. Do I make you uncomfortable?" she asked, sliding over to the wall opposite him.

"Not at all," he managed to say. "We're all adults here. Usually," he added.

She leaned back with only her head above the water and closed her eyes. He pretended to do the same. It wasn't as if he had never imagined what she might look like nude. After all, he was a man with a keen appreciation of the female form. It had been a good while since he had seen a nude woman. A year or more at least, he figured as he thought of an old acquaintance he had looked up on the spur of the moment while passing through Seattle. The two of them had been dancing around the bedroom for the better part of two decades. At the time, he was already having back pain and sensed a shoe dropping. His discomfort colored their lovemaking with a desperation that alarmed them both.

"Iris," Fumiko said, interrupting his thoughts. "I believe she uses drugs."

"You think? You should've seen her back in her heyday."

"Hay day? I am not familiar with that word."

"Her peak. Back when she was all rebellion and twenty-four seven hormonal storm."

"I will just say you must observe her. I believe she is a person who takes risks. Am I wrong?"

"Who doesn't take risks at that age? Something tells me you took your share."

Fumiko didn't reply at first, as if she were weighing the cost of revelations. "Yes, I took risks. With my life. With people I loved. On the other foot…"

"Hand. On the other hand. Shit, who taught you English?"

"Do not be rude. I was saying risk brought me to America. It sustained me through many things. Through nursing school. I believe one must take certain risks to get anywhere. Just as there are risks one should not take."

Leon nodded. "Jesus, Fumiko. That's the most information you've ever offered up short of your name, rank, and serial number."

"Perhaps it is because you talk so much. Always talking and dominating the conversations. Besides, you have never asked."

"Alright then, I'm all ears. Tell me something I don't know about Fumiko Sato, RN."

"And what is it you wish to know? The stories from my happy childhood? No? You wish to know of risks I have taken." She smiled. "You make up stories for a living, Leon. It would be foolish of me to disclose things you might one day use and then… What is the term you like to use? You will only embellish them."

A sudden quicksilver glint of memory rose to his mind. Lou Ann said something similar the day they first met. He made a twisting motion in front of his mouth with his hand. "Tick-a-lock. Just leave in a few good parts."

"I will share with you no more than I shared with my college roommate who was often intoxicated and therefore never remembered anything. I grew up poor and was raised by a single mother. That is almost a crime in my country. To be a single mother. The reason for this… her shame… is nothing I will discuss. I ran away from home at sixteen. I went to Tokyo and danced in clubs. Yes, topless clubs. Does that shock you?"

"Consider me shock proof."

She paused a moment before going on. "Someone saw me dancing and liked my face. I became a model, a minor celebrity among girls in their braces and knee stockings. Being a young, naïve woman, I was taken advantage of. I was cheated and then discarded like trash. I danced again. And then one night, I met this man. He offered to take me away from that life. He brought me with him to San Francisco. I was his wife. Or like a wife," she added. "Until I was no longer his wife. He left me one day. Everything else is of little interest."

Before he could formulate a comment, she went on.

"You have never spoken to me about Lou Ann. As I said before, it is not my business, but I believe you are still in love with this woman. Or should I say I sense there is a connection that once made is never really broken. Is that not the same thing as love? Iris told me about Tahiti, at least her mother's version. One day, I will allow you to smoke too much marijuana and you can tell me your version," she said with a smirk.

"I think we should try this. First, I tell a story, and then you tell me a story. There might be a…"

"Ms. Sato," a voice crackled from a small speaker concealed in a potted bonsai.

"Yes?"

"I believe you have a guest with you. A Mr. Riser?"

"Yes, that is correct."

"There is a gentleman here who says it is urgent that he speak with Mr. Riser."

Leon looked at Fumiko, and then shrugged and moved closer to the bonsai. "Who is it?" he asked.

A moment passed before there was a reply. "His name is Detective Ahrens. He says it will only take a moment."

"Well, I can either walk down to the lobby in my robe or you can escort him to our tub. Tell him he can leave his clothes on," he said, shooting Fumiko a mischievous grin. He climbed from the rub and slipped into his robe. A few moments later, there was a soft knock on the door. He opened it to find Ahrens standing there and gawking at the garden-like surroundings.

"I've never been up here," he said, turning to Leon. "I think I'll try it sometime." He tried to look past Leon, no doubt curious about Fumiko. "I hate to interrupt your soak. It's about your daughter. Hold on," he added in response to the look on Leon's face. "She's okay. Relatively okay,"

"What do you mean by relatively okay?"

"She showed up at Riordan's home this evening. There was an altercation of sorts. Short of a few bruises, I believe she acquitted herself pretty well. Unfortunately, Riordan wishes to press charges."

"So she's in jail?"

"No. I brought her back to the hotel. Consider it a courtesy. And her being an attorney and all. It wouldn't look good on her record. Besides, my opinion of Riordan grows less favorable with each passing day. I'll make sure she's charged with only a misdemeanor. Disorderly conduct. If Riordan knows what's good for him, he'll drop it. An unlicensed firearm was involved in the incident."

"Jesus." Leon shook his head and cursed under his breath. He looked back at Fumiko who had edged her way close enough to eavesdrop on their conversation.

"Ms. Catskill said it wasn't until Riordan threatened her with a gun that things got ugly," Ahrens said with what seemed a smile of amusement. "I like her side of the story."

"We were planning on leaving town tomorrow. Will that be a problem?"

"No, just as long as you keep me apprised of your whereabouts. Leaving town might actually be for the best. It might keep Miss Catskill from giving that asshole another thumping."

"Thanks. I owe you."

"Just don't forget to leave me some books." He made one final effort to look past Leon, and then gave him a two-fingered salute and disappeared through the shrubbery.

"Shall we go?" Fumiko asked.

"Hell no," he replied, shedding his robe. "Let her stew for a while."

"Stew?"

"Contemplate. Ruminate on her actions. Something I once tried to drill into her hormone- addled brain. Obviously, that lesson never quite took. She can wait," he said, hoping he didn't come off as uncaring.

They both fell silent for a long moment. "I believe you are a very conflicted man, Leon Riser," Fumiko said finally.

He didn't say anything. Fumiko was right that his connection with Lou Ann remained an open wound. His illness had brought so many things to a head. His mortality, his legacy as a writer, places he still wanted to see. And now Lou Ann seemed to have joined in the unbraiding of this life. After all, either she or his memories of her had consumed almost half of his life.

"Those many years ago. Did you follow Lou Ann on her tour?" she said, interrupting his thoughts.

"You're not going to let this go, are you?" He closed his eyes, and as always, edited his thoughts before saying more.

"We had this complicated courtship, for lack of a better word. We did these long two hour phone calls across different time zones. I'd meet her for a night or two somewhere on one of her tour stops. And then there was this time she came to this house I had rented on the Big Island. And afterwards, whenever she had a break I took her places. Oaxaca, Europe. Thailand. In the vernacular of the times, we were into each other. At least, I thought so. Is that the same as love? I don't know anymore. In retrospect, we should've left it like that. A long distance on and off love affair. I forget who it was that said that the perfect lover is someone who lives in another city, is a workaholic and has a great sense of humor. It all seemed to work for a while. All wine and roses," he muttered, recalling what Iris had said.

"Have you ever been in love, Fumiko? I mean to the point where all you do is think about the other person all the time. Ache for them at night. You're high on it. Intoxicated."

Fumiko seemed to carefully consider her reply. "I met someone after I left San Francisco. For the first time, I felt this... emotion that you describe. I believe it is much different for a woman. To feel that way."

"So what happened?"

"What often happens. It did not endure."

She looked away and he sensed she had no intention of offering more.

"Anyway, after a year or so of this, something in Lou Ann changed. Granted her life, her schedule was insane. The tours, the pressure on her to always come out with a new album. By then I had figured out she wasn't suited for that kind of life."

He lost himself for a moment before going on. "Iris might've told you her mom is bipolar, which never helped matters much. She self-medicated whether she needed to or not. In her defense, she wouldn't be the first diva who crashed and burned. She was a big star by then. Always on stage. Living in the fast lane. I think it changed something in her." An old

Billie Holiday song came to mind. "You've changed," he sang half to him-self. "The sparkle in your eye…."

"Does Iris know of those times?"

"Oh, every once in a while I'd provide her with little vignettes about her mother and I. But I assumed that at her age she'd have trouble wrapping her brain around the complexities of adult relationships, especially one like Lou Ann and I shared. At the time, it seemed Iris just took it all in and filed it away somewhere. Stockpiling for the next war is how Lou Ann used to put it." He smiled at the memory. "There are other things that if she knows, she never lets on."

"But you are not her father?"

"No," he said after a moment's hesitation. "And Iris knows that. I have no idea if Lou Ann ever told her about that period in her life, much less who her father is. That's a rock I don't want to turn over. I always thought bringing that kind of stuff up might make Iris judge her mother more harshly than she already does. Judge me, too."

"Harsher than you judge yourself?"

He let out a snort of laughter. "Lord, Sato. Are you wearing your shrink hat tonight? Maybe I should hire you as my muse."

"I am not sure of the meaning of that word."

"Muse. It means someone who gives me inspiration. Fuels my cre-ativity. Someone who asks all the right questions."

She frowned. "You are pulling my arm."

"Your leg. The expression is pulling your leg. No, I'm just compli-menting you on your intuition and insight."

"I would not take such a position as your muse person. Once your treatments are over, I will go back to Denver."

"Fine. Now that we've settled that, why don't we cease conversation and soak up these healing waters."

A minute later, he opened his eyes just enough to see that she seemed to be studying him with the kind of scrutiny one might use when first encountering some weirdly exotic creature at the zoo. He closed his eyes and began mentally flipping through the pages of remembrance, visiting places and scenes, some almost forgotten, others never far below the water-line of his psyche. Lately, he found himself indulging in that endeavor more often than he thought was healthy. Yet to his surprise and content-ment, these reflections neither annoyed nor comforted him. *C'est la vie*, he thought, slipping further down into the water.

Later, on the way back to the hotel, they stopped for takeout sushi at Whole Foods. He followed Fumiko to her and Iris's room with every inten-tion of confronting Iris, but a Do Not Disturb sign on the door dissuaded him. He simply was no longer in the mood. He bid Fumiko good night and started to turn away when she grabbed his arm.

"Do not forget to take your medicines. And…" She hesitated as if choosing her words. "It is good for friends to share things. Yes?"

Friends. He had never quite thought of her that way.

"Yeah, it was good to talk. *Oyasumi,*Fumiko." He almost hugged her, settling instead for an affectionate pat on her arm.

Back in his room, he took a split of Chardonnay from the fridge, unwrapped the tray of sushi and eased himself into the chair by the win-dow. As he nibbled on a California roll, he thought about the conversation with Fumiko. It had done nothing if not stir things up even more.

The amount of time he spent thinking of Lou Ann had lessened with time. It was only when he heard one of her songs or thought about some place they had visited together that she returned to haunt him. And then Iris showed up. He pondered what he had just disclosed to Fumiko and wondered if he had painted too critical a picture of Lou Ann.

He tossed the tray of half-eaten sushi onto the nightstand and unscrewed the cap off the bottle of Chardonnay. Taking a long pull of the wine, he thought how Lou Ann was like an uncompleted novel he kept in the bottom drawer of his desk. Always there, always begging to be taken up again, but never completed. This latest venture was forcing him to revisit chapters and edit the parts best left unwritten.

He switched off the table lamp and stared out the window. Wisps of cloud scooted across the full moon. His thoughts drifted back to another full moon, cloud-streaked night; a different chapter. One that was only slightly less painful to revisit than others.

# 16

*"Come all you people and see the show*
*Come all you souls, one and all*
*Do you see me now?*
*See the wounds?"*

-Lou Ann Catskill
Woman Down

**HAMAKUA COAST**

**THE BIG ISLAND**

**DECEMBER 1996**

The house was hemmed in by thick forest and sat atop a cliff some two hundred feet or more above the ocean. As a result, the nights this time of year often became quite chilly. Leon's landlord, an elderly Hawaiian gentleman, called this time in the islands *Ho'oilo-,* the time that passed for deep winter, for it could often be wet and cool, the sun sometimes absent for days at a time. Other than the welcome rains, nothing much good could be said about *Ho'oilo,* the old man said.

After an alfresco dinner of *poke* and tortilla chips, Leon had fetched a sleeping bag to share in the hammock where he and Lou Ann now lay entangled like a giant chrysalis. A full moon had just breached the forest canopy that rose up around the house. In the span of a minute, the dark ocean below appeared transformed; the whitecaps resembling a vast, blinking constellation of stars, the cresting waves like luminous ribbons. Other than a few isolated and small rain squalls drifting along the horizon, the night was mostly clear.

"Do you mind if I unzip this bag a little?" he asked. Their body heat was making him sweat

"Oh, baby," Lou Ann murmured. "Zip me up, zip me down. I like it both ways."

He unzipped the bag and settled in beside her. He could still smell the sea in her hair along with the musky perfume of their love making. They had spent much of the day on a secluded beach on the leeward side. The cliff house was located on the windward side of the island, and the surrounding coastline consisted mostly of cliffs and deep forested gulches. One had to drive almost to Hilo to find a decent stretch of beach, but even then, the leeward side had the finest beaches.

The landlord had turned him on to one of his favorites, a secluded cove that was a twenty minute hike across a lava field festooned with thick stands of thorny *kiawe* trees and the occasional clumps of bougainvillea. The effort rewarded them with a beach entirely to themselves. They spent a good part of the morning and early afternoon swimming and snorkeling. It was late afternoon before they returned to the cliff house, sunburned and dehydrated. They never even bothered to shower, but instead fell into bed and spent the better part of two hours having sex with hardly a word uttered between them,

"I swear I smell something burning," he said, lifting his head. "Shit," he cursed as he tried to untangle himself from the bag.

"I don't smell anything," Lou Ann said as she struggled to right the hammock.

"It's something on the table. The magazine," he replied, slapping the smoldering National Geographic on the edge of the table. "I think you missed the ashtray," he said, pinching a half-smoked joint from the small pile of ashes on the table. "I know you're tired. But let's try to avoid burning down the house," he said, slipping back into the hammock. Neither of them said anything for a long moment.

"I almost burned down our house once," she said finally. "I was nine and I was already having twisters in my head. That's what my mama called them. I put a lit candle underneath my parents' bed. They weren't in it of course. It was the thought that counted."

He turned and looked at her, unsure of how to reply.

"You've never told me much about when you were growing up," he said finally. "You've told me how you started performing when you were sixteen and everything else afterwards. Well, maybe not everything. But everything before that… what it was like as a kid. I'd like to know. Then again, maybe I should be grateful I don't know."

"There's nothing to tell." She wriggled deeper into the bag and turned her back to him.

"What's wrong?"

"Nothing, I'm just a bit out of it. Jet lag. I told you it was the middle of the night before I ever got back to the hotel in Sydney. I doubt I could've even made it to the airport if it wasn't for my manager. Did I tell you I changed managers? The new one, this guy named Riordan, has taken pretty good care of me so far. I never have to worry about anything except showing up."

"You never really told me about the show," he said, curling himself around her.

"It was alright. The venue was fine. We sold out the place. The only bummer was this Maori chick that opened for me. She was almost too good. She made me feel… I don't know. Inauthentic, I guess. All in all, it wasn't really my best gig."

She propped herself up on his chest with one elbow. "Are you going to watch me on Johnny Carson? I've never been on a show like that. It scares me shitless. I'm afraid I'll say something embarrassing. You know I'm real insecure, don't you? Shy, too."

"Oh yeah? Insecure for sure, but not shy."

"Did I tell you I'm seeing a new shrink? I'm not too sold on him yet. All he does is sit there and nod. He doesn't even take any notes. At least he refills my prescriptions. I'll give him that. You listen to me a hell of a lot more than he does. And you don't judge," she added when he didn't reply. "You don't seem to care whether I'm good or bad. You reward me either way,"

"I especially like to reward you when you're bad."

"Don't I know it?" she said, lowering her head onto his chest. A minute or so went by, and he wondered whether she had fallen asleep.

"Where are we going with this?" she murmured, stirring him from his own torpor. "You and me," she added when he didn't reply.

"Depends on where you want it to go," was his rather lame rejoinder. What he really wanted to say was does it have to go anywhere.

She lifted her head and looked at him, her expression unfathomable in the darkness. "I've never gotten too comfortable with a guy. You know, like in a real relationship. There's always all that needing," she said, settling back down. "Promises I can't keep. That's another thing about this new shrink. Whenever I tell him that I'm afraid of needing someone, he doesn't comment. He just nods some more."

"I think you need a different psychiatrist."

"Maybe once this next tour is over. I just needed a way to get my pills."

Neither of them said anything for what seemed a minute.

"Shit, Leon. I'm so tired of taking those pills. They make me feel…I don't know. Not myself. I can't write when I take them. And I'm always asking myself if this is just the way it's going to be for the rest of my life? Bouncing up and down. Take the yellow pill for this, the green one for that. I hate it," she added after a moment.

"Back in Tahiti, you…"

"Don't start. Yeah, I didn't need to take anything. But I was scared shitless the whole time. Don't you get it? That was a life I've never lived before. My other life… my real life is so different. On stage performing is where I live. But it's just play acting. Or at least I feel that way. It's like I'm wearing a mask. I always have to be the person the audience wants me to be. They think I'm one thing that I'm not. And so I give them what they want."

He could sense the rising tension in her body.

"Back in Tahiti, I didn't have to wear my mask. I wasn't performing. No manager, no record people hounding me. Just you and me. But it's not my reality. That wasn't really me, Leon. You don't want to see or be with the real me. She's not a nice person."

"So you wear a mask? Don't you see how wrong that is?"

"Goddammit, Leon! You're not hearing me. I'm afraid of being without my medications and without a mask. I've tried living without them before and I trashed my life. I don't trust myself. You want me to set fire to your fucking bed?"

After a moment, he realized she was crying. He pulled her closer.

"After I got back from Tahiti, I wouldn't let myself think about us," she said, choking back her tears. "I was afraid of you seeing the real me. I was afraid of needing you. Afraid that I might have to need you to make myself happy."

"Is that so bad? Someone making you happy? Christ, Lou Ann, it doesn't always have to be about needing, you know."

She didn't say anything at first. "I told myself," she said finally, her voice thick with her tears. "It would never work out, between you and me, because if I can't make myself happy, how could I ever make you happy? And that's what scares me the most." She swiped at her face and made a snorting sound that almost sounded like a laugh.

"The one and only time that worthless shrink ever raised an eyebrow was when I admitted that to him. And how pathetic is that? All those years of therapy at three hundred bucks a pop and I get one fucking epiphany. The bottom line is I'm afraid because you and I can't last. We won't make it. I get close to someone and I blow it. And all I do is ask myself the same old question. How is it… when is it going to end?"

"Then let's not ask that question. Let's just take it a day at a time. Let it go where it goes. Speaking of," he said, hoping to change the topic. "When do I see you again?"

She sniffled and wiped at her eyes. "I've got the Carson show next week. Then I have to go to Nashville to meet some record producer who says he wants to take over my career. This new manager of mine says this producer is quote, unquote, crazier than a pet coon. We should hit it off quite well then, don't you think? Then it's Miami in three weeks."

"That won't work for me. I'm due to go back to Bali to take another look at some things."

"I'm on Austin City Limits in February. Please please come." She chocked back what sounded like a sob. "Don't you see how hard that is? Me asking you for something? Oh God. I am so fucked up."

"Hey, I'll be there. I promise."

She didn't say anything but only clung to him more tightly, burying her face in his neck.

"Look," he said, tilting her face upwards. "If it makes you feel better, just know you don't have to need me. You just have to know I'm there. Is that enough?"

"Yeah. That's enough," she said without conviction.

She craned her neck and kissed his cheek. Neither of them said anything for a long moment, the silence filled with the chatter of the night birds and the static trilling sound of the *coqui* frogs. After several minutes, he heard her snoring softly.

As he lay there cradling her, he pondered his own vulnerabilities. He had always managed to avoid any relationship that might entangle him in commitment. The reasons for his reticence were perhaps not so different from hers. He had long ago come to the realization that being in a position of needing someone to feel complete engendered a weakness that harkened to his upbringing with a mother whose availability shifted with the wind. It was as if it was part of his DNA, his adversity to having to rely on something as tenuous as love to secure completion.

However, in spite of Lou Ann's volatility and baggage, somehow this time felt different. He had developed deeper feelings for her than any of his previous romantic relationships. Her vulnerabilities called forth a sense of responsibility and commitment on his part that he had never been willing to offer up. Was that the beginning of love? He struggled with that thought in mind for a while longer before he managed to stir her just enough for them to stumble to bed.

# PART TWO

# 17

*"The first time we met*
*You told me there was two of me*
*One the woman you met at the bar*
*And then the one you say you want*
*But the one you want isn't the woman I am*
*Ain't I lucky at love?"*

-Lou Ann Catskill
Miss Lucky

## LLANO COUNTY, TEXAS

## APRIL 12th

Lou Ann unfolded the tattered road map and turned it this way and that until she felt oriented. She traced her index finger along the margin and then stabbed at the center so hard it ripped a hole along the crease,

"Okay. It has to be right about here. Just outside of town on this side road. Maybe another five miles or so."

She turned to look at Sudd who seemed intent on adjusting the side mirror in an effort to better study the young woman at the adjoining gas pump. Lou Ann had noted Sudd's apparent interest the moment the woman sauntered out of the convenience store. She wore a tube top one size too small and a pair of brief shorts with the word PINK emblazoned across her ample rear end.

"Dammit, Sudd! Pay attention." She clicked her tongue in irritation. What was it about middle-aged men and their fascination with twenty-year old booty? It's just the skulking shadow of mortality is how a friend explained her husband's adolescent indiscretions.

"I heard you. Ten miles or so out of town," he muttered, his attention still focused on the mirror.

"I said five."

"You're not worried that he doesn't know we're coming?" he asked, finally turning to look at her.

Lou Ann stared at him and wondered how it was that Sudd managed to look even more dissolute than when he appeared at her door in Santa Fe four days ago. The skuzzy beard, the greasy, shoulder length hair. At least, he still dressed like a dandy in his stovepipe black corduroy jeans and fancy white pearl-button Western shirt. Then again, a certain amount of his so-called appeal was a carefully groomed and practiced persona. My look of depraved indifference, he liked to crow. Catnip for the ladies, he would always add. As much as she hated to admit it, she herself had once fallen for his bad boy allure.

"Just drive. If my memory serves me right, the cutoff to his place is next to an old abandoned gas station."

"You're sure you've been there before? You never mentioned ever coming here."

"Do you think I tell you everything? You don't work for me anymore, Sudd. You're not my ...whatever."

"Are you forgetting who rescued you?"

"Rescued me? Sudd, all I asked for was a goddamn ride. I rescued myself." She made a half-hearted and unsuccessful attempt to fold the map before finally wadding it up and hurling at the windshield. "Just drive," she said, tossing her eyeglasses onto the dash. "Please. I'm tired and hypoglycemic as hell."

He cranked the ignition, slipped the van into gear and then paused to look at her.

"Maybe you should take one of your chill pills."

She glared at him. "There aren't going to be any chill pills on this trip. I need to stay focused." Focused and unyielding, she reminded herself. And pissed off.

"Oh, God. In that case, I'll mind my Ps and Qs and tread softly." He shook his head and snorted. "I wish I would've known that before I drove all the way out here."

"And miss all the fun? Stop whining and drive. And watch for an abandoned gas station on the left. At least, I think it's on the left."

He turned on the ignition and stabbed at the radio a half-dozen times until he came across Jackson Browne singing 'These Days.' She suddenly recalled performing that song in a duet with Browne at a benefit concert in Palm Springs. She rolled up the window and sang the lyrics in her mind before softly whispering the lyrics.

"These days …" And counting the time, she thought.

She closed her eyes as her mind drifted back to that show. She remembered Sudd driving her to Palm Springs after playing two road shows in three days. She had hardly slept in that entire time, running on coffee, Ritalin, and mania. And as she remembered it, that duet was really pretty good. At least, Browne thought so. These days. Those days. And then there were freaking days when the only thing that ever changed was the scenery. Just counting time.

"I don't have to wear a mask, do I?" Sudd asked, interrupting her thoughts.

"A mask?" she said to herself, her mind elsewhere. Do I need a mask? Not anymore, she thought, rolling the window down again. Now you get what you see.

"Did you hear me? Is that old fart going to make me wear a mask?"

God, he was insufferable, she thought, not bothering to reply. Three days cooped up with him in the van and in the motel in Amarillo was working her last good nerve. At least, she had managed to make him spring for separate rooms. Even then, the cheap bastard made her promise she would reimburse him.

"Just wear the goddamn mask if he asks, okay?"

He retreated into sullen silence. Sure enough, after fifteen minutes or so, they found the old Sinclair gas station. The green Brontosaurus on the faded sign was riddled with bullet holes. Beneath the sagging portico, four toppled gas pumps lie in perfect rank as if they were casualties of some unfortunate tragedy.

"That's it," she said. "I remember."

Sudd slowed and turned onto a narrow dirt road that appeared little used gauging from the knee-high weeds that almost obscured the track. A short ways further, they encountered a closed wooden gate. A rusty chain with an open padlock hung draped over the top of the gate, more an invitation than an obstacle.

"Hold it," she said. "Back up a bit to that mailbox," she said, pointing at the battered excuse for a mail receptacle nailed to a waist-high stump beside the road. It was missing the door. She retrieved what appeared to be a month's worth of water-stained advertising flyers. She separated out an envelope that looked like some kind of a bill, slipped on her glasses and peered at the address.

"I told you," she said. "JB Coonts. And from the looks of the date on this postmark, I'll be surprised if they haven't cut off JB's electricity." She rifled through the rest of the mail. "Come on. Drive," she said, tossing the pile onto the floorboard.

"Remind me again why we're going here," Sudd said, rolling up his window to block the dust.

"I told you. JB owes me money."

"Did you ever hear of a bank transfer?"

She didn't reply. Sudd wouldn't understand the art of solicitation; or obligation either for that matter. He never had. For that matter, a good argument could be made that neither did she. Issue number four, her latest therapist called it. Not honoring obligations, especially to those who care about you.

She flipped down the sun visor, took off her sunglasses, and studied herself in the small rectangle of mirror. She would have to settle for lip gloss and a run at her hair, she decided as she rummaged through her handbag. The way Sudd was barreling down the deeply rutted road precluded any serious attempt at applying makeup. She leaned into the mirror and dabbed at the corner of her right eye, her finger tracing the fine delta of wrinkles. They seemed new. Or had she just never noticed them before? Living with Kevin could do that. Make you not notice things.

Twelve days ago, she had turned fifty-five. By all accounts, she thought the years had treated her kindly. Her esthetician liked to tell her that good genes went a long way. Just don't forget the sunscreen, she would add. Lou Ann ran the brush through her hair and gave it a fluff. She still wore her hair long, and other than the hint of gray at the temples, it remained just as jet black and voluminous as when she was sixteen and first began performing at county fairs and roadside bars.

They drove for perhaps a mile through pastures choked with mesquite and the occasional clump of scrub oak. Between the trees, wide swaths of Bluebonnet and Paintbrush competed with the native grass for any toehold in the sandy soil and jumbled outcroppings of pink granite. The landscape appeared both desolate and pleasingly pastoral. Its relatively untrammeled appearance suggested JB didn't run any livestock. A gentleman rancher, she reckoned, flipping the sun visor up, only half content with her appearance.

They drove across a dry creek bed, the concrete slab spanning it cracked and uneven. The road then rose sharply before topping out atop a granite ridge. In the far distance, Lou Ann could just make out the immense granite dome of Enchanted Rock. She had gone there once with Sue Mendez after a show in Austin. She recalled it was in the spring and the horizon was awash with bluebonnets as far as the eye could see.

Sudd paused at the top of the ridge. In the wide swale of the valley below them sat a sprawling structure that was all glass and dun-colored stone, its roof covered in reddish clay tile. The edge of a swimming pool peeked out from its rear, the turquoise water in sharp contrast with the surrounding granite landscape. What appeared to be a Land Rover sat parked in front.

"What are you waiting for?" she asked when Sudd made no effort to drive on.

He lit a cigarette and took a deep draw. "Nothing," he said, exhaling and slipping the van back into gear.

"Then go."

They drove down a steep and deeply rutted road before pulling to a stop behind the Land Rover. The only attempt at anything resembling landscaping was a patchy gravel pathway that ended at a small, unpretentious portico. Sudd had no sooner turned off the ignition when a short, pudgy man in a wide straw sombrero and brandishing a rifle rounded the corner of the house.

"Maybe you should stay here," she said as she flung open her door. She hesitated a moment before dismounting. The man let the rifle drop to his side, but made no effort to approach them.

"JB."

"Lou Ann. My God, ain't this absolutely cosmic?" He slung the rifle over his shoulder and limped towards her while she waited in the knee high grass. "It wasn't more than an hour ago that snake of a husband of yours called. He wanted to know if I heard from you or seen you. And here you are in the flesh."

"So he called? He's just missing his piggy bank."

"Speaking of snakes. You probably shouldn't loiter in that grass. I shot a rattler there a week ago."

"Oh, shit," she yelled, dancing her way to a patch of dirt.

"So what's it been? Five years, maybe?"

"Longer," she replied, stopping a couple of paces away. Even though he wasn't much older than her, he looked weathered and sun boiled. His beard, the hat and his thick bifocals obscured most of his face. He wore faded jeans, a grimy T-shirt and scuffed and cracked cowboy boots. His smile revealed more than a couple of gold crowns.

"Yeah, I remember now. It was after that shit show in Phoenix when you threw a hissy fit and fired me. I hope you realize I didn't have that coming."

"You're right. You didn't. And I want you to know I never once said a slanderous word about you."

"I just wish you would've waited and let me produce that last album of yours. I could've done a better job than that Nashville bozo." He looked past her at the van. "Who's the shaggy dog?"

She glanced over her shoulder at Sudd who had made no effort to get out of the van.

"Sudd Kiehne."

"No shit? If he knows what's best for him, he'll stay put. That sorry little piss ant still owes me two grand from a poker game. He even had the gall to say you were good for it."

She approached and started to give him a hug, "I'm vaccinated," she said.

"And I'm probably the only person in all of Llano County who took the needle. Come here," he said, opening his arms. She leaned into him. He smelled of old man sweat and cigarette smoke.

"Let me look at you," he said, stepping back. "You're a little broader in the beam, but you're still a fine looking woman."

"And you still closely resemble a pederast."

It was true that thanks to bearing Iris, she was fuller in the hips than in her prime. Still, she knew that her figure still rated a second glance from any male over the age of forty.

"How about we leave Sudd to simmer and come around back and have a drink. I always keep a jug of martinis in the ice box."

He led her to the rear of the house to a large flagstone patio. The kidney-shaped swimming pool appeared not to have been cleaned in quite some time. A tumble weed bobbed and drifted in the breeze at the pool's far end. A large, somewhat tattered umbrella provided the patio's only shade. JB produced a pair of folding aluminum chairs from the recesses of the back porch and plunked them down next to the table.

"I'll be right back," he said and disappeared into the house.

A large trash can sat against the back wall, its rim overflowing with beer cans. A half-dozen or so bulging plastic trash bags shared a corner with an assortment of garden tools and a rusty power mower. All in all, the place looked a bit neglected.

JB reappeared, carrying what looked to be a pair of crystal martini glasses and a quart size Mason jar of clear liquid. He noticed her scrutinizing the back patio.

"I'm sorry to say the inside doesn't look a whole lot tidier. I never was one for housekeeping and these days I've got no one to please. This little old Mex gal comes every once in a while and cleans up. She's overdue," he said with a grin. He brushed some leaves off the table before unscrewing the lid of the Mason jar and pouring them each a drink.

"Sorry, but I'm out of olives."

She heard the van start up, and a moment later saw it edge its way to a spot beneath a stand of live oak a short distance from the house. Sudd cut the ignition, but still made no effort to get out.

"He's scared I'm going to ask him for that money. If he knows what's good for him he'll stay put. There's always lots of snakes and poison ivy amongst those live oaks." He raised his glass in a toast and took a long sip. "The name Sudd. I never figured out if that was some sort of diminutive or it was his Christian name, though Sudd doesn't sound remotely Biblical."

"It's short for suddenly. His Mama started to call him Sudd after he suddenly strung two words together when he was about three. It seems she was even more impressed when he suddenly stopped crapping in his pants."

JB hooted with pleasure. "That sounds about right." He took a pack of cigarettes from his shirt pocket and lit one with the same gold plated Zippo she remembered from their recording days. "So how are you?" he asked, exhaling.

"In general or might you be referring to my mood disorder?"

"Is that what they call it these days? Hell, my mood's been disordered most of my life. I don't need to see your mood ring to know you're not quite yourself," he added when she didn't say anything.

She glanced at the martini but made no effort to pick it up. "I just spent the better part of the past month locked in my bedroom counting train wrecks. You know how I can get."

"Sure do. It means that I'm going to get the short end of the stick. The last time I saw you, I got poked with that stick. Can I get you something different?" he asked, nodding at the untouched martini.

"I'm on the wagon. But I still like to look at it," she said, forcing a grin.

"I doubt you came all this way to gaze at my liquor. What's up?"

"I need some cash. I thought maybe you would front me some. If you recall, that last album you produced went platinum. I made sure you got your cut. I figured maybe you owe me."

JB nodded and took another drink. "Does this have anything to do with Kevin? I swear when I heard you married up with him, I couldn't believe it. You sorely disappointed me. You know that, don't you?"

"What can I say? I can always blame it on my mood disorder. Anyway, he's history. I left him. And I don't want him finding me," she added.

"Let me guess. Kevin's got you mixed up in one of his shady deals."

"Something like that. He owes me a small fortune. Me, his creditors and his so-called business partners. That's why I need cash. I need to drop off the grid for a while and I don't want him tracking me."

He spread his hands and looked around him. "Is this far enough off the grid for you? At least I got hot water and a satellite dish." When she didn't reply, he downed the rest of his drink and reached for her glass. "Maybe I should just loan you my rifle instead."

"Believe me. It's almost come to that. Come to think of it, I will take a handgun if you have one lying around. I seem to remember you always used to pack a little pearl handled revolver in the back of your waistband."

"It's yours. Fitting, too, since all I ever use it for is to shoot snakes." He took a sip of her untouched martini before going on. "What do you hear from Leon?"

His question caught her off guard. She held his gaze for a couple of seconds before turning away. Leon. Her spirit demon. That's what she called him. But that wasn't quite fair. He was a demon only in the sense that he haunted her relentlessly. In the darkness of her soul, she implored him to go away. And when her mind had settled, she realized she almost welcomed his visitations.

Iris had more than once offered to give her Leon's phone number. And each time, she had either refused or deleted it from her email. Her last psychiatrist had led her to believe that her need to punish herself far outweighed her fear of reconnection. That epiphany only served to harden her intransigence.

Iris had also mentioned that Leon was living back in his cabin in Colorado. She could never quite screw up the courage to ask if he was alone. Not that it mattered. Both of them had always felt alone even when they weren't.

"We haven't spoken in a long time," was all she could manage to say. She looked back at JB.

"I heard tell he was sick," JBe said. "A guy I know up in Denver said he ran into Leon at a hospital up there. No details. He just said Leon didn't look well."

"That's too bad." She started to reach across the table for the martini but stopped herself. "So do you have any cash lying around or not?"

"Are you writing?" he asked, ignoring the question.

"Don't change the subject, you cheap bastard."

"How much do you need?"

"Ten grand would work. It might be enough to see me through until I get Kevin off my back."

"It's Saturday. The bank won't be open until Monday. Can you wait that long?"

"Can you put me up until then?"

"Sure, but I'm not so sure the welcome extends to Sudd."

"He's having a pity party. I'll bring him a beer and some cocktail nuts and he'll be good."

"Maybe I should go ask him for my two grand."

"Leon and I," she said, filling the ensuing silence. "We didn't make it for lots of reasons. The least of which was that I never thought we could make it in the first place. We broke up once… twice actually. Or was it maybe three times? I just knew that after that second time, I couldn't do it again."

"Didn't you write a song along those lines once?"

"More than one I think. And they all sucked."

"Should I be asking where you're headed?"

"I have to go to Austin first. Iris lives there. I haven't told her yet what's going on."

She didn't know why she hadn't returned Iris's calls. She convinced herself that it was because she feared Iris would be disappointed in her. Disappointed that another of her mother's relationships had floundered. The truth was she was disappointed in herself. It was bad enough allowing Kevin back into her life. What was even worse was the price she paid for a foolhardy stab at conventionality. It would be easy enough to blame it all on a fit of delusional mania. That or was it simple desperation?

"How about I rustle us up some dinner?" JB said, interrupting her thoughts. "I can thaw out some rib eyes. Bake some sweet potatoes. I might even deign to break bread with Sudd. Meanwhile, we can talk about the good old days since the new ones never seem to quite measure up."

"The good old days. Was there ever such a thing?"

"As I recall, when you were flying high and wide, everything seemed golden."

"That just goes to show you were never one to pay attention to detail. That was the reason I fired you. Well, one of the reasons. Do you have plenty of hot water? A long hot shower would be nice."

"Can I watch?"

"Still a pervert and a voyeur, are you? I'm going to get a change of clothes and tell Sudd to make his bed."

"Watch for snakes."

She stood up and started for the trees. The lowering sun had turned the granite ridges a russet hue. The air had cooled and she could smell the sweet perfume of the bluebonnets. For the first time in a long while, she felt hopeful. Free of her demons. Or was it all only delusion?

Her cell phone suddenly chirped. She pulled it out and looked at the screen. It was Iris again. She started to put it away and then noticed Iris had sent a text message.

**Where are U? Would U please pick up or call. Worried. I'm with Leon.**

Dammit, Iris. What did you do? And why was Leon with you? Now she regretted not calling her the day she left Santa Fe. I'll call her tomorrow, she thought as she began picking her way through the grass to Sudd's van.

# 18

*"My heart is open to wrongdoing*
*But when will it ever be open to right doing?"*

-Lou Ann Catskill
Wrongdoing

Lou Ann flicked on the lamp and squinted at the alarm clock on the nightstand. 3AM and she still hadn't fallen asleep. She regretted jettisoning her Ambien along with her other medications. Then again, she figured she had slept plenty over the past month. Back in the day, she had made full use of these spates of insomnia, writing music and lyrics that more often than not passed muster in the light of day. But she wasn't writing anymore. She hadn't for a year or more, at least not since she married Kevin. Living with him proved to be more of a soul crusher than her life on the road.

She had almost fallen asleep several times, only to begin ruminating on Iris's text message. And then there was JB's mention of Leon. Once Leon managed to invade her monkey mind, the recrimination, the regret, the fantasy, the false hope, it all went around and around. Then it was set, match, game over. Sleep would come some other time.

She flung off the blanket, grabbed her glasses, and slipped into the musty, threadbare robe JB had fished from the closet and then headed for the kitchen, only to find JB and Sudd sitting at the table playing cards.

JB looked up from his hand and nodded, but Sudd scarcely seemed to notice her.

"Who's winning?" she asked.

"Considering Sudd here started off two thousand in the hole, we're neck in neck, I'm sorry to admit,"

"Do you have anything sweet to eat?"

"Check the freezer, There might still be some Dulce de Leche ice cream."

"That'll do nicely."

She went to the fridge and opened the freezer, removed the carton of ice cream and wandered into the living room. JB was right. The interior of the house appeared just as cluttered and ill-attended to as the patio. A dozen or so sealed cardboard boxes were stacked haphazardly along one wall. A faded bathrobe and a pair of blue jeans were draped over an exercise bike. A baby grand piano sat in one corner, its top heaped high with magazines and books. The only other furnishings were a cracked leather recliner and a massive stainless steel coffee table that held a television the size of a child's mattress.

The bone-colored limestone walls were bare with the exception of the wall behind the piano. It displayed a dozen or so framed platinum and gold records. She picked her way through the rubble and inspected each of the records as she licked a spoonful of Dulce de Leche. Four of the records were hers, two of them were platinum.

She dropped back onto the piano bench and set the ice cream carton on the floor beside her. Wiping her hands on her robe, she allowed her fingers to gently graze the keys before tapping several of them. The piano badly needed tuning. She paused, and then started to play a slow, disjointed melody that had lingered unfinished in her mind for longer than she cared to remember. It began slowly, the chord dropping and then increasing in tempo before dropping again.

"I followed you…. Stole for you…Cared for you. Then…"

She stopped. The lyrics no longer came as easy as they once did. They hadn't in a long time. She rested her fingers on the keys and stared at the records on the wall before lowering her gaze to take in the stack of books and magazines on top of the piano. Something about the spine of one of the books near the bottom of a pile of magazines caught her eye. She tilted her head in order to make out the title.

*Nights on the Ganges – A Pilgrim's Journey to the Kumbha Mela.* It was one of Leon's earlier books. She remembered reading it while on her first European tour, shortly before she and Leon had broken up the first time. His description of fifty million Hindu pilgrims camped on the banks of the Ganges had both enthralled and unsettled her. She had found Leon's account of bathing in the river at dawn amidst the hordes of crushing humanity especially compelling.

At the time, reading it had made her realize that for far too long, she had focused too much of her energy on her own travail. Leon's narrative had forced her to question her place in the larger picture. But rather than place her life in some kind of comforting perspective, the resulting introspection had unnerved her, sending her spiraling into a month long depression. The only way she managed to finish the tour was to run the gauntlet of uppers and downers. It was only when Leon rescued her and took her grizzly bear watching in British Columbia that she felt she could breathe again.

She dug the book out from beneath the pile of magazines and examined the cover for a moment before opening it to a dog-eared page of text. She held the open book to the light and began to read.

*I awoke the second morning to the now familiar chorus of coughing and hacking, the rattling of cooking pans, and the muted birdsong of conversation coming from the makeshift shelters crowding me on either side. The occupants of the large tent on my right consisted of a group of pilgrims of every age, station, and gender – men, women, the elderly and children. Some of them appeared plump and well fed, their clothes and adornment suggesting an elevated station in life, while others, some of the children especially, seemed almost cachectic, their swollen bellies and skeletal limbs rendering them cartoonish in appearance. It wasn't clear if they were members of an extended family or had merely sheltered together out of convenience.*

*The tent to my left, a far grander affair, was constructed of heavy canvas, complete with an ornate portico decorated with strands of brightly colored silk and garlands of marigolds. The previous night, I observed its sole resident, an elderly swami, as he held court, granting absolutions to the various passersby. He wore only a loin cloth and a wreath of desiccated marigolds around his neck. His long gray hair and beard were braided together and draped over his shoulders like a cloak. He sat cross-legged upon an elevated platform surrounded by a circle of flickering candles. The passing supplicants placed coins, paper bills, plastic bottles of tea, and paper cones of saffron rice at his feet as he pleaded their cases to the various deities....*

*As I lie in my thin cotton sleeping bag, I suddenly became aware of a sort of throbbing, almost humming sound that I soon realized was chanting. A moment later, I felt the ground begin to tremble. An earthquake I thought, such was the magnitude of the tremor. In near panic, I stuck my head out of my small pup tent only to see a horde of people streaming through the narrow pathways of our densely packed encampment. Most of them wore white clothing, the women in saris, the men dressed only in loincloths or a white shroud draped over one shoulder. As they passed through the tents, they separated into tributaries and then reformed, only to separate again.*

*I chugged the last of my water and grabbed my belt bag and camera and crawled out of my tent. I immediately found myself being swept up in the tide of humanity, bobbing like a cork in a raging stream, the current gaining velocity with every passing moment. The throng flowed on as if without purpose or direction, weaving this way and that through the tents, an organic entity driving ever forward.*

*By now, the chanting had grown to a roar, an almost vibratory sibilance unlike anything I had ever heard before. At times, it was all I could do to avoid losing my footing and being trampled. And all the while, this river of pilgrims flowed on, joined by another rive of supplicants, and then another. And then without warning, the flow slowed, and I found myself knee deep in the warm waters of the Ganges. I stopped and glanced over my shoulder and saw only a seething mass of my fellow pilgrims pressing on, forcing us further into the river. Finally, waist-deep in the tepid water, I lifted my gaze and saw on the far horizon, the blood red orb of the rising sun cloaked in the dust and the smoke of the thousands upon thousands of campfires. And at that moment, I felt reborn and knew that nothing would ever be the same.*

Lou Ann turned the next page to a photograph portraying Leon wearing only a pair of khaki shorts and standing knee deep in the muddy brown water. A Hindu priest, clothed in a flowing gold robe, appeared to be anointing Leon with water from a tin can. Leon stood there, eyes closed, head bent, hands folded in piety, and all around him were pilgrims in various states of dress, all partaking of the same rite. She studied the photo for a long moment, her fingers lightly caressing the image.

"Oh, Leon," she murmured as she fought back her tears.

For whatever reason, reading this passage gave rise to an unexpected epiphany. How could you be so sure about something, and yet be so wrong, she asked herself as she struggled to contain the wave of emotion engulfing her. Invariably, her thoughts carried her back to that night in Nicaragua and the beginning of the end. Or it had merely been the end of the beginning? Her confusion gave way to a surge of memories about that time in her life -the pain, mostly self-inflicted, and the hurt she had caused Leon. And she recalled something a close friend had once imparted to her on the event of her first divorce. Love doesn't always last, but that doesn't mean it didn't happen, her friend had said with an earnestness that almost seemed genuine.

She sat there a moment longer before taking the book and retreating to her bedroom. Reading Leon's accounts might keep the demons at bay. But she doubted it, for she knew all too well that her insomnia would be tinged with regret.

# 19

*"I can't be unfaithful*
*But neither can I be true*
*'Not to you, not to myself."*

-Lou Ann Catskill
Regrets

## LAGO APOYO, NICARAGUA
## MAY 1998

They wound their way down to the lake along a muddy, deeply rutted track, its edges hemmed in on either side by thick forest. Several times, they encountered large pools of muddy water, their unappreciated depths requiring Leon to negotiate the pickup truck along what passed for a shoulder. It had been near dusk when they turned off the main highway that led to Granada and onto the poorly maintained road leading to the lake. Soon enough, the murky darkness pressed around them. The abrupt arrival of the tropical nightfall always left Lou Ann feeling claustrophobic and anxious, and now she felt doubly so.

Occasionally, they could see flickers of light from deep within the trees. Otherwise, there seemed scant evidence of habitation. Ever the travel writer, Leon felt it necessary to relate a running commentary regarding the flora and fauna of the region and also reminding her that they were driving into a volcanic caldera that formed the deepest freshwater lake in Central

America. He had traveled to the lake on more than one occasion in the early eighties, back when the Contra rebels still controlled parts of the back country. Fortunately, Lago Apoyo had always remained behind the lines and securely in Sandinista hands.

Leon had arranged for them to stay at a small hostel on the far side of the lake. He warned her ahead of time that getting there would require leaving the car at the end of the primitive road and hiking a half-mile or so through the forest. He also cautioned her there would be no electricity or hot showers. When she revealed her displeasure by not commenting, he reminded her that she had explicitly requested he take her some place where no one knew her.

The flight from Houston to Augusto Sandino Airport in Managua had taken five hours, just enough time for her to catch a long nap. She had just come off a brutal trans-European tour. Consequently, she couldn't recall the last time she had slept for more than a couple of hours at a time. In between fitful slumbers, every waking moment of the past several weeks had been consumed by an endless parade of seemingly identical airports; a different stage every other night, and the requisite attendance at interviews and backstage parties. And then three days ago, she awoke alone in a house overlooking the Hollywood Hills. No purse, no clothes, and no memory of how she had gotten there. No faces, no names. It was all a blank.

As she stood that morning by herself on the deck of the empty house, she recalled the advice offered to her by a well known studio musician she had once known. He had a penchant for rum and any kind of white pill. Once, on a whim, he had decided to accompany her on a road tour. At the time, she took his unsolicited counsel for nothing more than drunken bluster.

"If you can't out run your demons," he had told her while sucking down the last of a bottle of Flor de Caña. "You might as well make them your closest friends."

Hadn't one of her psychiatrists told her something much the same? Both of these would be gurus were now long dead, one from a heroin overdose, the other by suicide. Embracing her demons had always been her modus operandi. And what had that ever gotten her? The psychiatrist told her it would help her to know herself; to recognize just where those demons came from. She doubted the rum-besotted studio musician had meant it quite the same way.

To her irritation, self-discovery had led more to self-loathing than enlightenment. And as far as intimacy with her demons went, this familiarity led her to feel more secure in their companionship than any of her doomed relationships ever had. And then there was Leon, a demon of an altogether different cloth. A demon that consumed her and offered a temptation that in her heart of hearts she knew would only end in pain. Hadn't she written enough songs about just that very thing?

So where did that leave the two of them? In that dark moment of introspection while standing on the deck of a strange house overlooking a city built on fiction and illusions, she feared that she had caged herself in a prison of her own fiction, and escape would now require crossing the Rubicon without any hope or possibility of turning back.

In a pair of filched overalls, she had hitchhiked to a service station and called Sudd. When she called Leon later that day, she should've canceled the trip. Instead, she gave in to inertia and her usual reticence to deal with confrontation and agreed to meet him in Houston in two days time. To her credit, if it could be remotely called that, she told Leon she would meet him at the departure gate rather than spend a night with him at his hotel. Once at the gate, and after the usual endearments and Leon's attempts to engage her in conversation, she claimed fatigue and fell asleep soon after boarding.

During the subsequent drive from Managua to the road leading to the lake, little had been required of her beyond the occasional nod and banal comment on Leon's lengthy tutorial on Nicaraguan history. Once they reached the cutoff to the lake, Leon also retreated into silence, either because he had read her mood or because of the tedious driving conditions.

Her hypoglycemia and a migraine only aggravated the tension. At Leon's urging, she had left behind all of her medications. Nicaraguan customs, he warned her, was notorious for declaring any medications as contraband and confiscating them. To her despair, she realized she was on her own without so much as a Tylenol. There would be no little white pills to help her sleep, no rainbow colored capsules to level things out. Her support system was securely tucked away in her medicine cabinet back in LA.

They had been driving for perhaps a half an hour down the muddy track when three men suddenly emerged from the dark shadows and into the high beams of their headlights. Two of them brandished rifles. All wore a mix of camouflage and mufti. One of them, the tallest of the three, wore a broad brimmed sombrero; the other two wore baseball caps. The tall one motioned for Leon to stop. Lou Ann could see the man had a handgun stuffed into his belt. Leon slowed and then slipped the truck into neutral.

"What are you doing? Don't stop," she said, doing her best to conceal her anxiety.

"It'll be alright," he replied, his eyes fixed on the three men blocking their way.

As the tall one approached Leon's window, he cocked his head in an attempt to look into the cab. His right hand had dropped to rest on the butt of his handgun.

"*Buenas noches,*" Leon said as the man leaned into the window.

The man didn't reply at first, but instead took his time scrutinizing them, his gaze lingering on Lou Ann.

"*¿A donde vas?*" he said finally, straightening and stepping back.

"*Vamos a la casa de la Señora Aronda.*"

"*¿De donde eres? ¿Americano?*"

"*Si,*" Leon replied after a moment of hesitation. He then proceeded to offer the man what sounded to Lou Ann to be a lengthy explanation in Spanish. The man seemed to consider this for a moment before launching into his own long winded monologue.

"*¿Dólares o córdoba?*" Leon asked the man.

"*Los dólares son los mejores.*"

"Relax," Leon said, turning to Lou Ann. "These guys are just the neighborhood watch. Do you still have some dollars?"

"Sure."

"Who would've guessed this is a toll road," Leon said. "Give me a twenty if you have one. Better yet, the more ones you have the better."

Lou Ann dug into her bag and came up with a wad of US currency which she handed to Leon who scrutinized the money for a moment before handing it all to the man. Leon said something to the man who stood there for a long moment staring at Leon as if expecting something further. Finally, he nodded and stepped away from the window.

"*Puedes ir, amigo,*" he said before shouting something to his companions who also moved to the edge of the road. Leon slipped the pickup into gear and slowly edged past them.

"Forty bucks will make sure the truck's still there when we leave. Ten years back I might've taken them for Contras. For all I know, they might've been. For now they're just some guys trying to make a living."

They drove in silence another fifteen minutes or so before the road ended abruptly at a large pile of brush and fallen tree trunks. "We're going to have to walk from here," Leon said, cutting the ignition.

Lou Ann didn't reply, nor did she make any effort to get out. Leon also sat there staring straight ahead. The only sound was the ticking of the hot engine and the staccato trilling of the insects.

"Are you okay?" he finally asked.

"Yeah," she said absently.

"You're sure? It seems like something's bothering you. Is this too Third World for you?"

"It's just those guys back on the road. You seemed so blasé about it. I'm beginning to believe you when you said you were in the Foreign Legion. Jesus, Leon. How did you know they weren't going to hijack us and leave us for dead?"

"I really didn't know. All I could think was whatever was going to happen, would happen."

"Oh, goody, now we're both fucking fatalists."

They set off, Leon carrying his small backpack over his shoulder and clutching Lou Ann's carry on. His headlamp cast just enough light to see only a few meters ahead on the narrow, rain-soaked path. The static of the insects and screeching of night birds seemed at times almost deafening. At one point, Lou Ann startled at a loud hooting that erupted from the trees above them. Howler monkeys, Leon explained.

As they walked, Leon recounted how he met their hostess. A minor Sandinista official Leon had befriended first introduced them. Señora Aronda had been employed by one of the dictator Somoza's ministers as a cook. After the revolution, someone had denounced her as a collaborator and she was imprisoned for a short time by the Sandinista government. It was only due to the intercession of Leon's contact, a close relative of hers, that she was eventually freed. Now she hosted the occasional off the beaten path tourists, mostly Canadians and European backpackers.

Soon the path widened, and in a clearing ahead, they came upon a rustic stone structure shrouded in darkness except for a single strand of anemic, multi-colored Christmas lights looped across its front. Lou Ann could hear the flatulent chugging of a generator from some distance away. As they approached, a dog began to bark, and a woman appeared in the doorway, the faint light from the interior revealing only her short, stout silhouette.

Leon and the woman greeted each other effusively with kisses and embraces. Lou Ann received the same greeting. In the light leaking from inside, Lou Ann saw that the woman appeared quite old, her face deeply wrinkled, her hair almost entirely white. She could also tell the woman had no teeth. Leon had informed Lou Ann earlier that Señora Aronda spoke only Spanish. Lou Ann watched the woman's face as she listened to Leon's introduction. At one point, she arched her eyebrows and smiled at Lou Ann broadly.

"I told her you were a famous American songstress. She seems duly impressed."

The old woman said something and gestured for them to follow her inside. Her voice sounded stronger than one might expect, her words somewhat muddled, perhaps due to her lack of teeth. At first glance, the house seemed to consist of only one room. The room's low ceiling was composed of cross- hatched tree limbs, the walls a sagging patchwork of stone and stucco. What appeared to be some sort of ivy snaked up the wall in one corner. The room obviously served as both the kitchen, dining room, and gauging from the two sagging and well worn sofas along one wall, it also served as the living room.

"Don't worry. We have a little casita to ourselves down by the lake. She wants us to eat first. *Truchas en salsa verde. Su especialidad,*" he added to the woman's obvious delight. "We're eating out here," he said, guiding Lou Ann through a low, narrow doorway that opened onto a small lantern-lit patio corseted by tall stands of bamboo intertwined by morning glory vines. A small *nicho* carved into the adobe wall beside the doorway displayed a statuette of the Virgin Mary, a handful of marigolds, and a burning tea candle. A gingham tablecloth covered the small rough hewn wooden table. Two candles and a glowing mosquito coil graced the table along with a small bouquet of flowers in an earthen vase.

"It's lovely," she said, turning to Leon. "Thank you." She grasped his hand and raised it to her lips.

"You're not in Kansas anymore, Dorothy. More like in the middle of bum fuck nowhere,"

Señora Aronda appeared with a bottle of white wine and two glasses. "*Disfrutar,*" she said offering them each a smile.

"You've been awfully quiet," Leon said, pouring them each a glass.

"You're the one who told me to leave my pills behind. So what you see is what you get."

"Is there a subtext there?"

"A subtext? No. I'm just tired."

She took a sip of the wine. It was too sweet, but quite cold, and she wondered how Señora Aronda kept it so cold. The lake, she guessed. She emptied the glass in one swallow, fortifying herself for what she was about to say. She waved Leon's hand away, refilling the glass herself. She tilted back the glass and emptied it in one long swallow. Here goes nothing, she thought to herself.

"You have this magical life, Leon. Do you realize that? The travel, the adventure. You live... outside of yourself. Your world is so much bigger than mine. Hold on," she said when he started to interrupt. "You and everyone else think my life is so exciting and glamorous and interesting. Well, it's none of those things. Believe it or not, my world is much smaller than yours. Like you told me before, I live too much in my head. That's just the way it is," she added, filling the ensuing silence. "You keep telling me to just drop out for a while. Live it differently. I can't do that. Don't ask me why. It's just the way it is."

Leon poured himself some more wine, but didn't say anything as if waiting her out.

"I guess what I'm trying to say is that you and I both have such different lives," she said, breaking the silence. "We want different things. You want things I can't give you."

"How do you know what I want?" he asked with an edge in his voice.

She shrugged. "Maybe it's what I want. Please. Leon. Hear me out. We can run with this all we want, but we'll never make it to the end of the road."

"Spare me the shitty lyrics. Lou Ann, you just need to step back and see your life differently. That's all I'm saying. That's all I've ever wanted for you."

She considered this for a moment before continuing on. "Leon, it's not that I don't... My God, do you realize what it costs me to say I love you? I've never... I've never said that to anyone. "

"Then don't say it unless you really mean it. Look, I get it about you and intimacy. How you're afraid of being vulnerable. It's the why that I don't get."

"The why? Because I'm unstable is why. And that's the nice way of putting it."

"And that's supposed to make you unworthy of love?"

"Shit, Leon. It makes me unreliable. Missing in action. Unfaithful. A risk. Sooner or later I crash and I burn everything down around me." She looked away, suddenly unsure if she wanted to go on. "I'll burn your bed with you in it," she said turning her gaze back. "And I can't do that. I won't do that. Not to you."

When he didn't say anything, she went on. "I just think we need to be apart. Just for a while. Give each other some space. Look at it this way. How many couples are lucky enough to realize early on that things aren't working out? It saves a lot of time and hurt."

"So that's it is? Fine," he said, pushing his chair back. "Maybe..."

Before he could finish what he was about to say, Señora Aronda appeared bearing their dinner. She set their plates down and offered Lou Ann a smile. "*Bon appétit,*" she said in her deep, graveled voice.

"*Gracias,*" Lou Ann replied, returning her smile.

Leon murmured something in Spanish before looking up and nodding at Señora Aronda who smiled and withdrew. They ate in silence, any rapprochement hindered by what had been left unsaid. The trout had been baked to perfect delicacy and tasted of wood smoke and some herb she couldn't place. It was only when their hostess interrupted to present them with a small cake that Leon's mood seemed to soften. He smiled at Lou Ann and asked if she wanted another bottle of wine.

"Sure, if we can take it back to our room. It might help us write some music," she added, reaching her hand across the table.

He smiled without humor and after a moment, opened his palm and took her hand.

"You're breaking my heart," he said. "You know that, don't you?"

"Yeah. I've hurt you. And I'll just hurt you again."

He shook his head in what seemed great sadness. "*Señora. Una botella mâs de vino, por favor,*" he shouted over his shoulder. He looked up at the dark pitch of sky before turning to her.

"This is all beginning to sound like some good material for a song. Just promise me you'll write in a part about you leaving me with my dog and my pickup," he said without obvious amusement.

She tried to laugh but couldn't manage more than a grim smile. In her mind, she spun the wheel. He loves me. He loves me not. I love him. I love him not. Any place she landed seemed to engender more pain than pleasure. She finished her wine and stared past him at the flickering shadows cast by the candle in the *nicho*. And she wondered why this pain felt so different.

# 20

*"Once in a while we can play*
*This love game*
*Why is that so hard?*
*Why is it such a mystery?*
*Why are there always more questions than answers?"*

-Lou Ann Catskill
Vase of Hearts

It was shortly after sunrise when she ventured into JB's kitchen. She found him leaning against the counter, a coffee cup in one hand and a bottle of Jack Daniels at his elbow. He slurped and nodded.

"Any more of that left? The coffee, that is," she added.

"Have you been up all night reading?" he asked, pointing at the book tucked under her arm.

She held it up to show him the cover.

"That was a wild one. Though it didn't exactly make me want to quit Nashville and paddle up the Ganges. But he sure can paint a picture, can't he?"

"So how did the card game turn out?" she asked, tossing the book on the counter.

"That sumbitch Sudd's up a thousand."

"In that case, maybe I'll have to hit him up for some money."

"You don't really think I gave him anything other than an IOU? At least, I didn't tell him you were good for it. Are you going somewhere?" he asked, nodding at her overnight bag.

"I've been thinking about going on into Austin. I've got enough cash to last me for a few days. I need to see Iris."

"I still plan on getting you your money. Just let me know how I can get it to you."

"I imagine Sudd could be persuaded to come back out here on Monday, seeing as how you owe him. Or you could drive into Austin yourself and join the reunion. Iris says Leon's with her," she added.

"Leon's in Austin? It would be good to see him again. How about yourself?"

"You mean how do I feel about seeing him? I don't know." She poured herself a cup of coffee and opened the refrigerator. "Do you have anything to eat?" The fridge contained only a Tupperware container of something grayish, a small carton of half and half and a cantaloupe. "Any eggs?" she asked, opening the bins.

"It's been a while since you've seen him, right?" he asked, making no effort to aid in her scavenging.

She straightened and looked at him. "I told you. We quit for good. Leave it at that."

"I probably have some frozen chorizo. Your only other option is this nice little diner in Fredericksburg. They serve up a pretty good breakfast. Or you can go back into Llano…"

The sound of her cell phone chirping interrupted him. She fished it from her pocket and glanced at the caller ID. It was Iris. She tapped the phone.

"Iris."

JB picked up the bottle of Jack Daniels and strolled out of the kitchen.

"Mom, where the hell are you?" Iris sounded frantic. "I was worried that…"

"I'm fine," Lou Ann said, cutting her off. "Look, I'll be in Austin later today."

"I'm not in Austin. We're just now leaving Santa Fe. Leon and I," she added when Lou Ann didn't comment. "And Fumiko."

"Fumiko? Who's Fumiko?"

There was a moment of silence. Lou Ann envisioned Iris glancing at Leon for an answer. Leon's latest paramour, she guessed. Leon was never without a new woman. Was that really a fair judgment?

"It's a long story," Iris said. "I'll tell you when I see you. Why are you going to Austin?"

"To see you, of course. Some things have happened." When Iris didn't say anything, she went on. "Why is Leon with you?"

"Look, Mom. He wanted to help."

"Help? With what?"

"With finding you."

She fumbled for something to say. "Finding me? Okay," she said finally. "I plan on seeing Sue Mendez. Call me when you get into Austin," she said and disconnected.

Why was it that whenever Iris thought her mother was in trouble, she sought out Leon to come to the rescue? It was no different than when Iris herself was in trouble, whether it was the school suspensions, the boyfriends, the girlfriends, the DUIs. Iris had never come to Lou Ann once to seek her help. She had always gone to Leon. It had always been a bone of contention between them, and no doubt contributed to her and Leon's final breakup. Leon had assumed the role of father for how long? All of six years? It wasn't as if... She caught herself and quickly cast the thought from her mind. She started to slip the phone back into her pocket and instead dialed another number. It rang for almost a minute before the voice message came on.

"This is Sue. You know the drill. Leave a number."

"It's Lou Ann. I did it. I left Kevin. Look, I'll be in town in a couple or three hours. I'll call you then. Listen... Leon's going to be there," she blurted. "I thought you should know."

She looked up to see JB standing there looking at her. She hung up and slipped the phone into her bag.

"Is everything all right?"

"It's fine."

He handed her an envelope. "In there's the sum total of cash I've got lying around. Might as well take this, too," he said, offering her a pearl handled revolver. "Feel free to use it with minimal discretion. The gun, that is."

She tucked the money and the gun into her bag and then hugged him. ""Thanks, JB. I'll call you," she said and walked out.

# 21

*"And some nights pass without you*
*I'll take those nights*
*Nights when it all seems right*
*Even when it's wrong."*

-Lou Ann Catskill
Woman Down

**AUSTIN, TEXAS**

**APRIL 13th**

Sue Mendez awoke to the muted ringing of her cell phone, followed by a long silence, and then a pinging sound. Someone had left her a message. She nudged the cat off her pillow, and squinted at the alarm clock. 7AM. Only then did she remember she wasn't alone. Glancing over her shoulder, she saw the form wrapped in the bunched sheet. That was a mistake, she thought to herself. She pulled the covers over her head and went back to sleep, or at least gave it an attempt. A half hour later, she flung off the covers and sat up. Her cat, Chica, lifted its head but made little effort to move. She swung her legs over the side of the bed, and paused just long enough to orient herself as to what day it was. The half-dozen or so tequila shots she had consumed last night made it difficult to focus. She felt pretty sure it was Sunday. She was also pretty sure that she badly needed a glass of water and some Tylenol.

She shuffled into the bathroom, filled a glass with tap water and plopped down on the toilet to pee. Chica studied her from the doorway with what she interpreted as judgment. She sat there for a minute before finally pushing to her feet, flushing and then refilling the water glass. As she gulped the water, she studied herself in the mirror and decided she had done a pretty sorry job of removing her makeup the night before. She set down the glass, wet a washcloth and gave her face a few perfunctory swipes or two before tossing the washcloth into the sink.

She brushed her long blonde hair out of her eyes and took another look. Her eyes were bloodshot and puffy. There was no point in further appraisal, she decided and turned away. It was no longer the face of a beauty queen, even though she had once reigned as the Alpine Rodeo Queen. She had also once been the runner up for the 1991 Miss Texas crown. Her singing talent had almost put her over the top. She lost out to a Farah Fawcett look alike that couldn't sing a lick, but did offer up a rather spirited soliloquy expounding on the virtues of being born and bred a Texan.

She shook out a couple of Tylenol, downed another glass of water, and went back in the bedroom. Billy hadn't stirred. Moving as quietly as possible to her closet, she grabbed her kimono from the hook before changing her mind and snatching a pair of Lycra running tights from a pile of dirty laundry. She needed to jog. It might help her hangover. She rummaged through the laundry again until she found a sports bra, and then followed the cat into the kitchen.

She took a moment to pull her hair back and knot it in a bun as she surveyed the wreckage from last night's birthday postmortem. Several of her friends had taken her out on the town to celebrate her big four five. *Chile rellenos* at Matt's El Rancho had led to a circuit of night clubs that ended at Antone's to catch a midnight gig by a local blues band whose name escaped her.

Gauging from the frying pan on the stove and the stack of egg yolk-smeared plates in the sink, someone must have fried some eggs, although for the life of her she couldn't remember. A half-dozen beer bottles lined the counter beside a half-empty carafe of coffee. After retrieving a cup from the sink, she filled it with the cold coffee and launched it into the microwave.

As she waited for the coffee to heat, she slipped into her workout clothes and then looked for her phone. It took her a moment or two to remember she had most likely left it in her jacket. It took her another moment to find her jacket beneath the pile of her and Billy's discarded clothes. As she dialed up her messages, she retrieved the coffee mug from the microwave. One swallow proved enough. The coffee was lukewarm and tasted soapy. Someone must have made a half-ass attempt to wash the cups. She dumped the coffee into the sink as she scrolled through the messages. There were three voice mail messages.

"Coffee," a voice growled from the hallway door.

Billy stood there in his boxer shorts, his hair askew, his face reflecting a look of intense desperation. He needed a shave, something she hadn't noticed or perhaps had just ignored the night before. She preferred her men clean-shaven. His body wasn't that great either. Not enough muscle tone and again too much hair. She wondered why it was that men always looked so unappealing the first thing in the morning.

Giving into her irritation, she pointed at the carafe of coffee on the kitchen counter, half-hoping he would take a soapy mug from the sink. When he instead retrieved a clean one from the cupboard, she turned away.

The first message was from her dentist reminding her of her appointment on Monday. The second was from her niece wishing her happy birthday. She deleted it and went on to the third.

"Where's the sugar? Every time I come here..." Billy muttered as he rifled through the cabinets. "Sue. Where's the damn sugar?"

She held up her hand to shush him and turned away. To her surprise, the message was from Lou Ann. All Sue managed to hear was something about Kevin and Austin. She didn't catch the last part over the din of Billy slamming drawers. She walked into the living room and listened to the message again.

"Shit, no," she whispered. Lou Ann and Leon. Were they back together again? Was that how she was reading it? She listened a third time before walking back into the kitchen. Billy was in the process of shoveling coffee beans into the grinder.

"I'm going to buy you one of those machines where you just pour in the beans the night before and in the morning... *Voilà!* Fucking coffee."

"I don't want a machine," she replied,

"You're not really going to the gym, are you?"

"And what if I am? It's none of your goddamn business."

"Get your claws in, girl. I was just asking. Jesus."

"You should go. I'm sorry," she added in response to his look of what she interpreted as relief rather than hurt. "I mean I'm not feeling all that great and a friend is coming by in an hour or so." When he didn't say anything, she went to the sink and began washing a cup. Billy just stood there and watched her. "Look," she said, turning and looking at him. "I'll call you later and we can talk about the gig. Okay?"

"Sure," he said and retrieved his clothes from the living room floor and turned for the bedroom.

Billy was a small time music promoter she had known for years. The night before, he had offered her a job touring on the West Coast with an up and coming jazz singer. The money sounded good, but the rest of the commitment not so much. Billy had intimated that he wanted Sue to travel with him on the tour. As a companion was the way he put it – translation eye candy and fuck buddy.

It wasn't that she didn't find him sexy and entertaining. He had a nice face, at least when he bothered to shave. He had the sort of blue eyes and full lips that when he smiled, always reminded her of some movie actor - Brando, maybe. Or maybe that old timey French actor, Yves something.

Her reservation over taking the job wasn't that she hadn't accepted similar arrangements in the past. It was more that her head was simply not in a place for complications or obligation, no matter how appealing touring the West Coast sounded. Her last romantic entanglement, a dentist with a surfeit of oral fixations, had taken the wind out of her sails. For now she was content with hanging with her girl friends and the occasional club date.

A minute later, Billy emerged from the bedroom. He still hadn't combed his hair and it made his head look lopsided. He came up beside her and attempted to give her a kiss on the neck, but she pulled away and laughed.

"Let's not get anything started we can't finish," she said. "I told you. I have company coming." She made an uncertain attempt to comb his hair with her fingers.

"I really want you to come along on this tour," he said.

"And I might. Let me think about it," she said, touching his lips with her fingers before turning back to the sink.

"You do that," he said, patting her butt before walking out the door.

She stood there a moment staring out at her neighbor's barricade of overgrown oleander before going and picking up her phone. She listened to the message again, hoping she could read between the lines. What did Lou Ann mean when she said Sue ought to know Leon would be in Austin? Maybe she shouldn't be reading anything into it. All she knew was that after all this time, she would be crazy to rake through those coals again. She went into the bathroom and looked at herself in the mirror. "Shit, Leon," she muttered as she attempted to smooth out the wrinkles around her eyes.

Why did she suddenly feel like a teenager who had just been asked to the prom by your best friend's boyfriend? She went back into the living room and walked over to the fireplace mantle. The small, unframed black and white photo had been clipped to a larger photo of Lou Ann's band, The Imperfections, the name more appropriate than one could ever imagine. She glanced at the smaller photo for a few seconds longer and then slid it behind a vase of dried flowers.

"Shit, shit." She turned and headed for the shower.

# 22

*"Pay no mind to me.*
*Your love is not for me*
*It's only in the chorus of a song."*

-Lou Ann Catskill

**BRADY, TEXAS**

Leon waited impatiently in the 4Runner for the two women to return from the gas station's restroom. He had made a half-hearted attempt to peel himself from the front seat of the 4Runner and stretch, an inclination quickly dispelled by a sudden spasm of back pain. It had been a long day, and after nine hours of driving, they were still a good two hours or more from Austin's outskirts. He regretted not taking anything for pain since that morning at the hotel in Santa Fe, his rationale being that the pain kept him from ruminating on other matters. Or was it merely his version of self-flagellation?

They had managed to leave Santa Fe at seven sharp after breakfast at a drive through burrito place and a pit stop at Starbucks. For the next two hours, their conversations had consisted of nothing more than grunts, yes, no, and maybes. Even Fumiko had said little beyond her usual utterance of contented endorsement. *Sugoi,* she had proclaimed after her first ever bite of a egg and chorizo burrito.

Leon could only assume Iris knew that Ahrens had filled him in on her altercation with Riordan. Her reticence to volunteer anything led Leon to wonder if she believed some deal had been cut with the cops allowing her to leave Santa Fe. If that were indeed the case, she knew bringing it up might lead to the offer being withdrawn. Her reliance on Leon to pull her ass out of the fire had always been a dynamic in their relationship. As the morning progressed, his annoyance grew. After a good five years apart, she still expected him to be her fixer.

It wasn't until outside of Fort Sumner that Iris broke her silence. She had volunteered to drive the first leg over Leon's cursory protest, her reasoning being she was a morning person.

"I'm tired of driving," she announced. "This countryside sucks."

"I wouldn't think that would bother a morning person." Up until now, he had feigned sleep, but he felt her comment deserved a smart-assed retort.

"Okay, Leon. Why don't you stop being so passive aggressive and ask me about last night?"

He took off his sunglasses and winced in pain as he struggled to sit upright. "Ahrens told me enough. I don't need a blow by blow."

"I wasn't going to let Kevin get away with not telling me that the dead woman in Grants wasn't Mom."

"So you settled up, did you? You're lucky he didn't shoot you."

She didn't have a rejoinder, and for his part, he had no interest in pursuing it further. They drove in silence for several minutes before Iris spoke up again.

"I talked with Mom this morning," she blurted out.

"You what?" He twisted in his seat with some difficulty to face her.

"I called her from the hotel just before we left."

"And when were you planning on telling me?"

"She's in Austin. Or will be. Look, I thought that if I told you before we left this morning you would've backed out."

"Damn right, I would've. So, what's the story? Is she off her meds? Manic? Or just stirring up shit for the hell of it? I take it then she's definitely not missing."

"I guess not."

Leon cursed under his breath, but didn't offer a reply, confident there wasn't any point. Iris didn't offer anything more either. They rode in silence for another hour or so, the only discourse between the three of them was the occasional commentary regarding the scarce evidence of any obvious civilization in the surrounding countryside. The gritty steppes of Eastern New Mexico gave way to the monotonous Texas plains. The small towns, with names like Muleshoe and Levelland and La Mesa, all seemed to offer little more than gas stations, fast food drive-throughs, and pickup and tractor dealerships. The landscape in between consisted mostly of dusty and barren cotton fields, the only disruption on the otherwise featureless horizon were the occasional derelict windmill and the rocking of the mantis-like oil pumps.

After another hour of banal commentary, Fumiko pestered Leon to entertain them with a travel story. Out of boredom, Leon acquiesced and regaled them with an account of a hitchhiking trip through the landmine-riddled landscape of Cambodia. When that story had run its course, he decided in a fit of pique to launch into a recounting of a long ago trip to Spain with Iris. Her behavior back then, a mix of adolescent angst and the fallout from her strained relationship with Lou Ann, led to more than a few tense interludes, leading Leon to more than once consider cutting the trip short and dumping her back in Texas. Iris's reaction to hearing this story for perhaps the fifth time led to the usual sullen silence that lasted until they stopped for gas in Brady, a small town on the edge of the Texas Hill Country.

While the two women were still in the restroom, Leon managed to reach into the back seat and retrieve his bag of bootleg medications and find his hydrocodone. As he rummaged around the front seat for a water bottle, he noticed Iris's open wallet on the driver's side floorboard. He picked it up and started to place it on the seat, but out of idle curiosity, he rifled through the contents. There were several hundred dollars in cash and little else other than her driver's license, a student ID, a coffee punch card, and a couple of credit cards. He started to replace the cards when his eyes settled on her driver's license.

The photo had been taken when Iris still wore her hair in a bleached buzz cut. For some reason, his gaze fell on her date of birth. He stared at it, first in confusion, then with a growing sense of unease and disbelief. The date was wrong. Her birthday was in April, the same month as Lou Ann's. The license listed her birthday as Feb 1, 1998. Why was the date off by two months?

He stared into the near distance for a moment before tossing the wallet onto the seat. He could still recall the birthday celebrations, the sleepovers, the mock *quinceañera* on the occasion of her fifteenth birthday, and the perennial gags since her birthday fell on April Fool's Day. So why was her birth month listed as February first? He counted backwards in his head. It didn't make sense. Or did it? His thoughts were interrupted by the two women's return.

"I will drive," Fumiko announced, sliding behind the wheel. She handed him a fistful of Slim Jims and a can of Mountain Dew. "Iris says we must eat Texas road food," she said without a trace of sarcasm. "Did you stretch?"

"Sure did," he lied. He glanced back at Iris as she made her nest in the back seat..

They drove for perhaps thirty minutes before Fumiko broke the silence. "Are you okay, Leon? I think we should have spent the night in that San Angelo city. Do you want some of your hydrocodone?" she asked when he didn't reply.

"Stop the car. I need to get out."

"Are you ill?"

"Pull over, goddammit!"

Fumiko slowed and pulled off onto the shoulder. Leon hardly waited for her to come to a complete stop before flinging open the door and stumbling out. He leaned against the 4Runner for a moment, grimacing in pain before turning and limping off in the direction from where they had just come. He had gone no more than twenty or so yards when he heard Fumiko open her door. He kept walking until he felt Fumiko grab his arm.

"Leon. What is the matter?" she asked, tugging at him until he faced her.

"I need to… Shit. Leave me alone."

He fumbled in his shirt pocket for the joint and the lighter he had sequestered there that morning. With trembling hands, he struggled to light it. Fumiko finally grabbed his hand to steady him. He took a long drag from the joint and pulled his hand away in irritation.

"You are angry. Why?"

He turned and looked back at the 4Runner. Iris hadn't stirred from where she slept in the back seat. He took another long hit off the joint, exhaled and began to take another but Fumiko snatched the joint from his grasp. Before he could protest, she licked her fingers and snuffed it out.

"Enough," she said, tossing the joint out onto the highway.

He turned his back on her and stared out at the pasture land on the other side of the barbed wire fence. He had forgotten how splendorous the Texas Hill Country could be in spring. The warm, moist air, the brilliant green of the mesquite along with the lush carpet of grass and wildflowers transformed the rugged landscape into something almost benign. He felt the initial buzz of the marijuana, and with it, a fleeting sense of serenity that turned quickly to anxiety. Fumiko stood next to him, waiting him out.

"Her birthday…." The pot allowed his mind to drift back and forth slipshod to a different time. He started over. "There was a time when I used to fantasize about Iris. What it would've been like if she had been my daughter, and I would've been something other than some fucking convenient surrogate." He paused as a couple of eighteen wheelers roared by. "I'd wonder if it would've changed things between us. Between Lou Ann and me."

"I do not understand, Leon. Where does this come from?"

At the moment, he wanted nothing more than to just lie down in the knee-high Johnson grass and sleep, but something told him he might never get up. He leaned over, his hands on his thighs, and grunted in pain.

"I told you this would be too long to drive. Too much," Fumiko said, placing her hand on his back.

"This whole fucking thing is too much." He straightened and started walking back to the 4Runner.

Fumiko hurried ahead of him and opened his door. "We will go back to Brady," she said. "I saw a Holiday Inn there. We will spend the night and rest. Tonight, I will give you a massage and your hydrocodone. You will sleep. Tomorrow will come no matter what."

Leon pushed her hand away as she tried to help him into the seat. As she walked around to the driver's side, he fished the hydrocodone out of his shirt pocket and dry swallowed it. He turned and looked over the seat at Iris who hadn't awakened. If he asked her about her birth date, what would she say? Why had she never mentioned to him that her birth date had inexplicably been changed? One way or another, the truth would come out - if not from Iris, than from Lou Ann. That is if they ever caught up with her, a prospect that now offered him even less comfort. He settled into the seat and closed his eyes.

# 23

*"Have I lost you?*
*Or only myself?*
*Tell me.*
*So I can find my way."*

-Lou Ann Catskill
Isle of Hearts

Fortunately, the Holiday Inn Express in Brady had two remaining rooms, their capacity challenged by a Southern Baptist Youth convention being held at a nearby ranch. Typical for Texas, Leon's room was overly air conditioned and smelled of some sickly sweet floral air freshener meant to mask the underlying bouquet of Lysol and mold. In a near stupor from fatigue and the hydrocodone, he collapsed on the bed. He barely remembered Fumiko saying something about returning later with food. It was dark when he heard her slip into his room. He lifted his head to look at her. She wore a pair of running shorts and a sleeveless T-shirt.

"I brought you a pork chop, salad, and baked potato. You should eat," she said, sliding a Styrofoam container onto the night stand. "This is not healthy food, but comforting for you."

"I'm not hungry," he grunted.

"Eeeee! Why must you be so difficult? You have to keep up your strength. How is your pain?"

"*Mas y meno.* So so."

"I think this journey was a very bad idea. How are your legs? I told you that thrombosis is a side effect of the new medication. You have not moved enough today."

"My legs are fine."

She ignored him and began palpating his calves for any obvious tenderness or inflammation. "I think you should have your laboratory tests earlier than next week. Perhaps when we reach Austin." She muttered something under her breath,

"What?"

"I do not look forward to telling your doctor that we are traveling. He will fire me."

"He can't fire you. I hired you."

"Yes, but he will be very unhappy. He will report me to my agency or even the Board of Nursing."

"Don't worry. I'll deal with them."

"Remove your shirt and roll onto your stomach and I will massage your back," she said, retrieving a large bottle of lotion from her handbag. The handbag, a woven straw affair the size of a small duffel bag, contained everything from extra medications, a pulse oximeter, her stethoscope, and an array of other medical supplies.

He hesitated for a moment before complying. The hydrocodone had obviously done its job for he felt little discomfort as he flipped over. The effort however made him cough.

"Where's Iris?" he asked after catching his breath.

"Why do you cough so much today?"

"It's probably my allergies. It's spring time in Texas after all."

"Iris is hiding. She feels you are very angry with her." When Leon didn't reply, she went on. "It is obvious she loves you very much. She feels she has disappointed you, and that makes her very sad," she said, straddling his thighs. Her bare legs felt like a bank of hot coals.

He wasn't sure what to say. Yes, Iris had disappointed him, but not for the reason she assumed. Part of him was proud of how she had confronted

Riordan. The real source of his displeasure was her failure to ever disclose that her birth date had been changed and the reason why.

He flinched as Fumiko dribbled the lotion onto his back. She began to rhythmically slide her hands up and down his back. She paused to apply more lotion and began anew, this time leaning into him, her hands kneading his muscles almost to the point of discomfort.

The very first time she had given him a massage had been at the hospital in Denver. She referred to it as her audition. At one point, he had begged her to stop, partly because of the ravages of the multiple myeloma but also because she seemed unaware of the strength in her hands. All he remembered was that his back pain had almost subsided by the time she had finished. He hired her the following day.

After another application of lotion, she used her fingers and the sides of her hands to separate the muscle fibers in his latissimus dorsi, a maneuver that always made him tense up and grunt in pain.

"You must relax. Do not be a child."

"You keep that up and I'll be forced to tell you all my secrets."

"Yes? Perhaps, that would be a good thing. Is this better?" she asked, easing up on the pressure. "So? You will now confess to me your secrets?"

"Shit, Fumiko. Let's not go there." He tried to roll over but she pushed him back down.

"It will be better if you tell me. It concerns Iris. Yes?"

He didn't reply at first, content to have her continue her massage. "You never tell Iris anything about what we talk about, do you?" he asked.

She paused and sat back on his legs. "Of course not. That would be unprofessional."

He didn't say anything for a long moment. "I got triggered by something," he said finally. "Something I'd rather not talk about."

She leaned into him again and began massaging his neck and shoulders.

"She is on your mind all the time, yes?"

"Who? Iris?"

"And her mother." When he didn't say anything, she sat back. "It is good to talk about such things."

"You get off on this, don't you? Being my confessor?"

"Confessor? If you mean do I enjoy listening to your personal stories, then yes I do. And I believe you have a need to tell these stories. I believe it to be emotionally beneficial. Do you not agree?"

How much was he willing to disclose? The birth date discrepancy couldn't simply be a clerical error. So he was back to wondering what Iris was hiding. Or more importantly, what Lou Ann was hiding. Why had this never come up before in conversation with either of them? He and Iris had always been honest with each other, often painfully so. This poorly thought out search for Lou Ann was one thing, but now this birth date business had raised its ugly head. It seemed that with every passing day, he was being forced to exhume and confront more and more ghosts from the past.

His cancer diagnosis had triggered a great deal of introspection, and even more retrospection. It led him to dwell on chapters of his life that he would like to edit if not completely rewrite. Since receiving his diagnosis, reviewing some of those chapters had resulted in some of his darkest days. But there had also been days when his pain was bearable, that he would allow his mind to play back certain episodes that nourished the last of what remained of his *chi* as Fumiko had once referred to his life force. Oddly enough, his memories of Lou Ann seemed equally divided between the good, the bad and the ugly. And no matter the conclusion, he found himself consumed by the thought of her.

"You're sure that…" He had a sudden coughing fit that resulted in him having to catch his breath. He started over. "You're sure you want to hear this?"

"*Hai,*" Fumiko replied before slowly running her knuckles down his spine. It had always been her signature that the massage was over. He felt her crawl off the bed and then open the mini-fridge. "You should drink some water. It is almost time for your medications."

"I'd rather have some tequila first. Check my dopp kit," he said, not bothering to check out her certain look of disapproval.

She clicked her tongue in annoyance before disappearing into the bathroom, emerging a moment later clutching two mini-bottles of Patron. She twisted off the caps and handed him one. "Only one. This one I take," she said, sitting back down on the side of the bed. He sat up with some difficulty and took a swallow of the tequila.

"Okay. You want a story. The first time Lou Ann and I broke up was 1998. It didn't really surprise me that she wanted to end it. As screwed up as Lou Ann was, of the two of us, she was the clear thinker. She knew we were a dead end. That it would never work. Of course at the time, I didn't want to accept it."

He took another swallow, and she took a dainty sip of hers.

"I dealt with it by traveling a lot. I tried my best to stay away from the States. I didn't want to hear about her or see her on some magazine cover. If I happened to hear her music in a bar somewhere, I'd walk out. I spent almost a year in South America trying to convince myself I was working rather than hiding. Then one day I was stuck in the airport in Buenos Aires and out of boredom I picked up a People magazine someone had left. It was the Spanish version, mind you. It always has a lot juicer photos than the US version. Way more skin," he added, smiling to himself.

He emptied the rest of the tequila. "As fate would have it, there was an article about her. It said she had a kid. She wasn't married so there was the usual speculation about who the father might be. The article had these pictures of her and some rock star or an actor she had been seem with. It went down the list of all the usual suspects. Someone in her band, maybe." His mind flashed back to Sudd Kiehne. He thought for a moment and smiled. "There was this Nashville record producer she used to toy with. Coonts was his name, though I can't imagine he would have ever managed to get her into bed."

"Anyway, I didn't see her again until 2000. I was flying back home to Hawaii from Manila when I overheard somebody behind me talking about getting into Honolulu in time to catch a concert at The Shell. It's this out-door amphitheater in the park."

"Yes, I know it."

He tilted back the empty tequila bottle. "It turned out Lou Ann was playing there." He paused to edit his memory. "I was planning on catching a late flight back to the Big Island, but then I thought what the hell? I suppose I was just curious about her."

"And Iris."

He thought for a moment. "Yeah, I guess I was curious about her, too. She would've been two, two and a half by then." He paused, unsure if he really wanted to go on.

"Anyway, I met this young Filipina gal on the plane. A nurse who worked at one of the Honolulu hospitals. I charmed her into giving me a ride to Waikiki. I think she wanted more than to just give me a ride. She settled for a kiss and a promise I'd send her my next book."

He distinctly remembered the kiss, their fumbling embrace in her car, but not her name. The nurse let him off at the edge of Queen Kapi'olani Park.

As soon as he got out of her car, he heard the sound of a ukulele coming from deep inside the park. The music faded in and out with the breeze coming off the ocean that lay just across the avenue. And then he heard the wavering sound of a woman singing in Hawaiian, her vibrato clearly audible over the clattering of the palm trees.

He could close his eyes and still vividly remember that evening; the dark looming profile of Diamond Head backlit in the glow of a rising moon, the twinkling lights of the suburbs spilling down from the slopes of the Ko'olau. The soft moistness of the air. The raucous cackling of the mynah birds in the palm trees overhead. And the tang in the air from the ocean. In that moment, he found himself wondering why in God's name did he want to ruin this otherwise beautiful evening with what he sensed would be a reopening of wounds.

He leaned over and gently removed the bottle of tequila from Fumiko's grasp. "You don't need this as much as I do," he said and emptied it in one swallow. "So I walk up to the entrance of The Shell. And I just stood there for a long time just watching people, listening to the music of the opening act. And after a while, I realized this maybe wasn't such a good idea after all. I had just started to walk off when Mr. Jimmy spotted me."

# 24

*"Days pass and I keep waiting for you*
*Weeks pass, and I struggle just to remember your face.*
*And now you're here*
*And I just don't know."*

-Lou Ann Catskill
Woman Down

**HONOLULU**

**MAY 2000**

"Mistah Leon. Dat you, mon?"

Leon turned at the sound of the booming baritone coming from just inside the entry gate. Leon hesitated and then waved. Jimmy motioned for him to come to the gate. As Leon approached, Jimmy leaned down and said something to the young man who was taking tickets.

"Come in. You got celebrity pass now," Jimmy said with a broad smile. "How you been, mon? Long time, yah?" he said as Leon cut through a file of incoming concert goers. Jimmy clapped him on the back and hustled him through the gate. "Jus' in time. Boss lady goin' on stage mebbe ten minutes."

Leon still had reservations about seeing Lou Ann, but felt helpless to resist Jimmy's firm grip on his arm as he pulled Leon through the crowd.

The Jamaican looked pretty much the same as he remembered. He wore white linen pants and a loose fitting aloha shirt. Leon recognized the shirt's busy pattern of pineapples and flora as a popular vintage style from the 50's. Its folds did little to conceal Jimmy's barrel chest. The only thing different about his appearance was the gold crown on one of his front incisors.

"How have you been?" Leon asked.

"I am very fine, mon. I tell you. Dese islands, dey up up. I see why you live here. And the ladies, Goodaz," he said. "You know how I mean?"

Jimmy ushered him past a pair of burly Polynesian security guards who nodded at Jimmy. They slipped behind the large concrete half-shell structure that housed the stage and through a chain link fence that opened onto a small parking area. The lot held a couple of moving vans and a double-wide trailer decorated with a mural of palm trees and a rainbow.

"Hold up, Jimmy," Leon said, grabbing the Jamaican's arm. "How is she doing?"

Jimmy gave him a look of confusion and then smiled. "She doin' big tings, mon. She a big star now."

"That's not what I meant."

Jimmy's face grew serious. "Her mood is what you ask, yah? She's okay," he said, wiggling his hand in a gesture of ambivalence. "When she take her medicine, she be fine. If not, den..." He threw up his hands. "I know one thing for sure. She goin' to be happy to see you again. I tell you dat for sure. Now come, not keep boss lady waiting."

Leon hesitated a second and then followed Jimmy. Just as they approached the trailer, the door opened and Sudd Kiehne stepped out. He obviously didn't recognize Leon, giving him only a cursory glance before turning to Jimmy.

"Make sure she's up there on time," Sudd said and walked away,

Jimmy gave Leon a look that telegraphed his disregard. "Pay no mind to dat waste man. Now go see the boss lady," he said and walked away in the direction of the stage.

Leon opened the door and stepped inside. A blonde woman he didn't recognize sat in a recliner at the far end of the trailer. She wore a pair of silky black pajama pants, a matching halter top that revealed a considerable amount of cleavage, and red high heels, one of which she dangled from her left foot. She looked up from the magazine she was reading and gave Leon a look of mild curiosity before going back to her magazine.

"Lou Ann," she said without looking up. "Are you expecting someone?"

"Here, zip me up," Lou Ann said, backing out from behind a dressing screen.

She was attempting to wriggle into an elegant looking, black gown that may have been one size too small. Her long black tresses were tied in a French braid interwoven with small red flowers.

"Be a gentleman," the blonde said, looking up from her magazine and cocking her head in Lou Ann's direction.

It was only then that Lou Ann turned and looked at him. At first, her face registered confusion, then a faint flicker of anxiety, and finally what he assumed might be pleasure.

"Yeah, Leon. Come zip me up," she said, raising a hand mirror and turning her face from side to side. "I still have that *défaut érotique*. Sue, you know how my face is all sorta crooked? Leon here called it an erotic flaw. Didn't you?"

"That I did."

He walked up behind her. She smelled of sandalwood. Still holding the mirror up to her face, she made eye contact with him over her shoulder. He lost himself for a moment in her gaze before zipping up her dress.

"I take it you two know each other," the blonde named Sue said.

Leon considered Sue more closely. Other than her bright red lipstick, she didn't appear to be wearing much makeup. She had intelligent green eyes that took his measure, as if disassembling him piece by piece.

"Leon's a coon ass out of Lake Charles," Lou Ann said, lowering the mirror and turning to look at Leon. "Aren't you?"

"Really?" Sue said, her eyes dropping back to the magazine. "As I recall, we played there once. Lots of coon ass down there in that neck of the woods." She looked back up at Leon. "You know a bar there called Tooties?"

No? It's a lesbian bar a few miles out of town. Only way to get to it is by boat. I talked my way into an invitation. Only out of curiosity, mind you."

"I'm sure," Leon said.

"Leon didn't come here to hear about your border crossing stories," Lou Ann said, tucking a stray hair behind her ear.

"On the contrary, I'm always keen to hear a good story," he countered.

"And I'm always keen to tell one." Sue looked at each of them in turn. "So tell me how you two know each other."

"Leon's my biographer," Lou Ann said, giving him a peck on the cheek. With her thumb, she wiped the smear of her lipstick. "He's already got some good chapters laid down, don't you, Leon?"

Before he could reply, the door opened and Sudd leaned in. "It's time, ladies. We got…" His voice trailed off when he recognized Leon. He muttered a curse and shook his head in annoyance.

"Sudd," Lou Ann said. "You remember Leon? Make sure he gets a good spot backstage." She looked back at Leon. "Don't run off." She patted his cheek and followed Sue and Sudd out of the trailer.

# 25

*"Step out of your head, you say*
*But step where?*
*Into another costume?*
*What good is that?*
*Step into my bedroom instead."*

-Lou Ann Catskill
Miss Lucky

Without so much as a word, Sudd passed Leon off to Jimmy and then promptly disappeared. Jimmy planted Leon just off stage at a vantage point where Leon would be able to clearly see the performance. He had seen Lou Ann perform perhaps a dozen times, but never with an eight piece band and four backup singers. He couldn't help but notice the keyboardist was none other than Sudd. As Lou Ann strolled onto the stage, the audience erupted in cheers. She held up both hands and gave the crowd the *shaka* salute, thumb and little finger extended, and the crowd went wild.

"Howzit, Honolulu?" she shouted, eliciting even louder cheering. "So good to be back in da islands. Yah? Give me chicken skin," she said, slipping into the local pidgin. "No talk story tonight. Sing story instead. Rajah dat?" The audience responded with hoots and whistles.

It was only when one of her stage crew handed her an electric guitar that the crowd began to settle. She started to strum the guitar before pausing. "Someone mentioned we have a Blue Moon tonight. So I thought it only fitting that I open with the blues, A couple of years back, I go ovah Big Island, yah? And when I left there I wrote this song. It's called Woman Down." A woman in one of the front rows yelled something unintelligible. Lou Ann waved at her and then began to strum a couple of cords before pausing to tune the guitar strings. "Thankfully, that mood didn't last too long. You see, I was in love. I just didn't know it at the time. Can anybody out there relate to that? Yeah?" she said when a chorus of cheers broke out.

She turned to Sudd at the keyboard and nodded, and then began playing a trilling bluesy guitar riff. And then she began to sing, her clear contralto voice filling the night.

"When my baby loves me

It feels so right

And it feels so wrong

You said hearts understand each other

But it seems I got no rhythm

In this dance we do

And it's as good as it gets"

The audience responded with screams and cheers of approval. And so it went for the rest of the evening. She played an almost two hour concert replete with her old songs, some of her new material, ballads of lost love, a handful of jazz and blues covers, and even some Billie Holiday. After acknowledging her band, she bowed and walked off to yells of "*Hana Hou! Hana Hou!*" the Hawaiian plea for an encore. Jimmy greeted her at the edge of the stage with a bottle of water and an orchid *lei* that a fan had left for her which he draped over her shoulders. She took a long swig and looked around until she spotted Leon. She held his gaze until one of her crew handed her back her guitar. As her band drifted back on stage, the applause grew louder. She stood there a moment before strolling back onto the stage. The audience roared in approval, taking almost a full minute before settling.

"I'm going to leave you with a song I wrote some years back. It's called Thunder in My Heart."

The song was a raucous, almost eight minute long rockabilly tune recounting searching for love and only finding pain. The last chorus brought the audience to their feet, their applause and cheers going on long after she had walked off the stage. Leon hung back for several minutes before making his way back to the trailer. He found Sue sitting on the steps smoking a cigarette.

"Good show," he said.

She turned her head aside and blew out a stream of smoke. "You're the writer, aren't you? I put two and two together." She gave him a long look before taking a final drag from her cigarette and then dropping it into the plastic cup at her feet. "You should know that she was pretty fucked up after you and her split up. Just saying," she said, getting to her feet. "She's okay now. Let's keep it that way."

Leon wasn't sure what to say, so he said nothing. Sue gave him a look that telegraphed something nothing short of menace. "She said you should wait for her," she said and walked off.

A couple of minutes later, Lou Ann emerged from the trailer. She had changed into jeans and a silky floral print blouse. She wore a pair of oversize sunglasses and a black fedora pulled low over her face. Without saying a word, she took his hand and started to pull him behind the trailer when someone shouted her name.

"Lou Ann! Where are you going? You can't leave yet." The owner of the voice hurried after them. "The writer from Billboard is supposed to interview you," the guy said, cutting off their retreat. He spoke with a Southern accent and wore a white long-sleeved Western shirt and jeans. It took a moment before Leon recognized him. It was her manager, Kevin something. Riordan if he recalled correctly. He remembered meeting him once briefly backstage.

"I'm off duty, Kevin. Reschedule him," she said, trying to walk around him, but he stepped in front of her and grabbed her arm.

"He flew out here just to talk to you."

She pulled away and pushed past him. "Comp him a room at the Royal Hawaiian and he'll get over it."

"Stop the primadonna shit and…"

She whirled on him. "I told you. Not tonight. Do your job and take care of it."

"God dammit! Listen to me. This is important."

Leon stepped between them. "Hey," he said, trying the best he could to keep his voice neutral. "You heard her. She's done for the night."

"Who the fuck are you?"

Leon offered him what an old acquaintance, an ex-cop from Dallas, used to call the all-weather smile. A response best used in certain situations that required both appeasement and intimidation. Riordan glared at both of them in response, muttered a curse, and stalked off.

Lou Ann took Leon's hand and dragged him off. They passed through a gate manned by a security guard and across a parking lot before cutting through a line of thick shrubs that opened onto a large expanse of open parkland. The light of the full moon had bathed Diamond Head and the surrounding trees and grassland in a gauzy white.

"I'm sorry about Kevin," she said. "He's just doing his job. He'll quit tomorrow. And I'll let him. Then he'll call me back next week wanting his job back. Any chance you'd want to be my manager?"

"I'd have to have benefits. Medical, vacation leave amongst other things. A booze allowance would be nice. Where are we going by the way?"

"Just across the park," she said, nodding in the direction of Kalakāua Avenue and the ocean. "I rented an apartment for the weekend. Someplace Kevin doesn't know about." She grabbed his hand more tightly. "I thought one of these days you'd show up. It took you long enough."

"One thousand and ninety-five days, but who's counting?"

"I'm sorry."

"You should be."

"You liked the show?" she asked, obviously wanting to change the subject.

"Sure did. It's been a while since I kept up on your music. You've broadened your repertoire quite a bit."

"Kevin thought most of what I was writing and singing was too dark. Too personal. I told him I write what I know. I guess I'd just about covered all there was to know about heartache and regret." she said, leading him across Kalakāua. "My daughter came with me," she blurted out. "I thought I should tell you before you came up."

"Iris, right? I read you had a daughter."

"We're here," she said, leading him through a small parking lot to an elevator.

The building was perhaps eight stories, and from the sound of crashing waves, he assumed it sat directly on the ocean. An elderly Asian couple joined them as they boarded the elevator. Nods were exchanged and glances politely averted. Lou Ann, still wearing her hat and dark glasses, settled against Leon. The Asian couple got off on the fifth floor. The elevator doors had no sooner closed, when Lou Ann yanked off her hat and glasses and leaned in for a kiss. He remembered her open lips and the way her tongue seemed to snake into his mouth. They kissed long after the elevator door to the next floor opened and closed. She fumbled blindly for the open button, their mouths still engaged.

"My floor," she mumbled, pulling away.

He followed her down a dimly lit hallway to a door at the far end. She knocked softly and a moment later the door opened to reveal a short dark-complexioned older woman dressed in a simple white cotton shift that was intricately embroidered around the neck and shoulders in a floral motif. The dress and her facial features suggested Mexico, Oaxaca perhaps gauging from her dress. She nodded a greeting.

"Is she asleep?" Lou Ann asked.

"Yes. For one hour maybe," the woman replied. She glanced at Leon. "I will go now?"

"Sure. If you like, my friend here can walk you to your door."

"*No necesito.*" She picked up a woven cloth handbag from the sofa and headed for the door.

"We will leave at eleven. Okay? *Buenas noches,* Nina," Lou Ann said. The woman nodded and left. The apartment wasn't large, and from what Leon could tell it consisted of a single bedroom, an open kitchen and living room and a lanai that he could see faced towards the ocean. Lou Ann tossed her things on the sofa and led Leon to the darkened bedroom. In the dim light from the hallway, Leon was able to make out a small form huddled on the bed. Lou Ann carefully covered Iris with a blanket, and then leaned over and kissed her on the forehead.

"It's too bad she's asleep," she said once they were back in the hallway. "Have you eaten? A girl's gotta eat."

"You have any fried chicken?"

She smiled. "You remember that, do you? You know that waitress Ruth always asks about you. My manager of Internal Affairs is what I called you. Remember?" She opened the refrigerator. "Great. I thought it was going to be Fruit Loops and bananas, but we've still got a little sushi and some fruit salad. No booze though," she said, turning to look at him. "I'm on the wagon." She handed him a platter of sushi and the bowl of fruit. "Take it out to the lanai and I'll be there in a minute."

The lanai was almost as large as the living room and offered an expansive view of the moonlit ocean and the lights of Waikiki. A large daybed occupied one end, a pair of rattan chairs and a coffee table sat on the other end. He set the plate of sushi and fruit on the table and leaned over the balcony. The booming of the surf crashing on the rocks below drowned out all other sound except for the clattering of a pair of palm trees, their fronds partially obscuring the view of Diamond Head.

After a minute or so, Lou Ann reappeared carrying a bag of chips and a couple of bottles of Perrier. Her hair hung loose to her shoulders and she had changed into a thin white shift.

"I'm toying with moving out here," she said, handing him one of the bottles. "It would be a little inconvenient, but it would give me some distance."

"Yeah, you always liked your distance."

She shot him a look that he had trouble deciphering in the dim light.

"Maybe I'd run across you a little more often than every three years," he said, making little effort to conceal his irritation.

"Please, Leon. Don't be bitter."

"I was bitter. For a long time. Losing you hurt more than I thought it would. Yeah, the worldly Leon Riser, the shameless and unrepentant horn dog gets burned by a woman he for once in his life wanted more than anything."

In the awkward silence that followed, Leon realized that admission was tantamount to tearing a scab off one of those kinds of wounds that for one reason or another always took forever to heal.

"I needed a break," she said after a moment. "And not just from you and me, but from everything. Maybe you didn't see it back then, but I was headed for a major crash. I saw it coming." She rocked ever so slightly back and forth as she stood there looking out at the night. He remembered her doing this whenever she was nervous. "And there was nothing that I, or you, or anyone else could do about it. You have to believe me when I say I did it for you as much as for me. I didn't want you to be the one to clean up the mess. To see me like that. I owed you that much."

"Pardon my cynicism, but that sounds like the lyrics to some bull shit song."

"And you didn't seem to care anyway," she said in a flare of what he took to be anger. "As I recall you didn't put up much of a fight. If you wanted me bad enough…" she said, the remainder of what she was going to say trailing off.

"What? You wanted me to beg you not to break it off?"

"I thought you'd understand what I was going through. Your mother…"

"Leave her out of it. Look, I get it. I do. And I imagine you had a rough time of it. You're right. I should understand. And that was then," he added. "Now, I'd just like to know how much of Lou Ann Catskill is still wearing that mask. Who am I dealing with right now, this minute? And how much of you am I allowed to see?"

"And that's a fair question." She reached up and touched his cheek. "I love you, Leon. I always will. But I can't do relationships," she said in a way that sounded as if she were thinking out loud. "They don't work for me."

"And Iris?"

"What about her?" Lou Ann sighed and retreated to the daybed. "Look, I know what you're wondering."

"Do I have reason to wonder?"

She didn't reply at first, but instead took a long swallow of her Perrier. "You have to realize that back then I was pretty far off the rails. I was bat shit crazy. Manic. I wasn't leaving any survivors. And I surely wasn't any vestal virgin. If you want to know the truth, I don't know who Iris's father is. It could've been any one of … " She shook her head as if ridding herself of something unpleasant. "So you want to know who I am right now? This minute? Which Lou Ann are you getting?"

He could tell she was smiling up at him. She reached for his hand and pulled him down onto the day bed beside her.

"Right here and now, this Lou Ann is doing really well. The meds seem to work. And yeah, I still wear that mask more than I like. But I'm… leveled out. Even, I guess. At least that's how my therapist *du jour* likes to put it. I'm even. I hate that fucking word. Even," she said, her voice betraying her bitterness. "You know what I mean? On the positive side, I know myself a bit better. But if you ask me whether that's the meds talking or I finally achieved some kind of breakthrough? I don't know. Someday I'll go off the meds and I'll see."

For some reason, he thought about his mother, and what she was like when she didn't take her medications. "And Iris? How are you dealing with motherhood?" he asked with more cynicism than he intended.

"Hey, Iris needs me. Needs me more than anybody has ever needed me. And she sucks the oxygen right out of my room. Do you understand what I'm saying? There's no more space for anybody else in my life. Can't you be happy for me?" she asked in the ensuing silence.

"I am happy for you. I just would like to think there's some space in that happy place for me."

"We can be friends. Lovers," she said, taking his hand. "Isn't that enough?"

"Friends and lovers. That sounds like the definition of a relationship."

"What more do you want, Leon? I can't give you more. Do you want to put a ring on my finger? Have a marriage certificate? Is that really what you want? To be tied to someone like me? I can't do that. I'm sorry, but I can't. You can't."

"I guess I should look on the bright side. I don't have to go along on any of your shitty goddamn tours. I don't have to bother with the mundane stuff like sharing utility bills, cleaning up the breakfast dishes. Or taking Iris to school. Hell, I should consider myself lucky."

"Don't be like that, Leon. Take what I can give you because that's all there is."

He stood and walked back over to the balcony. Someone from a boat offshore was setting off fireworks followed by an answering volley from one of the hotels in Waikiki. He felt her behind him, felt her body heat as she encircled his waist with her arms.

"That first time in Tahiti," she said, resting her head on his shoulder. "I knew after that first night that we'd always be friends. Maybe even soul mates. I knew that there would always be something between us. But I'm still not ready for more than that. So you have to choose, Leon."

He unwrapped himself from her embrace and turned to her. "Choose? Is that the deal you're offering? Well, I don't like the terms of the contract, but if that's all I get."

"You're sure?" she asked. "You'd choose me? And be satisfied with what you get?"

"Do you really have to ask?"

He lifted her face to his and found her mouth. After a long kiss, she led him back to the daybed. She slipped the dress over her head and took his hand and pulled him down beside her.

# 26

*"Every time I lose at love*
*It's like I'm blown apart*
*The place where our love lived.*
*And I feel a cold wind blowing."*

-Lou Ann Catskill
The Uneven Surface of My Soul

Leon looked at Fumiko who sat with her legs drawn up, her chin resting on her knees. His recounting of that night left him drained and feeling as if he had just lost a foot race. Fumiko held his gaze for a moment and then stood and went into the bathroom. She came out a moment later with a handful of pills which she held out to him.

"You do not have to tell me the rest. It is your memory," she said, extending her open hand. "I know you took one of your hydrocodone earlier. I count them. Here is ibuprofen. You should sleep."

He started to cough again.

"This cough. Are you ill?" she said, leaning over and touching his forehead. "You are hot."

She reached into her bag and retrieved her stethoscope and then proceeded to listen to his chest. "Come, Leon. Large breaths in and out."

She listened for a moment before moved behind him and listening again. "You are wheezing."

"I told you. It's my allergies."

She reached into her bag and presented him with his inhaler. "Now. Two puffs."

He complied with a minimum of resistance. When he was done, she again held out her hand to offer him his pills.

"We went on like that for quite a while. Maybe eight years. I forget," he said, ignoring her hand. "Friends and lovers, Sometimes we'd see each other fairly often. Sometimes only a couple of times a year. Sometimes she'd have Iris with her. Sometimes she'd leave her with a nanny." He paused to cough, a wracking cough that left him gasping for air. "And then just like always, something changed. We saw each other less and less. Her life, her career didn't leave much time for much of anything else. And I moved to Mexico."

"Enough, Leon. You have had too much to drink. That is on me. Isn't that how you say it? Yes?" She took his hand and dumped the pills into his palm. "Now sleep. You look terrible. I will check on you later," she said as she picked up her bag and headed for the door.

"She's not who you think."

Fumiko turned and looked at him. "Then tell me who she is. Tell me why you still love this woman? She has left you with nothing but sadness."

"That's not true. We had a lot of good times."

"And you still love her. Yes?"

"Maybe love isn't the right word. Obsession. More like a blind spot maybe."

"And you wish to see her again?"

He thought for a moment. "If you're asking whether I'd give anything to spend a week with her? Sure I would. And probably a week is all I'd get. That might be all I could handle."

He cleared his throat and coughed again and reached for a glass of water. He tossed the pills into his mouth and took a long swallow of the water before going on.

"That night back at that spa in Santa Fe, I asked you whether you had ever been in love. As I recall, you said just once, but it didn't last. Well, try being in love over and over again with the same person. And then losing that person over and over again. It's like fucking Ground Hog Day."

She gave him a quizzical look. "I do not understand. This ground hog day."

"Never mind. Unless you've had your heart broken a half-dozen times by the same person, you won't understand. The call of the siren."

Fumiko shot him a quizzical look.

"The siren. It's a mythical woman, a seductress who lures you to destruction with her songs. She lures you into the rocks. And you can't resist. The song. The light. You get too close to the rocks and you get banged up and drown." He lost his train of thought for a moment as he pondered that image. "Lou Ann's this creative, talented, funny, sexy, mercurial. And a fucked up hell bitch," he added. "But when it worked, I felt this high." He shook his head. "That's love, isn't it?"

Fumiko seemed to consider this for a moment before walking to the door.

"Tell Iris I'll talk to her in the morning. *Oyasumi*, Fumiko."

"*Oyasumi*, Leon," she said and walked out.

# 27

*"This vase of hearts*
*Thorns and blossoms*
*So bitter and sweet*
*Why must they always die?"*

-Lou Ann Catskill
Vase of Hearts

Iris rearranged her *huevos rancheros* on her plate, her gaze fixed on Leon. The eggs had grown cold while she waited him out. Now they were about as cold as he was. He had merely nodded when she approached his table and asked if she could join him. Since then, he had scarcely made eye contact.

She had knocked on his motel room door earlier, and after not receiving a response, found him sitting alone in the small diner near the motel. Fumiko had left early, ostensibly for her second jog in less than twelve hours.

As she waited him out, she took the opportunity to study him. He looked dreadful, his skin pale, his bloodshot eyes reflecting his fatigue. That, and whenever he shifted in his chair, he seemed to grimace. She suddenly felt guilty for asking him to come along. And now that she knew her mother was safe, she wondered why he hadn't simply turned back.

She dropped her fork on the plate and pushed it away which elicited nary a glance from Leon. In a fit of anger, she tossed her napkin at him which at least got him to look at her.

"Why are you being such an asshole? I told you I was sorry for going to Riordan's. That it was dumb of me. What more do you want?"

Leon took her napkin and dabbed his mouth with it. Without taking his eyes off her, he slurped down the remainder of his coffee. She noticed his hand shaking as he carefully placed the empty cup beside his plate.

"Let me have…" he started to say but then began to cough, a wracking, phlegmy cough that went on for ten or fifteen seconds before he was able to stop.

"Jesus, Leon. Are you okay?"

She glanced at a couple of women sitting at a nearby table who stared at them with more anxiety than concern.

"You've been careful about wearing your mask, haven't you?"

Leon waved his hand as he caught his breath. He took a drink of water before saying anything. "Let me have your purse," he croaked.

"What? Why do you want my purse?"

"Give me your purse," he said again, his voice betraying his irritation.

She reached down beside her and took her small handbag and tossed it onto his side of the table. He picked it up and removed her wallet, flipped through the contents and removed something. Without saying a word, he placed the item on the center of the table. She leaned closer and glanced at it and then looked up at him.

"You want to tell me about this?" he asked.

She picked it up and looked at it. "I don't get it. It's just my driver's license."

He cleared his throat as if he were about to cough again. The look on his face led her to wonder if he might be in pain.

"Your birth date," he said, his voice almost lost in the hubbub of the diner. "How come it doesn't say April first?"

"Wait. I don't get it. You know that April first wasn't my real birthday. Mom must've told you what happened. What?" she asked in response to his blank look. "She didn't tell you?"

"No. She didn't tell me."

"Shit," she muttered, shaking her head. "I don't get it. You must've noticed the change. How many times did you carry my passport around? And you never noticed? You must've made my plane reservations for me."

"Your Mom always did that. Maybe now I know why."

She began to quickly dissemble as she attempted to come up with an explanation. The look of bewilderment on Leon's face mirrored what she herself was feeling.

"Look, what happened was when I applied for my first passport we had to change my birth date. It had something to do with my birth certificate. Some typo Mom said. I think the number two looked like a four. Turns out I was born in February. That's what she always said. It was just a typo. But she said since we had been celebrating my birthday in April for all these years that we'd keep it that way."

"That's bullshit!" He started to cough again.

She waited until he stopped. "I'm sorry, but I'm confused, Leon. Why is this suddenly such a big deal? It's just a date for chrissakes. It's not like two months make a big difference."

He muttered a curse and tried to get up from the table, but faltered and dropped back into his chair.

"Are you sure you're okay?" she asked, reaching across the table for his hand. "You look sick."

He shot her a baleful look as he pulled his hand away.

"Have you taken your pain meds this morning?" she asked.

"Did your mother ever tell you who your father is?" he asked, ignoring her question.

She stared at him. She felt a creeping realization about where this was going. "She never would tell me. She said it was better if I never knew. She said it was to protect me. What are you getting at, Leon?"

"So you were born February first, not April first. So what I'm getting at is that it means you had to have been conceived in May."

"Meaning?" She almost felt afraid to ask. "Meaning what, Leon?"

"Your mom told me more than once that I couldn't have been your father. That she got pregnant after we broke it off." He held her gaze for a moment before looking away.

"What are you saying? That you might be my father?"

She stared down at the table, stunned by this sudden possibility. Had her mother been lying to her all this time? Why would she not tell her that Leon might've been her father? Hell, he was her father in so many ways. So why wasn't she told? She scooped up her driver's license and wallet, stood and started to walk away.

"Iris," he said, reaching for her.

She ignored him and stormed past a knot of people waiting for a table. Once she was outside, she looked again at the driver's license for a moment before crushing it into a ball and dropping it on the pavement.

"God, Mom. What have you done?" She swiped at her eyes. It all made sense. And it didn't. She stood there another moment and started walking back to the motel.

# 28

*"I may know the words*
*But not how to say them.*
*I may knowhow love feels*
*But not the taste.*
*Oh, love oh love*
*Will you teach me how to love?"*

-Lou Ann Catskill
The Siren's Refrain

**AUSTIN**

Sudd pulled up in front of Sue Mendez's house and cut the ignition. Lou Ann flipped down the visor and briefly studied herself in the mirror before reaching behind the seat and dragging out her overnight bag.

"You're staying?" Sudd asked.

"I told you. Maybe, maybe not. It depends on Sue."

"I thought you said the two of you haven't seen or spoken to each other in years."

"Makes no difference," she said, reaching for the door handle.

"No bad blood anymore?"

"Why would you say that? Because of Leon? Sue's the closest thing I've got to a sister. Look, Sudd. I appreciate all you've done. Go back out to JB's on Tuesday. He's holding some money for me. Just don't be getting into a poker game with him and gambling it away. Behave and I'll make sure you get a cut. Okay?" she said, climbing out and slamming the door.

As she watched him drive off, she tried to think of when exactly she had last seen Sue. To the best of her recollection, it had been at least five years or more. It was probably after the concert in Nashville. Sue had abruptly announced then that she was leaving the band. Sue had been ada-mant that Leon had nothing to do with it. Still, Lou Ann often wondered if Sue's leaving was merely a way of putting distance between them in order to make a play for Leon. At the time, that possibility had hardly been a blip on her radar for she had her hands full just keeping her own boat afloat.

She stepped up onto the porch and before she could even knock, Sue flung open the door. They looked at each other for a moment before Sue reached for Lou Ann's bag.

"Get in here," she said, yanking the bag from Lou Ann's grasp.

"Jesus. I didn't think you'd be this happy to see me."

Once inside, they both stood looking at each other in silent appraisal before Lou Ann embraced Sue who responded by dropping Lou Ann's bag and reciprocating.

"It's been way too long," Sue said.

Lou Ann stepped back and studied her old friend. Sue looked older, but then again who didn't. She still looked the part of the sassy, sex kitten backup singer standing there in a pair of tight leopard skin leotards and a silky black bustier. Her patent leather stiletto heels completed the look.

"My, my. Do you have a date? Or are you just playing dress up for old time's sake?

"I thought it might make you feel at home. All we need is Shiney and a couple of coffee mugs full of Jack and Dr. Pepper."

"Shiney," Lou Ann said, shaking her head. "I heard."

Shiney, a former gospel singer from Atlanta, had been one of Lou Ann's other backup singers. One of Lou Ann's former roadies had sent her a note last year that Shiney had passed away from ovarian cancer.

"What do you hear from Janie?" Lou Ann asked. Janie had been another one of her backup singers.

"The last I heard she was living with her daughter and grandkids in Dallas. You care for a drink?"

Lou Ann smiled. "The things I used to do, Lord, I don't do more," she crooned the line from an old Guitar Slim song. "No, I'm fine. Just some water will do. Or some sweet ice tea if you have it."

"Then sit. I'll be right back," Sue said, disappearing into the kitchen.

Lou Ann took the opportunity to look around the living room. A black leather jacket lay draped on the sofa. She briefly picked it up. It looked like a man's jacket. She walked over to the mantle above the fireplace and studied several framed photographs. Her eyes settled on a black and white image of herself, her head flung back and cradling a microphone in one hand and a cigarette in the other. Antone's New Year's Eve 2000 was scrawled across the bottom. Beside it was another photograph of her huddled with her four backup singers. She allowed her fingers to graze over their faces before studying the other photos. She didn't recognize anyone, Sue's family, she assumed.

It was only then she noticed the corner of a small, unframed photograph peeking out from behind a vase of dried flowers. Giving into her curiosity, she picked it up. The faded, somewhat curled photo showed Leon perched on the hood of Sue's old Corvette. He wore only a bathing suit and clutched a beer bottle in one hand. She picked it up and turned it over. Leon, Xmas Lake Travis 2015 Sue had scribbled in her familiar imprecise cursive. She turned it over and looked at the image again. Something about the way Leon stared at the camera reflected a sense of his unease,

"Here you go," Sue said, returning and carrying a glass of wine and a tumbler of ice tea, She noticed Lou Ann holding the photo, but made no comment.

"I'm sorry to drop in on you without much notice, but I need someone to talk to," Lou Ann said, replacing the photo.

"So I gather," Sue said, dropping onto the sofa and taking swallow of her wine. "You left Kevin," she said. "What took you so long? I would've thought you would've worn him down to a miserable nub a long time ago."

Lou Ann shrugged. "It took longer than I would've thought. I was hoping you would've come to the wedding and talked me out of it."

"When have I ever talked you out of anything?"

"Point taken. You know how I get when I'm buzzing."

"Oh, yeah, and I've still got plenty of photographic evidence to prove it."

"Do you have a cigarette?"

Sue reached for her purse and pulled out a pack and a lighter and handed it to her. "You look good," she said, watching her friend light up.

Lou Ann took a long drag and exhaled. "I'm clean. No alcohol or drugs. This is the first cigarette I've had in six months." She took another hit before grinding it out in the ashtray. "I'm only taking one medication. I took up yoga and mindfulness and got me one of these New Age therapists. She's got me micro-dosing LSD and doing this stuff called breath work. Hell, I hardly recognize myself anymore. The new old Lou Ann. I'm good, Sue. Really," she said in response to Sue's look of skepticism. "Five by five. Copacetic."

"Does that mean no more embarrassing tabloid articles? No mug shots?"

Lou Ann shook her head in amusement. "I'm afraid not. Hopefully, those days are over."

"Let's not be premature. I've corrupted my share of the righteous. Are you writing?"

"Not a lick. I haven't performed either in nine months, and even then it was only a benefit for the animal shelter in Santa Fe. I'm done singing the blues. It's all too... I don't know. My therapist thinks I need to sing some happy shit."

"There's such a thing?"

Lou Ann snorted. "At least, I'm under the radar. There hasn't been nary a mention of me in People Magazine in a year or more. I'm thinking most of my fans probably figure I'm dead. Or senile and in a nursing home." She took a deep breath and exhaled. "So here's the thing."

She proceeded to fill Sue in on life with Kevin; their shared addictions, the lies they told each other, Kevin's avarice, and his emotional abuse.

"What sealed it for me was when these two goombahs showed up at the house."

"Goombahs?"

"Wise guys. I figured Kevin's business associates must've sent them. They came by the house when Kevin was out of town. They proceeded to ask me about how Iris was doing. They asked how she liked living in Austin, Shit like that. That's what finally did it." She reached for the cigarette stub and stopped herself.

"Hold that thought," Sue said and got up and went back into the kitchen. She returned a moment later with a second glass of wine. "You mind?"

"No. I could use the temptation if you know what I mean."

"I'm sorry I walked out on you that time in Nashville.. It wasn't what you thought."

"You mean Leon? Look, that's water under the bridge. You have to know I never blamed you. Or Leon. It was just the way it was. And what I did… Well, it didn't have anything to do with either of you. I have to ask. When did you last see him?"

Sue took a swallow of her wine before replying. "A year or so back. We both happened to be in Denver. No, I didn't sleep with him if that's what you're wondering."

"Too bad," Lou Ann said with a smile.

"You said Iris was on her way here. With Leon."

"Yeah, with Leon. When you saw him, did he look okay? The reason I ask is I just saw JB Coonts, and he said he had heard Leon was sick or something."

"Huh. That's the first I've heard. Iris hasn't said anything?"

"It seems she and Leon haven't been exactly on speaking terms. Iris and I talk pretty often but not about anything important. You know, mothers, daughters. We dance around things. It's been almost six years and she hasn't forgotten. Or forgiven me. Or Leon either evidently."

Sue put down her wine glass and took Lou Ann's hand. "Do you forgive me? It wasn't my finest moment. I still…"

"It wasn't one of my finer moments either," she said, cutting her off. "I told you, the past is the past. Sure, we all knew better. Not that it would've changed anything. If it was anyone's fault, it was mine. Leon and I were already finished."

"Do the two of you talk?"

"No. I figure there's no point. I burned that bridge. Burned down the whole fucking house. Look, are you hungry? I need to eat."

"I'll call ahead to Guero's and get a booth in the back."

"Do you have clothes I can fit into? I'm not going out in a pair of sweats," Lou Ann said. "I have to think about my public."

"Who all think you're dead. Don't worry, I'll dress you. Even though both of our asses are fluffier, I'll find something. Let's retire to my boudoir. I think I've got a dress for you that'll leave them rocking."

# 29

*"I always asked you*
*To take me as I am.*
*Take my blues*
*Live with the twisters*
*But would you still know me?*
*Or would I just be a another dead exotic*
*In your vase of hearts?"*

-Lou Ann Catskill
Vase of Hearts

"Get over it, hon," Sue said, slurping her margarita.

Lou Ann shrugged. "I guess I should be grateful no one recognized me."

"Hey, you were wearing a mask when we walked in. Besides, our waitress hit puberty about the same time we hit menopause. The manager knew who you were though."

"Yeah, but that's only because you introduced me."

"All I'll say is we both got the horny eyeball when we came in. We haven't lost it, have we? You look fabulous by the way."

It had taken a half hour to peruse Sue's two walk-in closets, but they finally settled on a tight red leather skirt that Lou Ann still wasn't convinced was age appropriate, and an off the shoulder white cashmere sweater. By the time it came to selecting footwear, neither thought the red snakeskin ankle boots as being over the top. As a result, their entrance to Guero's hadn't gone unnoticed. The manager had gone out of his way to welcome them and escort them to a table in the very back. He paraded them through the packed restaurant as if they were some sort of exotic circus animals.

"You look like something from Dairy Queen. Cool and very lux," Sue said, making a show of smacking her lips.

"Like one of those soft frozen vanilla cones, right? Only with Lipitor sprinkles."

Sue laughed and ended up spilling half of her margarita on the table. "I was going to order another one anyway. You're still okay with the virgin?"

"No, but I'm sticking to my pledge. For now," she added. She took her phone out of her purse.

"What?" Sue asked as she noticed Lou Ann read something on her phone before quickly looking away.

"Iris," she said, looking back. "They just got into town. She's asking if I'm with you." She began texting a reply.

"And Leon's still with her?"

Lou Ann paused and looked up. "Leon and his geisha. Some new sidekick by the name of Fumiko. He must be needing to brush up on his Japanese. Another of his linguistic love affairs. You know, he used to…" Lou Ann paused and then smiled. She looked up at Sue and shook her head. "God that man fucked me up."

"And here I always thought it was you that fucked you up."

"Jesus, Sue. Woman down already. It's not like my life isn't hard enough without my best friend calling me out."

"You guys stayed together for what? Six years?"

"Did we? It was more like Leon and Iris made it together for six years, not me."

Their conversation ebbed as the waitress brought their enchiladas and fresh drinks. This time the waitress who couldn't have been older than eighteen, stared at Lou Ann for a long uncomfortable moment before walking off.

"She was looking at me like I was something out of the wax museum," Lou Ann said as she attacked her enchiladas.

"You've never really gotten over that last breakup, have you? The way it ended?"

"You mean the way I ended it?"

"Yeah, the way you ended it. God, Lou Ann."

She held up her hand to stop Sue. "I don't want to talk about that." She fell silent as she took another mouthful of enchilada. After several bites, she reached over and took Sue's margarita and emptied most of it in one swallow.

"You know I used to think there must be some kind of weird, perverted honor in failing at a relationship. Like it was a normal rite of passage, and I should get some kind of merit badge. To answer your question, no, I never got over it. And never got that merit badge either, although I got plenty of material for a new album."

"You can't tell me that you two only stayed together because of Iris. I was there, you know."

Lou Ann dropped her fork onto her plate. "Could I order a margarita?" She started to raise her hand to get the waitress's attention, but Sue pushed her arm down.

"You never told either of them, did you?" Sue asked.

Lou Ann offered a nod and a half-smile to a passerby before looking back at Sue.

"No and you know why."

"Because you were whoring around and it could've been any one of a number of assholes that knocked you up?"

"Jesus, Sue. Yeah," she said after a moment. "I slept with someone… maybe more than just one person at the same time that I slept with Leon."

"Have you ever heard of a DNA test?"

"It wasn't just that. If I knew for sure Leon was Iris's father it would mean I'd have to…"

"Get married? Or just feel obligated?"

"Shit, Sue. Look at my track record for god sake."

"There's still time."

"Is there? After all that's gone down between us? As time went on, it just became too easy to just not tell either of them. Can you understand that?"

"Refresh my memory. So the only reason you two started living together was just because of Iris?"

"It was about Iris, just not in the way you think. You know what it was like back then. The way I was on that one tour. We should've called that tour the Bat Shit Crazy Cavalcade of Stars. Sudd selling coke out of the back of the bus. Your assault charge. At least I had an excuse for how out of control I was."

"Oh, yeah. That convenient ACDC excuse. As I recall, you were too wired to finish the concert in Seattle. You were the reason the rest of the tour was canceled. You do realize that by then you had become a joke? The stereotypical burned out rock diva. Don't keep blaming it on your goddamn bipolar. You made choices."

Lou Ann lowered her fork and looked around at the nearby tables to see if anyone had overheard Sue's tirade. She took a deep breath before saying anything. "You're right. I own that. All of it. Canyon Lake. The works." She paused as if editing her thoughts. "But at the time, I needed someone like Leon to bring me back down. He was always good at that. If you remember, he always... Well, maybe you don't remember, but Iris was out of control back then. I mean really out of control. I couldn't handle her much less handle my own life. So there was always good old Leon to pick up the pieces. There simply wasn't anybody else."

She took a couple more bites and washed it down with her virgin margarita. "I can have one drink. I'm bipolar. I'm not an alcoholic."

Sue waved down the waitress. "One more margarita, please," she told her.

"How about you, Miss Catskill?" the waitress asked.

Lou Ann smiled up at the young woman. She couldn't have been more than eighteen. "Promise me you won't believe everything your parents say about me. And no, I'll pass on the margarita. I'll just have a sip of my friend's."

Sue could see the pain of some memory etched on Lou Ann's face and reached for her hand. Lou Ann responded by opening her hand and squeezing Sue's. Neither of them spoke until after the waitress brought Sue's margarita.

"Did I ever tell you how I talked him into moving in with us? No? Well, it took me a good while to hunt him down," Lou Ann said. "We hadn't seen each other or spoken in maybe a year. I had to call his agent to find out where he was. I figured there was no use trying to call Leon. He wouldn't answer or call back. So I swallowed my pride and just went to see him. He was living in Mexico. Needless to say, he wasn't happy to see me."

# 30

*"My lies, the crimes of the heart*
*But aren't they sweet? These lies?*
*They're never as good as when I mean them."*

-Lou Ann Catskill
The Siren's Refrain

**TULUM, QUINTANA ROO**

**APRIL 2012**

The taxi driver pulled up in front of a barricade of concrete pylons that blocked any further progress down the narrow alleyway. Someone had made a feeble attempt at landscaping by planting a pair of stunted, tired-looking palms between the pylons, the effort defeated by a knee high wall of weeds colorfully festooned with litter. Lou Ann could see a busy commercial thoroughfare not a half block down the alley.

"*La Pausa,*" the driver said, nodding with his chin in the direction of the street.

"Where? *¿Donde?*"

"*No está lejos. Es* very near. *Alli,*" he said, again pointing down the street "*La Pausa.¿Si?*"

"Why can't you drop me off there if it's not far? Never mind. *¿Cuantos pesos?*"

"*Ochocientos pesos, señora.*"

Lou Ann dug through her bag for the money and then held up a fist-ful of crisp paper bills to the dim light of a streetlight. She peeled off a sheaf of what looked like hundred peso bills and handed it to the driver over his shoulder. He glimpsed at it for a moment and then turned to look at her. She handed him another bill of unknown denomination and opened the door. The driver muttered something as she crawled out of the taxi, almost losing her footing on the uneven pavement. She stood there a moment as the taxi disappeared down a side street before she set out in the direction the driver had indicated.

She had wasted two hours in a different taxi searching for the house Leon's agent had lent him. When the driver finally located the *casita*, no one was there. She managed to rouse a neighbor, an elderly Canadian gentleman, who assured her she could find Leon at a downtown bar called *La Pausa*. She then had to wait for another taxi to find her and bring her back into town. By then, she had a beast of a migraine and felt sufficiently surly to curse at the taxi driver when he began driving in circles in a thinly disguised attempt to increase the fare.

Her whole day had consisted of such aggravations, beginning with her discovery of Iris's empty bed when she went to wake her for school. All her attempts to reach Iris on her cell phone came to naught. Iris going AWOL was hardly anything new. Lou Ann could only hope Iris's school hadn't called Child Protective Services again. She had sifted through her mind in an attempt to decide which story would satisfy CPS - that Iris had skipped school to spend the day with her seventeen year old boyfriend, or that her mother had skipped a recording session to fly to Mexico to look up an old lover. To both her relief and dread, CPS hadn't called by the time her flight left Austin. Her housekeeper would just have to deal with it.

So here she was eight hours later, picking her way across the littered, potholed pavement of a Mexican alley way that reeked of urine and rancid cooking grease. She stumbled momentarily as one of her high-heeled sling back sandals slipped on what might have been a piece of smashed fruit. At least, she hoped that was all it was. As she approached the corner, she saw the neon sign across the street announcing *La Pausa*. She waited a moment in vain for a break in the traffic before slipping off her sandals and making a run for it across the street.

The entrance to *La Pausa* was little more than a narrow archway that opened to an even narrower stone stair well that funneled the sound of laughter and conversation overlaid with what she recognized as the trumpet riff from a number by Buena Vista Social Club. If her memory served her right, Chan Chan was the name of the song. One of Iris's nannies had played the song over and over ad nauseum. As she paused to slip her sandals back on, she watched a couple of young girls dressed in nothing more than bikinis pick their way down the stairwell. Neither of them appeared to be older than eighteen at most. She shuddered to think how long before Iris would run off on a Mexican getaway with some burgeoning pederast.

The customers at the dimly-lit U-shaped bar were two deep, most of them young and casually dressed in aloha shirts, swimsuits and shorts. Lou Ann managed to wriggle her way to the waitress station and corner a young Mexicana arranging neon-colored drinks on a tray.

"*¿Habla Ingles?*" Lou Ann asked.

"Yes. How may I help you?"

"I am looking for an American who may be here. His name is Leon Riser. Do you know him?"

"*Si.* Of course. *Señor* Riser. He is on *el balcón.* Come. I will show you," she said, setting her tray aside and leading Lou Ann through the boisterous crowd.

The waitress escorted her to a large open deck furnished with a dozen or so wooden tables, all of which sat nestled beneath lantern-lit *palapas.* Most of the tables appeared occupied by groups of four or more people except for a table at the far end of the deck. The waitress pointed to the table and hurried off. It took Lou Ann only a moment to make out Leon's silhouette, his back turned towards her. He wasn't alone. A woman sat beside him, her head leaning close to his as if they were engaged in an intimate conversation.

Lou Ann stood there a moment watching them. The woman had long blonde hair that concealed most of her face. It was only when she pulled away from Leon's shoulder that Lou Ann was able to make out her profile. Even from ten feet away and in the dim glare of the lantern light, Lou Ann could tell the woman appeared young, at least younger than Leon.

She hesitated a moment longer and then walked over to the table. At first, Leon failed to notice her, though the woman turned and offered her a look of idle regard. Leon laughed at something, and only when he noticed his companion's distraction, did he glance up at Lou Ann. She saw him stiffen, his face suddenly devoid of the animation of a moment before.

"Hey, Leon," she said, edging around the table so she could face them both.

The blonde cut Leon a questioning look. She had delicate features with cheekbones almost too high to be considered attractive. Her almond-shaped eyes led Lou Ann to guess she might be Asian.

Leon smiled and stared up at Lou Ann. His eyes looked glassy. "Of all the gin joints. Isn't that the line?" He glanced briefly at the woman who continued to regard Lou Ann with mild curiosity. "You wanna beer? China, why don't you bring this lady a beer?" he said, turning to the blonde.

The woman smiled and rose to her feet. She wore a diaphanous dress that left nothing to the imagination. "Would you prefer something besides beer?" she asked, her voice devoid of any accent.

"A margarita would be great," Lou Ann said, dropping into the empty chair across from Leon.

They both watched the blonde walk off. "She owns the place," he said in explanation, looking back at Lou Ann.

"So she lets you run a tab?"

"Hell, no. And not for lack of trying. For some reason, she doesn't trust writers." His voice sounded somewhat slurred,

"Very sensible on her part. Especially for someone so young to be so wise," she added.

"She's young? I didn't notice. So what are you doing here?"

"I came to see you, of course."

"With malice aforethought, I'm sure. I imagine my agent told you how to find me. So what? A year goes by and you think you can just drop in? You must need something. Maybe some friendly enabling? Someone to dole out your pills for you? Or maybe someone to talk to your latest record producer and try to explain the many ways of Lou Ann Catskill." The anger in his voice was obvious.

"Leon…."

"No, just tell me why you're here."

The blonde appeared with a tray and two margaritas. She placed the drinks on the table and gave Lou Ann a knowing smile that could have easily been taken for a smirk before walking off.

"Did I interrupt anything?"

"You didn't answer my question."

She took a swallow of the margarita. "Do you remember that time in Tahiti when we thought we were going to drown in a tsunami, and you asked me what I would do if I had only one hour left to live? And I said I would write music. And you asked what if I couldn't. At the time, I couldn't imagine that. Not writing music. Well ,.." She paused to take another swallow. "I'm not writing. I couldn't if my life depended on it. Which it does. And I can't say much for my singing either. Or my mothering. Or managing my life for that matter. I can't live up to myself. My shrink's words, not mine." She paused, almost out of breath. "Is that an honest enough answer?"

"If you're telling me you're a hot mess, you're probably understating it by half."

She tilted her drink back, emptying the glass in one swallow. "So let me add to that confession that I always thought I never needed anyone."

"No, you were afraid of needing someone. There's a difference."

"Okay. I need someone. And there's no one else. Wait…" she said before he could say anything. "I know what you're going to say. And I don't blame you. I've hurt you. And I have no right to ask you for anything."

When he didn't respond, she reached over for his untouched margarita and took a drink. "Help yourself, why don't you?" Leon said, nodding at his margarita.

"I'm nervous. Okay?"

In the brittle silence that followed, she became aware of the sounds coming from the street below and the hum of conversation from the other tables. She looked around at the other tables and wondered what exactly she was doing here.

"What are you asking?" he asked.

"I guess what I'm asking is for you to be a part of my life. A part of Iris's."

"Iris's? I'm not her father. You went out of your way once to assure me of that."

"No, you're not her father, but Leon... God, how do I say this? I need you. I want you to come back. To live with us."

"Live with you? What the hell does that mean? You want me to be some kind of half-ass surrogate father to Iris? Someone to take care of things when you're off on some tour? And what else? Would I be your Minister of Internal Affairs again? I rather liked that title for as long as it lasted." He studied her for a moment, "Why do you think we'd work out now? What's different?"

"What's different is I need something more than just my music. I need someone like you in my life."

"Someone like me? That's not exactly a ringing endorsement."

"Okay." She took a deep breath. "I love you, Leon Riser. There I said it. I think about you all the time. You realize that?"

"I imagine your shrink might label that obsession, not love. Look, if you're trying to sell this, you're not doing a good job. Where's this coming from anyway? Did someone dump you?"

"No one dumped me. There is no one. I know this all sounds... opportunistic and self-serving. But I'm different."

"Oh. yeah?"

"All right. You want me to admit to being as fucked up as I ever was. Okay?" She finished his drink and shook her head. "Look, never mind." she said, getting to her feet. "It was wrong of me to come here."

"Hold on," he said, raising his hand. He reached over and took his margarita from her and downed the remainder in one swallow. "Have you even run this by Iris? I mean how is she going to feel about some guy she barely knows moving in? She's what? All of twelve?"

"Twelve going on twenty with more vices than Keith Richards. No thanks to me, I suppose. You saw what it was like when she was little. The tours, a different nanny every six months. Her having to put up with me. Yeah, I was… I am a shitty mother."

"And a shitty, vagabond father figure is your answer for that? You're still not convincing me."

"You could teach her things, Leon. Teach her about the world. About life. Things I can't."

"And you think the two of us playing house is the answer?"

"Yeah, I'm finally ready to play house if that's how you want to put it." She raised the empty glass and looked around. "Do they serve food here? I haven't eaten since breakfast."

Leon waved down a nearby waitress. "*Por favor. ¿ Le traerias a esta señora camarones en mojo de ajo?*

"God. *Camarones en mojo de ajo.* I remember you used to make that all the time at your place on the Big Island. We'd always stop at that same little roadside stand and buy shrimp. You remember?" She smiled at the memory of those long ago times and started to reach for his hand but stopped herself.

"Say I agree to do this. No guarantees. No commitment. So what are you willing to give me in return?"

"Leon. You know I've never done this. And I'd be lying if I said there'd be any guarantees. I just know that for once in my life I want to try. What do I give you in return? All that I can. If that's not enough…" She shrugged.

He slumped back in his chair and stared at her for a long time. "Where are you living these days?"

"I was in Palm Springs, but I just bought a house in Austin. Most of my band lives there. My record producer's there. Iris has a good school. At least, when she goes. Look, you can still travel as much as you want. Have your own life." She started to say have your own women. But then that wouldn't be what she was proposing. Or what she wanted.

"Say I start off by coming for a visit," he said after a time. "See if Iris and I click. No promises."

"What about us?"

He shrugged. "We've been down that road before. You tell me why you think it's going to be any different."

"I'm going to try. I'm ready," she said. "I…" She caught herself. She had almost added I think. She still wasn't sure if she had convinced herself. All she knew was that she needed him. But was that anything close to a commitment? All she knew was Leon always seemed to settle her and help her to figure things out. Could he do the same for Iris? And what if it all turns to crap?

She looked at Leon and wondered if he was thinking the same things. She loved him. Of that she was sure. But love and pain had always seemed two sides of the same coin. Hadn't that been a lyric to one of her songs? It would be so simple if love could be relegated to the bridge of a song. But there was always that same old chorus.

"Can I stay with you tonight?" she asked.

He uncoupled his eyes and looked off to the side. She followed his gaze and saw the blonde Asian woman watching them from the doorway. A moment passed before he looked back at her. "I guess there's no way I'm ever going to get the chance to run that tab."

# PART THREE

# 31

*"My heart is black*
*My soul a cold breath*
*And wish it were not so*
*But it is what it is..*
*What is there to do?"*

-Lou Ann Catskill
Wrongdoing

**SOUTH AUSTIN MEDICAL CENTER**

**APRIL 14th**

Iris got up from her chair and readjusted the oxygen saturation monitor on Leon's finger. For some reason his saturation level had suddenly dropped to eighty-seven. Then she realized the nasal cannula providing Leon's oxygen had slipped from his nostrils. As she reinserted it, he opened his eyes and shot her a look of irritation.

"Don't be difficult," she said, dropping back into her chair.

"I wouldn't have it any other way," he said, grimacing as he shifted onto his other side to reach for his water glass. He cursed when he couldn't reach it.

Iris clicked her tongue and leaned over to hand it to him. "Fumiko told you," she said, "Just ask. No moving around."

He took a sip of water before dropping his head back onto the pillow.

"For chrissakes, Iris. Pull up your mask. You don't know what's floating around in here."

Iris readjusted her mask and sat back in her chair.

"Where is she? Fumiko? I thought she would be back by now," he said,

"Who knows? I think she felt uncomfortable."

He looked at her, his expression telegraphing something she thought might be due to pain, but she sensed it was more reflective of some private torment. "Uncomfortable," he muttered under his breath.

"I think she left us alone so we could talk," she said. "We should talk, you know."

Neither had uttered so much as a half-dozen words to each other on the two and a half hour drive from Brady to Austin. Even as they sat waiting in the ER treatment room for another two hours, she had said little unless asked something by Fumiko or the ER nurses. She and Leon had also done their best to avoid eye contact, and it was only when he seemed to fall asleep that she allowed herself to look at him.

She was his daughter. She was sure of it. In retrospect, everything made sense – the way her mother tiptoed around any discussion of who her father might be; Leon's seeming reticence to play the role of anything more than her part time caretaker and quasi-home school teacher. Now she understood it all. And she had to admit just how much of Leon she now saw in herself, a fact that neither annoyed nor comforted her.

"Dad," she blurted, surprising herself.

He looked at her and arched his eyebrows. "You're sure you want to call me that?"

She shrugged. "Why not? Don't you think you've earned it?"

He started to say something, but instead began with one of his coughing fits. She lifted her gaze to the oxygen saturation monitor above his bed. For a moment, it dipped into the eighties; something Fumiko said was not good. He stopped coughing and took a deep breath.

"I should've pushed it," he said. "Made her tell me the truth. I wonder if maybe I didn't want to know the truth. If I was really your father, then… why couldn't I act like one? And if I wasn't your father, then I didn't want to deal with how I felt about you. Does that make any sense?"

"It doesn't matter."

"Don't be so hard on her," he said after a moment.

"The hell, I won't. She needs to explain to me. She needs to make me understand. God, Leon… Dad… She's my mother and I don't know her. I only thought I did, but now… " She chocked back her tears and reached for his hand. "Don't leave me, Leon."

"Leave you? Look, enough of this maudlin shit. One, I'm not going anywhere anytime soon, and two, welcome to adulthood and the realization we're all imperfect assholes. We don't always get it right." He paused for a moment before going on. "When you get to be our age, you suddenly have this… epiphany. You start to see all the things you should've done different. And we didn't for some reason that now doesn't make sense. I'd lay odds that's occurred to your mother by now. You said she was going to Sue's. Well, go see her. Talk to her," he wheezed and coughed again. "Make her come see me," he added. "You'll do that?"

"Sure. I've always been good at guilt tripping her. I'll tell her you have an hour to live."

Leon shot her an odd look and smiled. "Yeah, you tell her that. I've got one hour to live.. We just have an hour. You tell her that."

Iris leaned over, slipped down her mask, and kissed him on the forehead and walked out. Suddenly, everything that had occurred the past three days, the memories, the retrospection, it all flowed together seamlessly in his mind, like a story that finally made sense. He closed his eyes and out of habit, began editing.

# 32

*"Well its half past midnight*
*Half past caring*
*Half past love*
*And you say you still care*
*But it's half past our time*
*Can you stop the time, baby?*
*Turn back the clock? "*

-Lou Ann Catskill
Lucky At Love

Leon drifted in and out of twilight sleep, his reveries littered with luminous fictions. A small cove, the water an impossible blue. A shoreline thick with palm trees. A gauntlet of women in neon *mumus* lined the beach like some multi-beaded necklace. They were singing a despairing dirge, their arms beckoning. And then the apparition faded from the screen of his consciousness. Only the faint sound of the women's mournful refrain remained before it too slipped away. And then he thought he heard a voice bidding him good evening.

It took a few seconds for him to realize where he was. The steady, muted beeping of the monitor on the shelf above his head oriented him in a manner not wholly comforting. He stared at the ceiling for a moment longer, attempting to recall the images in his dream, but to no avail. Finally giving up, he glanced around the dimly lit room, trying to make sense of the shadows.

"Good evening, Mr. Riser," someone said from the foot of his bed.

It was the doctor that had evaluated him in the ER. His name was Mac something or other. He had exchanged his mask for a transparent face shield, allowing Leon to finally see his face. He appeared to be quite young and had a pallid face that suggested he hadn't seen the outdoors in weeks. His bearing projected a nervous intensity that Leon found off putting. A first year resident, he remembered the young man telling him as an introduction.

Leon looked around the room and saw that Fumiko had also been awakened. She sat up and flung off her blanket and began rubbing her eyes.

"Your tests are all back," the resident said, placing his laptop on the night table at the foot of the bed. "First, your x-ray," he said, spinning the laptop around for Leon to see. "You have a touch of pneumonia, Mr. Riser. The good news is there is no evidence of consolidation or opacities which one might expect with COVID. These perihilar interstitial infiltrates that you see here suggest it is most likely another, more benign viral pathogen. RSV, perhaps. Respiratory syncytial virus. Or perhaps metapneumonia. We will test you to make sure." He glanced at Fumiko as if expecting some rebuttal and then spun the laptop back around. "Your COVID test was negative but the PCR will not be back until morning at the earliest. You are fortunate for the head pathologist is an admirer of your books, therefore he is attempting to rush your results. On the other hand, you are somewhat dehydrated which explains the protein in your urine and why your Glomerular Filtration Rate is low."

"How low?" Fumiko asked.

"Sixty," he replied without looking at Fumiko. "Not so bad. You are also anemic which is not surprising considering your diagnosis. We will give you a unit of blood and…"

"What is his hemoglobin?" Fumiko interjected.

He hesitated, his annoyance obvious. "Seven. I think a transfusion will make Mr. Riser feel better."

"And his white count?"

"His white count is fine. As are all his other blood tests. I think…"

"In light of his diagnosis," Fumiko interrupted, "I think it best you consult the oncologist on staff."

He muttered something under his breath and glanced down at his laptop before looking back at Fumiko. "I wish to schedule a CT scan in the morning. We should…"

"Hey," Leon cut in. "Talk to me, not her. I'm the patient. And no, I don't want any scans. I've had enough already." He glanced at Fumiko who nodded.

"Very well," he said his exasperation obvious by his tone of voice. "I shall consult with the oncologist on call. Meanwhile, I will order some antibiotics as a precaution, monitor your oxygen levels, give you some nebulizer treatments and begin rehydrating you. My guess is you will feel much better in the morning."

"What about my pain?"

The resident whispered something into his hand. He took a deep breath before replying. "Your nurse here informed me you have tolerated hydrocodone in the past, but it may cause respiratory depression. In light of your pneumonia, I think it best we see if Ibuprofen will suffice for now."

"Then just give me something for sleep."

"Very well. Now if you don't have any other questions," he said, as he turned to walk away.

"And you will consult with the oncologist," Fumiko said.

"Sure, first thing in the morning," he said, glaring at Fumiko who offered him a smile. He turned and left.

"Thanks, Fumiko."

"I have your back. Is that not the expression? Now you are in my debt."

"I'm not giving you a raise if that's what you're getting at. How about travel pay?"

"You must tell me how it ended."

What? Between Iris and I?"

"No, between you and her mother."

"I have to pee."

"Are you sure you can walk?"

"Come on, Fumiko. Don't treat me like an invalid. Of course, I can walk."

She lowered the guard rails, took hold of his IV pole and held his arm as he scooted from the bed. "Sit on the toilet. Do not stand," she said, guiding him into the restroom.

"Yes, Nurse Sato. You want me to pee like a woman. Are you coming in with me?"

She shut the door behind him without replying. He stood with both hands leaning on the wall and urinated, finishing with a prolonged fit of coughing. When he opened the door, she stood there waiting. He ignored her efforts to support him as he shuffled back to bed.

He slumped back onto his pillow and tried to edit what he was about to say. In the end, he gave up, more out of resignation than anything else. "I guess you've figured out Iris is my daughter. I don't think she knew. Not until yesterday."

"How is she dealing with this?"

"How do you think? She went to see her mother." He closed his eyes and retreated into a silence that continued for almost a minute before opening his eyes and looking at Fumiko.

"We had some good years. Lou Ann and I. Iris and I had some good years, too. But like always, Lou Ann started unraveling. The pressure, the touring began to chew her up.". He paused at the memory and grimaced.

"So she stopped writing her songs. And then she got lost. The alcohol and the pills didn't help matters much. She'd find a new therapist every few months. And for once, I couldn't help her because I was almost as screwed up as she was."

He paused again, fumbling for an explanation which after all this time he had still not sorted out clearly in his mind.

"I stopped writing, too. You could say my tank was empty. I'm not sure why exactly. Iris figured into it. She was a handful. Then I had this thing with Sue, the backup singer. It wasn't so much the cause of the break up. It was more like a symptom."

"And the two of you do not speak of any of this?"

"I think we're both afraid to lock horns and get tangled up again. And there's no starting over."

"Even if you still love one another?"

"Maybe that makes it even harder. There's always that risk of it failing again. I don't think either of us could handle that."

"Will you have regrets?"

"You mean when I die? Doesn't everyone?"

"But now that you know about Iris?"

He thought for a moment as he tried to sort out the conflicting emotions and motives. "You want to know how it ended. That last chapter. Okay, but when I'm done I want you to give me some Ambien and my hydrocodone. I need to sleep and I don't want to dream. I promise I'll keep breathing. You're going to be watching over me anyway, aren't you?"

She considered him for a moment before reaching into her bag and retrieving two small vials. "I am not a very good nurse. I think I will change professions," she said, shaking a pill from each vial. "Maybe I will become your muse. But first, your story."

He took a deep breath as if clearing himself. "She got this crazy idea that her mother was in the audience. She'd swear she saw her right there in the front row. Mind you, Lou Ann never spoke about her mother or much about her family. And I knew better than to ask. I'm not sure what it was all about, this delusion about seeing her mother. I figured it was the pills. Why she was coming apart. I could see where she was going. But like I said, I was in no shape to rescue her like I usually did."

He paused as he played it all back in his head. "I was with Sue when Iris called me," he said, finally. "She said Lou Ann had called and she sounded real bad. Drunk, high maybe. She wasn't making much sense, but she wanted to talk to me. Iris tried to give her my cell number but wasn't sure she'd remember it. So Iris called me."

# 33

*"When it's right as rain and wrong as sin*
*How do I start?*
*How do I end?*
*Make your move, you say."*

-Lou Ann Catskill
Right As Rain

**AUSTIN**

**July, 2016**

Leon opened the door and quit the oppressive Texas heat and humidity and stepped into the cool, dim interior of The Continental Club. He stood there a moment to allow his eyes to adjust to the club's dim interior. The only lights in the seemingly empty bar were the neon beer signs above the bar. The one proclaiming Shiner Bock blinked frantically. He could just make out some tables and upturned chairs that had been pushed to the side. After a few seconds, he saw someone sitting alone at one of the tables. The figure turned and looked in his direction, and only then he realized it was Sue.

"What the hell?" he asked, approaching the table.

"They cancelled at the last minute," she replied, her voice husky.

Leon had agreed to meet her and watch her audition for a spot as a backup singer for an upcoming tour of an Austin Blues Revue. He could see she was holding a small shot glass. She took a sip of whatever it was she was drinking, and with one foot, scooted an empty chair in his direction.

"There's no one here?"

"Just Angie the bookkeeper and the janitor. So I helped myself from the bar. I'm sorry. I should've called," she said after he sat down. She leaned over and planted a moist kiss on his lips. She tasted of gin and cigarettes. She reached for the bottle of Bombay at her elbow, refilled her glass, and handed it to him.

"No thanks, So did they reschedule you?" he asked, plucking the glass from her grip and setting it on the table.

She didn't say anything. Instead, she picked up the glass and took another sip.

"I need that job," she said, downing half the glass.

He took the glass away from her again and moved it out of her reach. She murmured something he didn't catch and reached for the pack of cigarettes beside her. She flicked on her lighter and leaned into the flame, her face momentarily illuminated in the flare. Her cheeks were wet, and he realized she had been crying. He reached over and wiped the tear from her cheek.

"It means that much?" he asked.

She didn't reply right away but took another drag of her cigarette. "You know why I want that job."

He kept his counsel before answering. He knew why, he just didn't want to acknowledge it. "No, I don't," he said, his denial transparent.

"What the fuck are we doing, Leon? I'm too old and cynical to be lying in bed at night trying out your last name."

He regarded her silently for a long moment. "I thought you told me you didn't want anything out of this but an accomplice."

She laughed, but it came out sounding bitter. "An accomplice? Yeah, I guess we're criminals. Gangsters of love. Wasn't that the name of a song? Or is this like I once heard some asshole say? Something to the effect that often times sex is like a crime, One percent motive and ninety-nine percent opportunity. Is that what I am? Opportunity?"

In his mind, he laid out his possible answers like cards before replying. "What do you want me to say?" he said finally, giving into his discomfort. "Look, it happened for a reason. We both needed... someone. Intimacy. Forgive me if that sounds trite, but Lou Ann and I..." He let what he was going to say trail off.

"Where is she, by the way?"

He shrugged. "I haven't seen or heard from her in four or five days. You know as well as I do that even when she's here, she's not. But you're here. That says something."

"Yeah, here and conveniently available."

"That's not how I meant it."

"No? Look, Leon. It's just that she's my friend, even if she is fucked up and not here. For either of us," she added. "But you and I ... She'll always be there lying between us. So what's the point?"

The discomfort of their intimacy made him reach for the glass of gin. He emptied it and pushed the glass away.

"You know, the two of us don't talk much anymore," he said. "And when we do, it's like... I don't know. Like we can never get past the... the past. There're times she's like the old Lou Ann, and then she's gone. It's not like you and me haven't seen this before. She's headed down that same black hole. And there's nothing either of us can do about it."

"And what we're doing is supposed to help? You know that she knows about us? After that last show in LA, she walks off the stage, comes up to me, and pats me on the cheek and says, 'You deserve each other.' She didn't say it in an ugly way either. She meant it."

"Jesus."

They sat there in silence for almost a minute, each seemingly lost in their melancholia. He felt suddenly powerless, much like one might feel standing on a shore and watching as a ship sunk slowly in the distance. He still wasn't ready to quit. He wanted her, but had no inkling of what might save them. His cell phone ringing interrupted these thoughts. He retrieved it from his pocket and glanced at the screen. It was Iris.

"Yeah?"

"Leon, Mom called. She sounds bad, like she's real drunk or high or something. She wanted to talk to you."

"Why didn't she call me?"

"'I don't know. She sounded confused. She said she had lost her phone."

"Did she say where she was?"

"No. I kept asking. And then she hung up."

"Look on your phone. Tell me what number she was calling from."

The number didn't sound familiar, nor was it an Austin area code. He repeated the number, committing it to memory.

"If she calls again, make sure she has my number and tell her to call me. Okay?"

He hung up and dialed the number. It took several seconds before anyone answered.

"Sundowner Motel," a raspy, high-pitched voice answered.

"Do you have a Lou Ann Catskill staying there?"

There was a long moment of silence. "No sir, No one by that name is registered here."

"She just called from there. She's fifty, long black hair. Maybe she's with someone."

"Sorry. I couldn't say. Are you sure…"

"Where are you located?"

"We're between San Marcos and Canyon Lake just before you get to Fischer if you know where that is. Would you like a room? We don't have any lake views but we do have a creek that's real nice."

He disconnected and looked at Sue. "I have to go. She's in the hole."

"I'm coming with you,"

# 34

*"The pill on my tongue*
*The infection in my soul.*
*The slow bleed, the abscess in my heart.*
*Why does this take so long?"*

-Lou Ann Catskill
Woman Down

Leon drove Sue's BMW in the hope they would make better time than if they took his twenty year old pickup truck. In the end, it made little difference as the traffic leaving Austin going towards Dripping Springs was unusually heavy. It wasn't until they turned off to Wimberley that the traffic thinned.

Neither of them spoke much, each consumed by thoughts of how this new drama might affect their tangled, triangulated relationship. It wasn't until they turned onto the highway cutoff to the lake that Sue finally spoke up.

"Are you sure we shouldn't be calling someone? The sheriff, maybe. Or EMS?"

"And tell them what? That she's loaded in a motel room? Maybe with someone? She doesn't deserve that kind of publicity. Iris sure as hell doesn't. Face it. We've both been there when she pulls this shit. We're the cleaning crew."

"We don't even know if she's still there. You said the clerk didn't know the name or anyone fitting that description."

Leon didn't reply. All he knew was that he couldn't do this anymore. Couldn't or didn't want to. It was the same thing. Part of him felt he was only doing this for Iris, for he didn't owe Lou Ann anymore. Their connection these past six years had run the gamut from close affection and something almost akin to a stable loving relationship to fractious tolerance and everything in between. Was that maybe how relationships were meant to be? A landscape of summits and deep dark valleys. He had never been in a long term relationship, and thus didn't know the rules, or what to expect, or how to maneuver through a landscape littered with mines. Nevertheless, he had persevered, partially out of concern for Iris, but also because in some perverted way, Lou Ann fed something in him, completed something in him. He still wasn't sure if that was the definition of love.

It was late afternoon before they pulled up to the Sundowner Motel. It was one of those stereotypical 1950's style motor lodges with a small swimming pool surrounded by a chain link fence and sported an out size sign in the shape of a setting sun. Gauging from the lone car in the potholed parking lot and the motel's faded exterior, Leon guessed the Sundowner was far from a thriving enterprise. The one car in the lot was an older model Camaro. The place had no more than a dozen units in a L-shaped formation surrounding the pool.

They parked and went inside to find a wizened figure of indeterminate gender sitting behind the counter and engrossed in what appeared to be a game show displayed on a television the size of a shoebox. The clerk wore a camouflage-patterned smock over a Dallas Cowboys T-shirt

"I called about whether you had a Lou Ann Catskill registered here," Leon said.

The clerk turned and gave Leon a look of silent regard. "Sure. And I told you nobody here by that name." It was the same raspy, high-pitched voice from earlier.

"Are you the only clerk?"

"Daytime."

"So she might've come in the evening?"

"Not under that name."

"You mind if we look at the guest ledger?"

The clerk made a smacking noise with his or her lips, thought about it for a moment, and then pulled a grimy, somewhat tattered ledger from beneath the desk. Obviously, the Sundowner had not joined the technological revolution. The clerk slid it across the counter. "Help yourself."

Leon flipped it open to the last pages that appeared to have been filled in. There were no more than a half-dozen names on the last page. He ran his fingers down the list, paused and passed the book to Sue. The last name was Sue Mendez.

"I guess you don't ask for an ID?"

"This ain't that kinda place."

Leon looked at the list again. Sue Mendez had taken Room 12. "Do you have another key for Room 12?"

The clerk gazed at Leon without expression for a moment before turning and glancing at a board on the wall behind him. The room numbers had been crudely painted above a line of small hooks.

"Guess not. Maybe this lady wanted both keys. Or maybe that was the only one."

"You have a master key?"

"Yeah, but I can't give you that."

"Would you rather I kick in the door? No? Then give me the goddamn key. Look, this woman may be in trouble. We just need to check on her. I doubt you want to sully your motel's sterling reputation by having the cops show up. "

"Giving you that key is against policy. I could lose my job."

Sue placed her wallet on the counter. Opening it, she took out what appeared to be three twenties and laid them on the counter. "Will this help?" she asked.

The clerk eyed the bills for a few seconds before reaching under the counter and removing a single key attached to a wooden fob. "You realize this ain't no deposit," the clerk said, picking up the bills. "And I need that key back."

Leon snatched up the key and they both quickly made their way down along the front of the motel to the last room. He started to insert the key, and then thought better of it, and knocked instead. When no one answered, he knocked once more and then unlocked the door.

The room was dark. The heavy shades had been drawn and there were no lights on, but the light from the open door was enough to see a figure on the bed wrapped in a blanket. Leon could see an empty Jack Daniels bottle on the night stand along with several medicine vials. One of them was overturned and a few white tablets were scattered on the night stand's surface. With some trepidation, he approached the bed, and then leaning over, pulled back the blanket.

Lou Ann lie curled in a fetal position. She was nude and drenched in sweat. Her long hair was matted and clotted with what Leon assumed was vomit. He rolled her onto her back and brushed her hair out of her face.

"Wake up, Babe," he said, patting her cheek. "Lou Ann. Come on. It's Leon."

She made a faint, guttural sound and blinked. He slapped her this time, but without eliciting any response other than a moan. He turned and looked at Sue who had already taken her cell phone from her purse and was dialing.

"Don't go yet," he said, leaning over and whispering into Lou Ann's ear. He turned her onto her side and then lay beside her.

# 35

*"If there's more, I can't see it.*
*So when's ever enough?*
*It's just so quiet in here.*
*So quiet."*

-Lou Ann Catskill
Regrets

Fumiko said nothing, honoring Leon's silence for as long as she could. "And that was the end?" she asked finally.

He looked at her as if surprised by her presence. "Not quite." He coughed and cleared his throat. "I stayed away from the hospital. I'd drop off Iris and..." He faltered and seemed to slip away for what seemed almost a minute. "Once they discharged her, I tried to see her, but she told Iris not to let me in. I went anyway. They must've had her doped up pretty good because she was pretty withdrawn. She wouldn't make eye contact, wouldn't talk to me."

"She was perhaps embarrassed."

"No, that wasn't it. And it wasn't about Sue and I either. Sue apologized to her, but Lou Ann wouldn't hear of it. Said that had nothing to do with it. She even told Sue to make it work with me. She said her and I had had reached the end. Run our course. It was over. When Sue asked her why, she wouldn't say."

"That must have been very painful for you."

He didn't reply at first. "Something broke," he said after a moment had gone by. "In me. In her. I was angry. I was tired. And I just gave up, Maybe, I finally saw her point. We weren't going anywhere. We hadn't for a long time. And it wasn't just her fault. We both went AWOL Absent without leave. Gone," he said in response to Fumiko's look of bewilderment.

"I could've blamed it on her lifestyle, her bipolar, on Iris, on simple fatigue. But at the time, I knew she was right. Sometimes when you lose something that you think you can't live without, well later, when the fire's out and your wounds have healed, you realize that person never meant as much to you as you thought. I felt that way for a long time. It was how I dealt with it. And then… this," he said, glancing around the room. "Coming down with cancer changes a lot of things. You remember what it was all about in the first place. And you find yourself wanting to do it over. Make it work out different. You want to hold on to it because that's all you've got. But then you realize there's no going back. Life doesn't work that way, does it?"

Fumiko wasn't sure what to say. In retrospect, she now realized how much pain he had been in all this time. And not just the physical pain of his cancer, but the profound sense of loss and regret he had been dealing with all those months.

"There is still time," she said.

"Is there?" he asked, looking at her. "I want to sleep. Give me my meds."

She handed him the two pills and his glass of water. "Do not worry. I will watch over you. Now sleep well."

# 36

*"Peel off my skin*
*To the muscle, to the bone*
*See my heart*
*Is it still black?"*

-Lou Ann Catskill
The Uneven Surface of My Soul

It started to rain as Iris pulled up in front of Sue's house. She sprinted up to the porch and startled at the two figures sitting on a swing in the dark. It was Sue and her Mom.

"Iris," Lou Ann said, obviously surprised to see her.

Iris wiped the rain from her face and looked at each of them in turn.

"I'm going in," Sue said. "Iris, can I get you anything? Wine or something?"

"No. I'm fine." She watched Sue retreat inside, but remained standing.

She and Lou Ann looked at each other for a moment before Lou Ann got up from the swing and held out her arms as if inviting an embrace. Iris didn't move. After a couple of seconds, Lou Ann lowered her arms.

"I guess I'm on your shit list again," Lou Ann said, dropping back onto the swing.

"As a matter of fact, you are. I just found out Leon's my father."

Lou Ann seemed to take an audible breath in and looked away. "He told you?"

"He saw the birth date on my driver's license and figured it out. Do you realize what it would've meant to me to have known that? Growing up? Why, Mom? Why didn't you tell me? Or Leon, for chrissakes? I'm trying so hard to understand. And I want to think you had a good reason for doing it. I just want to understand."

A minute might have passed before Lou Ann finally said, "Do you know how hard it is to let people in?"

"That's your excuse? That's a cop out, Mom. Maybe you should tell that to Leon. He's in the hospital, Mom."

"Why? What happened?"

"He's sick. Pneumonia, maybe. He's go cancer. Multiple myeloma. It's this kind…"

"I know what it is," she said, cutting her off. "How bad is he?"

"He was apparently doing better before this trip."

"You said he came with you to help find me. For one thing, I didn't need finding, and two, why would you ask him to do that?"

"Because I thought you were in trouble and I thought he might give a shit about you. I didn't have anyone else to ask."

"Sit down, Iris. Please."

Iris hesitated and then came and sat next to her. "You know, Mom," she said after a moment of silence had passed. "Who are you? You realize don't you, that I don't know anything about you. About who you really are. I mean, sometimes I think I do, and then something like this and… I look at you and I don't know. You've never once told me about your childhood. About your parents. Your life that no one ever sees. Everything before me, before Leon. It's like it it's off limits. All my childhood memories are the parties you'd drag me to. And all the hotels. Never staying in a house for more than a few months at a time. But no stories about your childhood. Or your mother. Nothing. I have to know things to understand who you are. Who I am. Don't you get that?"

Lou Ann stared straight ahead and said nothing.

"Mom…"

Lou Ann raised her hand, interrupting her. "Wait." She sat motionless, staring straight ahead, her expression blank. After almost a minute had passed, she cleared her throat and looked at Iris.

"My father left my mother… left all of us. He left my mother, me, my sister. He actually left us four or five times. At least, those were the times I can recall. And by left, I mean we didn't see him for six, nine months at a time. My mother told me once that he had another family stashed somewhere."

She waited a long moment before going on. "I was six years old the first time I called an ambulance for my mother. She had overdosed on Quaaludes. She wasn't breathing so my little sister and I took turns blowing on her lips. That wasn't the last time," she added so softly that Iris wasn't sure she had heard her correctly.

"You have a sister?" Iris asked when Lou Ann didn't go on.

"Had. Her name was Mattie. She died from an overdose when she was fourteen."

Iris stared at her mother, unsure how to respond. "And your mother?"

Lou Ann appeared to ponder her answer for longer than seemed necessary. "After Mattie died, my mother…" Lou Ann seemed to lose herself for a moment. "I came home from school one day and she was gone. I never saw her or heard from her again. I was sixteen. My father used to always promise us he would come back. And he usually did, until he didn't. Neither of them ever came back."

Iris turned away, stunned by this disclosure. After a moment, she reached for her mother's hand. Lou Ann hesitated before grasping her hand.

"How come you never told me any of this?"

"I never thought you would understand. You were either too young or by the time you were a teenager… I just couldn't. It hurt me too much to think about it much less tell anyone. I couldn't risk it."

"Risk what? Admitting you had a fucked up childhood? That you struggled? Like you were the only one that had to deal with that kind of shit?"

"I told some of this to the first psychiatrist I ever saw. Ten minutes into my first session, he tells me that I had difficulty trusting others, and that I had abandonment issues. I thought that if it was that easy for him to figure me out, I surely didn't need him. The next psychiatrist gave me some pills. This was only after I told him how I had spent the previous two weeks buying clothes. Morning to night. Going to one store after another. I'd stay up all night trying them on and then return them in the morning and then I would start all over. And then I'd crash. Lock myself in my apartment for days. That story must've impressed this shrink because he told me I needed medication. He called it my condition," She looked at Iris. "Have you heard enough?"

"No. Now I need to hear everything,"

Lou Ann took a deep breath and sighed. "Everything. There's not enough time for everything," She grasped Iris's hand tighter. "The pills kept me from pulling everything down around me, but they still didn't let me trust anyone. I finally found this psychiatrist who actually listened to what I told her, but at the time I didn't want to hear what she had to say. I wasn't ready. And I wasn't ready for a long time. So I went…." She started over. "I could never trust anyone. Not even myself." She turned her face away. "It's why I could never tell Leon about you. I thought he wouldn't stay." She looked back at Iris. "Or that I wouldn't stay. Do you realize what I'm saying? That there were times I almost walked away from you. What kind of mother does that?"

"But Mom, you didn't leave."

"No? Iris, I tried to kill myself. Because I wanted to leave. I almost left you then. The truth is that I left you long before then. I left you with Leon, where you were much better off."

Neither of them spoke for a minute so. The rain had stopped, and the only sound was the rain sloshing down the gutters. "It's never too late, Mom," Iris said finally.

"That's what Sue said." She brought Iris's hand to her mouth and kissed it. "Do you forgive me?"

"No."

"But you will," she said, putting her arm around Iris's shoulders and pulling her close. "You'll see."

"Leon wanted me to tell you that he wanted to see you and that he only had an hour to live. I don't think he was serious."

"An hour. That's what he said?"

Iris detected a smile as Lou Ann shook her head.

"Then for god sakes we'd better go," she said.

# 37

*"If I let you in*
*To that secret place*
*By the river of the past*
*Where I write my songs.*
*Will you know me then?"*

-Lou Ann Catskill
Isle of Hearts

Fumiko awoke with a start. She had fallen asleep, lulled by fatigue and the steady beeping of Leon's pulse monitor. She rubbed her eyes and reached for her glass of water. Only then did she notice the figure sitting in the chair on the other side of Leon's bed. Whoever it was sat with their head resting on Leon's arm. At first, Fumiko assumed it was Iris, based on nothing more than the cascade of long black hair. The shadows cast by the room's only illumination, a small bed lamp, made it difficult to be certain.

Whoever it was, must have heard Fumiko stir for she suddenly looked up. The dim light made her face appear ghostly pale, especially in contrast to the tangled frame of her dark tresses. She wore a surgical mask that concealed everything but her eyes. In that brief first instant of eye contact, Fumiko sensed the woman measuring her. She also realized it wasn't Iris after all. The woman's penetrating gaze forced Fumiko to momentarily look away.

The eyes, the hair, and the woman's pale complexion, elicited a sudden childhood memory. Fumiko's mother had often reprimanded her for her transgressions by promising a visit by the *yuki-omma,* the snow woman, a mythological figure with similar features to the woman sitting across from her. In Japanese folklore, the snow woman was a sort of vampire, a soul eater. Perhaps, I am only dreaming, Fumiko thought

Fumiko's expression must have telegraphed some degree of angst for the woman cocked her head in what seemed bemusement. She pulled down her mask, her face revealing a somberness that Fumiko found even more discomfiting. The woman glanced up at Leon's face.

"Is he in a coma?" the woman asked, her gaze still fixed on Leon.

"No. He is merely sleeping. A sedative," Fumiko offered as further explanation.

The woman nodded and looked back at Fumiko. "You must be Fumiko," she said.

Fumiko nodded deeply as if this were some formal introduction. "And you are Lou Ann. Your daughter has your eyes. This is how I know."

A brief smile organized Lou Ann's face before she again grew solemn.

"If you wish I can try to awaken him," Fumiko said.

"No, please don't wake him. Can he hear us?" she asked as an afterthought.

Fumiko shrugged. "He will hear some things. At least, his mind will register them. It is my belief that what one hears when they are sleeping is stored away in the same realm of one's dreams. Yes, I believe he can hear us."

Lou Ann appeared to consider this for a moment. "How is he?" Lou Ann asked almost in a whisper. "Please, tell me."

Fumiko took a moment before replying. "His oncologist in Denver is pleased with his progress. He says that Leon is almost in remission. Something like this though," she said nodding at Leon, "I do not know. Infections are never good in his condition."

Lou Ann looked back at Leon's face "He shouldn't have come," she muttered quietly.

"Have you spoken to Iris?" Fumiko asked.

Lou Ann rubbed her eyes with the heels of her hands. "Yes, she's waiting downstairs. She told me things," she added.

Neither of them spoke for a moment. The only sound was Leon's sonorous breathing and the relentless beeping of the monitor.

"Perhaps, you could return in the morning when he is awake?" Fumiko said, breaking the silence.

Lou Ann looked at her for a moment before replying. "No, that won't be possible. I can't stay." She hesitated and looked at him again for a moment before turning away. "I can't see him," she said so quietly that Fumiko thought she only imagined her words. Lou Ann looked at Fumiko. "I don't blame you if you don't understand. If you judge me. What I mean to say is…"

Leon appeared to stir, his eyes opening for a second and then he took a deep breath and was still again. Both of the women waited to see if he would awaken. When he didn't, Lou Ann went on.

"Part of it is that I'm a coward. I'm not sure I can deal with this," she said, her voice breaking. "And, I don't…. I can't do that to him again. Walk out on him." She looked at Fumiko. "Do you know about us? He was never one to reveal a lot of things. Maybe he's different now."

"He has told me certain things. Things of your time together. Some, but not all."

"Then you must know that our relationship has been difficult, I have been difficult. I have wronged him terribly." She ran her hands through her hair. "He loved me and I held him away. Pushed him away because I thought that I could never be what he wanted me to be. And I hurt him." She gently lifted his hand and brought it to her lips. "He never forgave me, and I have no right to ever ask him to. It's too late." She swiped at her nose with the sleeve of her sweater and sniffled.

Fumiko looked away, overcome by what she thought might be compassion, or a sense of intrusion, but also a fleeting realization of her own confused feelings for Leon. After a moment, she reached over and touched Lou Ann's hand.

"I think you are wrong about him not forgiving you. I have not heard him say such things in our conversations, I sense that he does not bear you ill will. That he perhaps still loves you."

Lou Ann looked at Fumiko, her eyes moist with tears. "Maybe once he could've forgiven me, but not now. Iris told me Leon found out that he's her father. And I never told him. How do you forgive someone for that?" She raised her hand to her mouth and stifled a sob. A moment passed before she seemed able to go on. "Someone told me once that hate…bitterness… destroys your spirit. It weakens your life force. I can't do that to him. Not now. Do you understand? He doesn't need me in his life."

Fumiko nodded. "This is true. About bitterness. But I also believe forgiveness helps heal us. I also know that it is often very difficult to forgive one's self for the pain you may have caused to people you love."

Lou Ann appeared to consider this for a moment. "Aren't you the wise one?" she said without any obvious sarcasm. "I have to go," she said, getting to her feet. "I would only make things worse. Tell Leon… " She took a deep breath. "Tell him I came to see him, but I couldn't stay. He'll understand." She leaned down and touched his cheek, and then gave Fumiko a nod and walked out.

Fumiko sat there, torn between the impulse to go after Lou Ann and berate her, perhaps plead with her, and her own confused sense of relief and guilt. It took not a minute before Lou Ann swept back into the room. She hesitated and then leaned over Leon's bed, lowering her face to within inches of his. And then she began to sing, at first a faltering whisper, before her voice grew stronger. Fumiko leaned closer, struggling to make out the words.

"You said love fades

Fades in the wind

Fades in the tempest of our hearts

You always said…"

Lou Ann's voice broke. "You always said love fades," she said and kissed Leon on the lips. "Well, for once you were wrong," she said and turned and was gone.

# 38

*"I look in the mirror.*
*And ask, do I know you now?*
*Are you safe?*
*Do you still feel it?*
*The weight?*
*No matter, it's quiet."*

-Lou Ann Catskill
Isle of Hearts

## HOLBOX, THE YUCATAN

**Four Months Later**

The dawn broke in a wash of neon orange and pink and rose. "Red sky in the morning, sailor ... Expect a shit storm," Leon muttered to himself.

A tourist Leon had encountered at the Arena Hotel bar the evening before had brought word that a hurricane by the name of Ida was heading into the gulf. Ida's my wife's hane, he remarked with no hint of obvious affection. He was a lineman from Alberta, and gauging from his boiled complexion, he was intent on stockpiling enough Vitamin D and ultraviolet light to sustain him through the long Canadian winter. He said he had decided to ride out any approaching storm in Holbox in the hope he would miss his flight home.

Leon stood on the beach watching the light on the water change from gray to silver flecked with the gold of the burgeoning dawn. Too late to evacuate even if he wanted to, he thought. Just like the Canuck at the Arena, he had more reasons for staying than going. He had done his best to urge Fumiko to leave while she still could. There was still time to take the morning ferry and catch a flight from Cancun to Houston.

She had only been here for four days with the intention of staying a week. It wasn't that he didn't enjoy her company, for visitors were far and few in between. Iris had come twice over the summer. His agent had even dropped by for a long weekend to discuss a possible book deal, but that was the extent of his guests.

Earlier that summer, Fumiko had seen him through another stem cell transplant. Afterwards, the oncologist had commuted his sentence and declared him in remission. At least for now, he cautioned. Leon took the good news as a sign that it was time for Fumiko to move on, for she had lingered in his employ far longer than was necessary. At first, she resisted on the grounds she was still needed. They both knew there was more to it than simple professional concern. In the end, both of them did their best to avoid delving too deeply into the bond that had developed between them.

Fumiko offered him frequent reminders of her need to maintain professional distance, although Leon knew women well enough to sense that someone like Fumiko would never wear her emotions on her sleeve. As for himself, in his moments of increasing clarity, he admitted to a degree of selfishness on his part; self-defense perhaps being a more apt portrayal. His prognosis carried with it a shelf- life; an impermanence that led him to shy away from any relationship deeper than mere friendship. Anything more would only mean that at some point he would be forced to let go of one more thing that he cherished.

He watched the sunrise for a moment longer before wading out into the warm water until it reached his waist. His progress stirred a school of flying fish, their frantic flight momentarily drawing the attention of a passing pair of brown pelicans that momentarily banked towards him before resuming their course down the length of the beach.

He lowered himself and began a slow and deliberate breast stroke. It had only been in the last several weeks that he felt a semblance of strength returning. Walks on the beach were still tiring. Swimming wasn't much easier, though he now could make it to the edge of a reef a good fifty yards offshore. To his dismay, all his exertions exhausted him to the point he found himself falling asleep soon after sunset. His doctors and Fumiko had cautioned him against overdoing things. And as usual, he paid their counsel little mind. It is what it is, became his new mantra. His well-honed fatalism told him that when, not if he relapsed, he would've lived the remainder of his life on his own terms.

By the time he turned back to shore, the rising sun had breached the bank of thick clouds forming to the east. Without bothering to look, he knew Fumiko would be watching him from her usual station inside the screened porch. The house, a patchwork of crude, weather beaten wooden planks and corrugated tin siding sat perched on stilts at the edge of the beach where the sand gave way to the forest. He had purchased it many years ago as a retreat to write uninterrupted by visitors, and thus, it lacked anything resembling modern conveniences. It had survived several large storms, but its flimsiness lent it an aura of impermanence, not unlike his own state.

As he drew near to shore, he saw Fumiko picking her way down to the beach bearing a cup in each hand – espresso for him, green tea for her. She wore a gauzy white, loose fitting caftan, beneath which she wore her usual conservative black one piece swim suit. She plopped down into one of the beach chairs and waited for him. As he waded out of the water, she tossed him a towel. They sat there slurping their coffee and tea, weaving through the silence in the manner only close friends could.

"Have you thought any more about leaving early?" he asked after some time had passed.

"Iris just texted me. She said the storm is going to Louisiana. So I will stay. I have no class until next week."

Leon couldn't help but smile at her mangled pronunciation of Louisiana.

"How come Iris is starting her classes earlier than you?"

Fumiko shrugged. Both of them had enrolled in graduate school - Iris in journalism, and Fumiko in the nurse practitioner program. They also had become roommates, their friendship quickly cemented in the month leading up to Leon's stem cell transplant. He wondered whether the two of them were perhaps more than just friends, but he never broached the subject with either of them.

"No jog this morning?" he asked.

"Perhaps later. I have a great deal of reading to do. School is difficult for me, you know. Not just the language. I had a learning disorder as a child. It is why I left school early to become a *geisha*," she said with a slight smile. "Iris calls me *geisha* gal. That is also how her mother refers to me. Leon's *geisha*. You realize she asks about you quite often," she went on when Leon didn't say anything.

"Who? Lou Ann?"

"Yet, you do not ask of her."

He looked at her. "Yeah," he said, simply. Before he could say more, a small single engine plane passed low overhead. Some high roller was flying in from Cancun. The only other way for a tourist to reach the island was by way of two hour shuttle to the village of Chiquila and then a fifteen minute ferry boat ride to Holbox.

"Does Iris ever mention where she is?" he asked.

Fumiko took a moment to reply. "You should not be angry."

"About what?"

"Iris also said that her mother was coming here. Today," she added with some trepidation.

"She's coming here? To Holbox?" He tossed what was left of his coffee into the sand. "And nobody bothers to ask me first?"

"All I will say is it is not right."

"No. It isn't."

"What I meant is it is not right… this play acting… this dance between the two of you. I told you about the night at the hospital and how she feels about you. It is quite obvious."

He started to push up out of his chair. "I'm going to take a shower."

"No," she said, her tone admonishing. "You are like children with your hurt feelings and stubbornness. It should end."

"It will. End," he added, looking down at her.

"That is not how I meant."

"Drop it, Fumiko."

"She loves you," she said but he paid her no heed and made his way up to the house.

# 39

*"I keep passing that open door, waiting*
*But you said love never lasts*
*So why this thunder in my heart?*
*This same tempest blowing?*
*You still think we can run to the end of the road?"*

-Lou Ann Catskill
Isle of Hearts

It was near dusk before Lou Ann finally made her appearance, her arrival no less over-the-top than her usual entry on stage. Since there were no cars on the island, the only modes of transportation for tourists and residents alike, were boats, motorbikes or small four wheelers that could manage the few rudimentary roads. Ever the diva, Lou Ann chose to arrive at Leon's isolated casita by boat. In this case, a sleek forty- foot, candy apple red cigarette boat that was forced to draw up twenty or so yards offshore.

Alerted by the sound of its engines, Leon and Fumiko stepped out onto the screened porch and watched the boat approach. Hardly a word had passed between them since their conversation earlier that morning on the beach. Leon had retreated into stubborn, sullen silence, his reserve fueled by contradictory emotions – a mix of anxious anticipation and dread that over the years had become his usual state of mind when faced with Lou Ann's unexpected insertions into his life. As for Fumiko, Leon sensed her silence stemmed from her own ambiguities as much as from her frustration with Leon's reticence to reveal his true feelings for Lou Ann.

They watched as Lou Ann exchanged a few words with the boat pilot before swinging her legs over the side. She paused to slip off her shoes before sliding into the water which fortunately was no more than a couple of feet deep. The pilot handed her an oversize woven cloth handbag like the kind one might have purchased in the airport curio shop. She wore a pair of red Bermuda shorts, a matching bikini top and a baseball cap. As she began wading ashore, the memory of her striding down the pier that first day in Papeete crept into his mind. The boat pilot hesitated a moment before accelerating away in an ear-splitting roar.

Leon glanced at Fumiko who shot him one of her usual impenetrable glances before retreating inside. He made no effort to walk out onto the beach to greet Lou Ann, but instead stood patiently watching her from inside the porch. It had been almost six years since he had last seen her. The distance, both physical and emotional, seemed an unfathomable chasm. He suddenly felt as nervous as a teenager on a first date.

Lou Ann paused at the water's edge and slung the bag over her shoulder. Still barefoot, she trudged up the sandy incline until she was within hailing distance of the porch. She glanced in either direction before looking up at him and smiling.

"How come you never brought me here?" she asked, raising her hand to block the sun that was just beginning to graze the tops of the palms that sheltered the house.

"I did ask you once," he replied through the screen. "You said you were too busy."

She nodded and then strolled up to the bottom of the stairs and removed her cap. He marveled at the fact that she hadn't seemed to have aged much. A streak of gray at her temples, the creases of her smile a bit more pronounced, but all and all, she appeared preternaturally youthful. He counted in his head. She had to be fifty-five, six maybe. Good genes had always been her explanation. More likely a deal with Beelzebub had always been his rejoinder.

"How are you, Leon?"

The voice hadn't changed much either– the same husky contralto that some writer from Rolling Stone had described as the kind that broke up homes. The Siren's Voice was how another writer had referred to it when reviewing her first jazz recording.

He considered her a moment before replying. "I'm curious why you're just now getting around to asking," he said, making little effort to disguise the edge in his voice.

She grimaced and looked away, her discomfort obvious. "Friends are supposed do that, aren't they? Ask after one another." When he didn't reply, she cleared her throat before going on. "I didn't know about your cancer. Not until Austin. Then it was too late. I rather doubt you were expecting me to linger at your bedside. Or that you'd really even want me there. The truth is I didn't want to complicate your life, Leon. I thought I was doing you a favor."

He couldn't help but laugh. "Complicate my life. That's quite the understatement."

"I suppose you and I were never a good idea from the start, were we?"

"That has come to mind."

"Yet somehow we managed to get way past the good idea part. That says something, doesn't it? I'm just not sure what." She took one step up the stairs and stopped. "Are you going to open the door and invite me in or not?"

He hesitated a moment before swinging the door open and taking a step back.

"I don't blame you for being angry," she said, slinging her bag onto a nearby chair. "I've been a grade A bitch."

The silence built for a moment before he said anything. "And Iris? I'd appreciate if you would help me understand. The not telling me. Not telling either of us."

"Not telling you was wrong. I know that. It was unforgivable. But I thought... God, Leon. I thought ..." She seemed to struggle with what to say. "I was losing her. You saw the way she was. I thought if I was going to lose her, I wanted to lose her to you. I would've thought you'd have figured that out. Me handing her over to you like that. I didn't think I needed to spell it out."

"You could've just said something. Come clean."

"I was afraid that…"

"That what? That I wouldn't have wanted to be part of her life? That I'd walk away from that? You don't…"

"I thought you wouldn't want to be a part of my life," she blurted. "The way I was. Why in god's name would you? Why would anyone?"

He didn't know what to say, his emotions strangling him. He let his eyes slide past her to the horizon over her shoulder. The sky had darkened to the north and he could see a wall of towering cumulus clouds, their shadows traced by an occasional scintilla of lightning.

"Is that fancy boat coming back for you?" he asked, still unable to sort out his feelings.

She shrugged. "I didn't ask him to. Should I have?"

"Would you like a drink?" he asked after a moment.

"I'm not supposed to."

"Neither am I."

"Well then I'll follow your lead," she said, stepping further inside the porch. "What about Fumiko? Will she be joining us?"

"Unlikely. You should know she's probably the only one on your team these days."

"Oh yeah? Iris thinks she's carrying a torch for you."

"Fumiko's my friend and my nurse. Nothing more."

"I'll have to admit she's been really good for Iris. Like the sister she never had."

"Do you think there's more to it?"

"If there's more there, I sure wouldn't complain."

"Tequila, okay?"

"Sure."

"Pull up a chair. I'll be right back."

He went into the kitchen and leaned against the sink in an attempt to collect himself. Who was it that said resentment was just as strong an emotion as desire, their heat interchangeable? Over the years, he had spent many a sleepless night measuring that heat and fantasizing about the prospect of seeing her just one last time. A day, an hour. And then what? He straightened and took a deep breath. And now here she was.

He suddenly remembered that he had come into the kitchen to cut up a lime, although his need to regroup was the real reason. As he sliced the lime, he watched her, the way she sat leaning forward in the chair, her arms crossed over her thighs, expectant, edgy as always. And he wondered why she had come.

He gathered the lime slices, found a pair of clean glasses, and grabbed the Patron from the cabinet beside his bed before going back out. To his surprise, he found Fumiko and Lou Ann laughing about something. He hadn't heard Fumiko come onto the porch. She had changed into a simple, embroidered white dress of the type the locals called a *huipiles*. She had a large straw handbag draped over her shoulder.

"Are you going somewhere?" he asked.

"I thought I would take the motorbike into town. There may be music at the Arena."

"You'd best keep an eye on the weather."

"If it should rain, I will get a room. Do not worry about me. Good night, Lou Ann," she said and nodded at Leon before disappearing around the corner of the house. A moment later, they heard the motorbike start up and soon its putting sound faded into the distance.

They sat and sipped tequila and watched the abrupt nightfall of the tropics, the darkness collapsing in the span of mere minutes. The swallows had given way to the fruit bats, the intensity of their squeaking at times unsettling. It would rain tonight, he thought. The storm was most likely a good couple of hundred of miles away, but he could already smell it.

"Why are you here?" he asked, finally.

"Iris said you were better," she said, obviously dodging the question. "In remission, she said. That's good. I know about multiple myeloma. A guy in my band had it."

"Then you know remission is like the two minute warning. It's nothing more than a pause for a commercial break."

"I thought there were better treatments these days."

"There are, but relapse is still a given. It could be a year from now. Maybe two years. Occasionally, someone makes it eight to ten, but no one gets out alive. I'm going up to Houston in a couple of weeks for follow up," he added, filling the silence. "Who knows? Maybe they'll tell me I'll outlive my reputation. I'll be one of those writers who when people come across my name they'll wonder whether I'm still alive."

She smiled, or he at least thought she did, for the porch now lay in deep shadow. He saw her raise the tumbler of tequila to her mouth and tilt it back.

"Another?" he asked, extending the bottle.

"*Juste un peu, monsieur.* I've been working on my French. I thought I'd try it out on the first Foreign Legionnaire I ran across."

"Where did you go after you left Austin?" he asked, tipping the bottle over her glass.

"Believe it or not, I hid out on JB's ranch for about a month."

"JB Coonts? I hope you kept your wits about you,"

"Twenty four seven. Anyway, after a month I went back to Santa Fe and made my peace with Kevin. And no, he's no longer a part of my life. I hired a French tutor and a new therapist. Yeah, I know what you're thinking, so don't say it. But I'm in a good place now."

She took a sip of her tequila but didn't say more until a long moment had passed. "I'm not the same person, Leon. My psychiatrist thinks it's finally about finding the right combination of medications. If you ask me, it's more likely due to menopause and getting off the horse."

"You mean giving up performing? The touring?"

"That's a lot of it. I have to work at staying balanced. Iris… our daughter." She shook her head. "Do you realize that's the first time I've ever referred to her that way? Our daughter. Anyway, Iris makes me toe the line. And then Fumiko gives me her fair share of sisterly advice and support. I'd be lying though if I said it was easy. I told myself that I wouldn't come here until I was feeling together." She made a snorting, laughing sound. "God, who would've thought it would take this long? Getting my life together."

"I wouldn't know. I'm not there yet. You never answered my question," he said, refilling his own glass.

"You mean the reason I'm here? To make amends for one thing."

"Before it's too late, you mean? I don't need…"

"I needed to come," she said, cutting him off. "For me if nothing else. Yeah, I know. As usual, I always make it about me. The bottom line was I couldn't bear the thought of you hating me."

"I'm long past that. Terminal illness can do that. Now it's just more about regrets. Another thing cancer does. It makes you take stock of things, especially the past."

They both fell silent again. "My god, would you look at that," she said abruptly. She gestured with her glass out at the near darkness. "What does that call to mind?" she asked

The clouds to the north and to the east had coalesced into a towering bank that extended the length of the Gulf's horizon. The setting sun had touched their summits, turning them a feathery crimson. Every few seconds, a jagged bolt of lightning further illuminated their contours. They waited in silence for the thunder, but the only sounds were the squeaking of the bats and the breeze stirring the palms. And he felt a rush of memory of that long ago night.

"Do you remember me asking you if we needed to move to higher ground?" she asked. "In case there was a tsunami. And you asked what I would do if I had just an hour to live."

He studied her profile in the darkness for a moment before replying. "If my memory serves me right, you said you would write a song."

"It's different now. Now, if I just had an hour…" She stared out into the darkness before looking back at him. "There are too many more important things. Is it too late to start over?" she asked in the silence that followed. "Live a different life?"

Leon looked at her but couldn't make out her face in the shadows. He felt a stab of something – melancholia perhaps tinged with misplaced optimism.

"A different life," he said. "It seems a little late for starting over. You have to realize I gave up on thinking in terms of the future some time back. I've cancelled all my subscriptions."

"That's good though, isn't it? To live in the present? You get older, and it seems it's all any of us have. We have that last hour. And we have to decide what to do with it. Which brings me to the other reason I came." She finished her tequila in one long swallow as if she were fortifying herself for what she was about to say. "Do you remember the sailboat I hired in Tahiti?"

"The Lost At Sea. How could I ever forget a name like that?"

"I bought it some years back. And I spent a shit load of money refitting it. I even learned how to sail a little. I thought maybe sometime we could go out on it." She seemed to reach for his hand and then pulled back.

"How come I'm envisioning a burial at sea?" he asked, finishing his tequila. "You're serious?"

"Yeah, I am. Look, I can understand why you'd say no. I've used up my quota of people taking chances on me."

"It's not that. I'm just not sure you realize what you're getting into."

"You mean like you going and dying on me?"

The bluntness of her reply gave him pause. "Yeah, there's that."

"One hour left, Leon. What's it going to be? Run for the hills or make music?"

"Why can't I do both?" he said after a moment's hesitation.

"Leon," she said, grasping his hand. *"La vie est la vie, et puis c'est parti.* This old guy I hired to teach me French. Well, he was a violinist. He had bad arthritis and couldn't play anymore. I'd go to his house almost every afternoon for a lesson. And when I'd leave, he'd always say that to me. Life…" She shook her head. "It's here and then it's gone. Come with me," she said, squeezing his hand. "Please."

He thought for a moment longer than necessary. "And when it's time, and I ask you to go?"

"I won't," she said. "I won't run."

"I might though."

"We won't let you. Me, Iris. Fumiko. We won't," she said, her voice thick with emotion.

"I can't give you any guarantees."

"None expected. There is one thing though. I do expect you to write. I even had this little folding writing table built for the boat."

"Write? You realize I don't write short stories."

She laughed. "I'll read to you then. How about trashy romance novels? I could be your muse. I just have to hit some bookstores when we get to Houston."

"I guess Houston can wait. Maybe we can't," he added, surprising himself.

"Well. Okay," she said, not bothering to conceal her own surprise. "Now that we have that settled, do you happen to have anything to eat?"

He shook his head in amusement and stood and opened the door to the kitchen. She shrugged her shoulders and grinned. "A girl's gotta eat," she said, brushing past him.

He stood there at the door a moment longer. He could hear her softly singing a melody that sounded familiar but he couldn't place. He looked back once more at the approaching storm and wondered if this would be the last time he would witness a storm on the gulf. And he wondered whether that really mattered anymore. And in that moment, he realized he wasn't ready. It wasn't that he was afraid of dying, but only of dying with the wrong regrets. He turned and went inside.

# THE END

**DENNIS JUNG** is the author of nine novels, four of which have been selected as a finalist in the New Mexico-Arizona Book Awards. His use of visual imagery and his strong sense of place are what make his novels as much an escape to a geographical location as the emotional landscape of his characters. Tapping into a background in anthropology, he weaves into his stories a sense of the mystical and the universal in the human experience – the drama and conflicts that consume us all, regardless of culture. The author lives in Santa Fe, New Mexico. Excerpts, essays about his books, and a biography are available on his website *www.dennisjung.com*